BLACK VELVET

A Black's Bandit's Novel

_____

LYNN RAYE HARRIS

All Rights Reserved. This book or any portion thereof may not be reproduced or used in any manner whatsoever without the express written permission of the publisher except for the use of brief quotations in a book review.

This is a work of fiction. Names, characters, places, and incidents either are the products of the author's imagination or are used fictitiously. Any resemblance to actual persons, living or dead, businesses, companies, events, or locales is entirely coincidental.

The Hostile Operations Team® and Lynn Raye Harris® are trademarks of H.O.T. Publishing, LLC.

Printed in the United States of America

First Printing, 2022

For rights inquires, visit www.LynnRayeHarris.com

Black Velvet
Copyright © 2022 by Lynn Raye Harris
Cover Design Copyright © 2022 Croco Designs

ISBN: 978-1-941002-73-5

Chapter One

Roberta Sharpe's long-awaited novel, The Vampire King, is a stinking, rotten mess. Everyone knows the author got divorced a few years ago, but did she have to let that affect her view of Damian LeBeaux? Readers everywhere have been in love with Damian since he first strode onto the pages of her debut novel, The Vampire Lover, *and they aren't going to take kindly to Ms. Sharpe's handling of Damian's romance with Velvet Asbury, who's calling it quits because she's suddenly in love with Neal Bolton. Neal!*

I mean the love triangle was okay and all for the past few books, but to fall for Neal over Damian? To choose a life of mediocrity instead of an immortal life with Damian, the man who worships you?

Give me a break, Ms. Sharpe! Just because your romance went sour doesn't mean you have to rip Damian and Velvet apart. They are meant for each other!

I don't know what went so wrong in your life that you have to torture the rest of us, but you need to make this right. Your next book isn't even coming out for a year, and now we all have to live with Velvet breaking Damian's heart and making him turn dark and twisted. She saved him, and you're killing him. Why? WHY?

I will never read another book of yours ever again if you don't fix it. One more shot, Ms. Sharpe. That's all you get from me!

— Damian&VelvetForever123 (From the Good Books Review Site)

———

YOU SUCK, *Ms. Sharpe.*
Sincerely,
A Former Fan

———

I HATE YOU! *You've ruined Damian and Velvet!*

———

NO WONDER *your husband left you! You're cold-hearted and cruel! Neal Bolton isn't the one for Velvet! Damian is the only one who really loves her!*

———

LIAR. *Thief! You deserve to die for what you did. You won't get away with it. I'll tell the world…*

———

THE DOOR WAS ALREADY OPEN.

Robbie had her key out, ready to slip it into the lock when she reached the back door, but it stood slightly ajar. Had she failed to tug on it hard enough when she'd left the house to take Lucy for a walk?

It was possible. The house was old, and though she'd had renovations done, the wooden door was particularly sticky when rain clouded the sky. If she didn't make sure it latched, it would start to swing open eventually. Which must be what had happened.

She swore. She was soaking wet because she'd failed to check her weather app before taking Lucy for a walk. In her defense, the sky had looked the same for days and it hadn't rained. Blue sky with random gray clouds that looked ominous but never did anything before moving on to drop rain elsewhere.

Not today, though.

Robbie hesitated on the step. No one had broken in. Not out here. She'd moved to Mill Landing on the Eastern Shore of Maryland precisely because it was remote. She hadn't seen anyone lurking around her house since she'd left the gated community she used to live in near DC five years ago.

She'd caused a shitstorm with her latest book, but that didn't mean a deranged fan had tracked her down and broken into her house. Or that her anonymous stalker had found her. She hadn't heard from that person in years anyway. Be a bit odd for them to start up again after all this time.

Robbie pushed the door all the way open. She just hadn't tugged it hard enough when she'd left. At least it hadn't blown open during the squall and soaked her wood floors.

She really needed to get the door fixed. When it was wet or humid, the wood swelled and the lock didn't always catch. She'd been putting it off because she didn't like talking to people. That had been Trent's job when they were married, but they weren't married anymore.

By the time Robbie got inside and found a towel to dry off with, Lucy had shaken a river of water all over the mudroom and left a trail of muddy paw prints as she escaped into the house.

"Lucy. Here, Lucy," Robbie called, but the beagle didn't return. Robbie prayed she wasn't making a beeline for the couch because that would be a hell of a mess to clean up. She'd probably have to give in and hire someone to get the mud off the fabric, which meant having a stranger in her house.

She really didn't like having anyone she didn't know around. People asked questions and she never knew what to say. She'd been an awkward kid, and she was an awkward adult. It was just easier not to deal with people if she didn't have to.

When Lucy started to bark, Robbie's neck prickled with warning. What if she was wrong and someone *was* inside?

Robbie grabbed the shotgun she kept in the mudroom and crept through the house, following the sound of Lucy's barking. She didn't hear anyone moving around, no one making noise as they tried to get away from Lucy. It was probably the cat. Lucy and Oliver got along just fine, but if Ollie was somewhere Lucy wanted to be—like the couch she'd probably bark at him so he'd vacate the premises.

Not that he ever did, but that didn't stop her.

Robbie made it to the living room where Lucy stood barking her face off at the piano. Ollie wasn't there, so it wasn't him.

"Hush, Lucy," Robbie said, walking toward the dog. Lucy looked up at her then turned and started to bark again.

The piano was a baby grand that Robbie had bought because it looked beautiful in the room, not because she played. Trent had told her it was a stupid waste of money, but she'd wanted it anyway.

Trent had thought a lot of things were a stupid waste of money until he decided to leave her and sue for half her earnings. Then he'd spent plenty of it on the kind of stuff he wanted, including a destination wedding to a twenty-five-year-old fitness instructor who looked stunning in everything she wore.

Robbie swallowed her bitterness. And then she realized there was something on the beautiful rosewood piano. Something that shouldn't be there.

Her heart skipped a beat as she crept closer. It was a box, Tiffany blue, and there was a pink rose that looked like it had come from her own garden lying next to it. *What the hell?*

Fear skated along her spine, pooling deep in her core. Someone *had* been inside. While she was out with Lucy, someone had broken in—or walked in if the door hadn't latched—and deposited these things on her piano. That person might still be here—

Ollie! Panic surged in Robbie's body as she lifted the gun and went in search of her cat. She had to find him. Her phone was in her back pocket, but help wouldn't get here quickly enough if she stopped to call. Besides, she had a gun and she knew how to use it.

She found Ollie almost immediately, sitting in the hallway leading to her bedroom, orange tail slashing angrily as if someone had disturbed him. He yowled when he saw her and stalked toward the kitchen, clearly expecting to be fed. Robbie's heart still hammered, but at least her pets were safe.

She took a deep breath to calm her racing heart then spent the next few minutes checking all the rooms, upstairs and down, gun in hand and Lucy at her side, until she was certain no one was there. She also double-checked the doors and windows to make sure they were all locked.

There was no sign of anyone having been in her home, other than the strange box and flower on her piano. She returned to the living room to take a closer look.

Robbie bent to examine the box. She knew better than to touch it with her fingers, so she retrieved dish gloves from the kitchen and gently pried the lid off.

It was a photo of her, but not any photo she'd ever had taken. She looked asleep, as if someone had snapped a picture of her in bed. It took her a moment to realize she was lying in a coffin rather than a bed. Fear twisted inside her.

Someone had been in her house, and they'd left this for her to find. She lay the photo aside with shaking hands and looked into the box again. There was a handwritten note lying beneath where the photo had been.

It was just a few words on a small square of card stock, but they chilled her to the bone.

You will die. Soon.

———

DAX FREED HIT the button on his steering wheel to take the incoming call from his boss at Black Defense International. He'd just gotten off a plane from London. It'd been a whirlwind assignment to meet with an informant and crack a security system on a computer, but he'd gotten the info and passed it to the appropriate agencies. Now he could use a shower and about twelve hours of uninterrupted sleep.

Still, when the boss called, you answered.

"Wassup?"

"Sorry to hit you with this now," Ian Black replied, "but I just got a call from Daphne Linden at Spring Books. It's time."

Dax groaned. Just what he'd wanted.

Not.

He'd been reading Roberta Sharpe's steamy romance novels for the past month. Ian had assigned him the books because she'd been getting death threats over her latest, which had only been out about six weeks. Up to now, Ms. Sharpe had been resisting her publisher's efforts to provide her with a bodyguard.

Since the threats had mostly been of the angry email variety, he'd understood. Clearly, something had changed her mind.

"What happened?"

"Someone broke into Ms. Sharpe's house and left a photo of her in a coffin along with a note that said she was going to die soon."

Dax blinked. "Well, that's kinda sick."

"Definitely. Look, I know this seems pretty mundane compared to what you've just done in London, but you're the man I want for this one."

Dax snorted. "Why? Because I've read all about Damian LeBeaux and Velvet Asbury, thanks to you making me?"

Ian laughed. "Good enough reason."

"I'm telling you, Ian, she really stepped in it with this last book. It's no wonder her fans are pissed off."

He wasn't exactly a romance reader, but he'd done the reading as ordered. Damian and Velvet's romance had seemed legendary—not to mention steamy as hell—for five books. And then, wham, Roberta Sharpe dropped a bomb and blew it all to hell.

"Apparently. I'm texting you the address. Get out there as soon as you can."

Dax sighed. "Ah hell, I was looking forward to a few hours' sleep."

"Sorry."

"You sure you can't send someone else?"

"Yep."

"What about Jared? He loves to read." Dax's teammate read huge tomes, not romance novels, but reading was reading. Besides, Jared's mother had been a big romance fan, and Jared still had the books she'd gotten signed by her favorite authors. Surely that would give him and Roberta Sharpe something to talk about.

"Jared isn't single."

"What's that got to do with it?"

"Ms. Sharpe is scheduled to speak at a conference in Las Vegas in a few days then embark on a ten-city tour. Daphne thinks that if Roberta is seen with a new boyfriend, it might take some of the heat off her personal life and how it relates to her writing."

Dax could feel his jaw slipping open. "Jesus, Ian—she broke up the relationship she's been writing about over six books. Years' worth of stories that people are invested in. What the hell will having a new boyfriend do to fix that? She's already disappointed her fans."

"I know. I've said the same to Daphne, but she doesn't want the protection angle to be obvious. Daphne would rather she be seen with a boyfriend than a bodyguard. Makes it less intimidating for the fans. I'll be sending Finn McDermott and Jamie Hayes along for the conference and tour. They'll join you in Vegas and blend with the crowd so they can keep an eye on things there."

Dax grumbled. He liked and trusted Finn and Jamie, so that part was good. It was the boyfriend part he wasn't fond of. He preferred the kind of ops where they hunted dangerous people—terrorists, traffickers, drug dealers, dictators, etc., and stopped them from hurting others.

But high profile protection was the cover story for Ian's real operation, and Roberta Sharpe was the kind of client they took on for that side of the business. Someone with deep pockets and a need for personal security.

"If you think it's the best way to do this, I won't argue."

"I think it'll be easier on the client. According to Daphne, she's skittish around people. You'll be able to help her deal with others if you're acting as her companion."

Dax let out a resigned sigh. "I have to stop at home so I can pick up more clothing and grab my weapons. Do you have any further info? A copy of the photo and note?"

"Not yet. I'll send those when I get them. She's expecting you."

"Great." He'd really been looking forward to sleeping in his own bed for a change.

"Cheer up, Dax. It could always be worse."

"Such as?"

"You could be crammed into a hot van by a wharf in Mexico with Rascal instead of installed in a famous romance author's guest room."

Okay, that was definitely worse.

Chapter Two

THE POLICE CAME AND WENT. THEY ASKED QUESTIONS, looked for signs of forced entry—there were none—and took the box with the photo, note, and rose as evidence. They didn't dust her home for prints, but they would dust the box and note. If they found something, they'd call.

Not immediately, because things like that took more time than on television, but sometime in the next few days.

Robbie was on the phone with Daphne for most of it. Daphne was the publisher of Spring Books, but she was also Robbie's editor. And her friend.

When the police left, she locked the door and closed her eyes as she leaned against it.

People exhausted her. She hadn't always been like this, but it was getting worse. She'd always been an introvert, always been rather shy, but she'd coped just fine. Since Trent had left her for Kimberlee, she'd felt herself pulling away from most interactions with others.

She could feel their eyes on her, questioning, and she didn't know what to say.

"Are you still there?" Daphne asked.

"Yes, I'm here."

"I called Ian Black. He's sending someone over."

"Daphne, no. Please. It's fine. I have Lucy and a shotgun. I'm not going to let some crank scare me."

Even though it was the first time anyone had broken into her home. Even though a part of her was scared spit-less. Who would do such a thing?

"Honey, listen to me." Daphne paused, and Robbie knew she was waiting for an answer.

"Okay, fine. I'm listening."

"BDI is a premier protection agency. They specialize in high profile clients. They can and will be discreet. Not only that, but I've asked for a very specific type of man."

Robbie's skin prickled. "What's that supposed to mean?"

"I asked for tall, dark, and handsome—and single. You need someone to go with you to Vegas, and this guy can do that. He'll pretend to be your hunky new boyfriend—"

"Daphne!"

"Hush. Hunky new boyfriend. Your readers will love it, and it might even help you get past this drama with *The Vampire King*."

Robbie didn't point out that since Daphne was her editor, she'd let Robbie make the drama in the first place. Not that she'd had much choice since the deadline and publication dates had been so tight. "I don't want a boyfriend. I'm done with men. And Autumn is going with me. She always does."

"First of all, your assistant is sweet but *not* what I'm talking about. You need a bodyguard. And honey, you are not done with men. You're done with cheating, lying, thieving SOBs like Trent, but you are *not* done with men."

"It's the same thing. My judgment is obviously flawed."

"Was flawed. Maybe. Trent is handsome, and you were young when you fell for him."

"Meaning I'm old now?"

"Meaning you are older and wiser. You would never make that same mistake again."

Robbie went into the kitchen and put on the tea kettle. It was spring, but with the rain and gray clouds, it was chilly. She needed something to warm her up.

"I wouldn't be so sure about that. Maybe I have a type. Maybe my type is inherently flawed. Cocky bad boy with muscles and a mischievous grin. That's Trent."

Daphne made a noise. "That man is not a bad boy. He may have pretended to be one, but he's not. He's just an asshole."

Robbie laughed. "He is that."

She'd thought it was going to be forever with Trent. She'd seen what she wanted to see, and she'd written so much of what she'd thought he was into Damian. Maybe that was why she'd wanted to strip Damian's soul bare in this last book.

Daphne had let her do it because she'd promised to redeem everything. But Robbie wasn't sure she wanted to. She was sick of Damian LeBeaux and Velvet Asbury. She wanted to write something else. A different story. A romance, because that was what she loved, but something besides a vampire for a change.

"I don't see why I need a new boyfriend. This is the twenty-first century. A woman can be happy by herself."

"I realize that. You're talking to someone who's never been married, remember?"

Robbie grumbled an acknowledgment.

"I think it will be better for the tour. I think having a big, bad bodyguard looming over you will send the wrong message to the fans. It will make people uncomfortable."

Robbie wasn't so sure about that, but she knew better than to argue with Daphne when she had her mind made up. Managing Robbie's brand was her job, and she did a great job at it.

"Hang on, just got a message from Ian…" Daphne said.

Robbie got out her favorite teapot and quilted cozy.

"Okay, he says his guy will be there in about two hours. His name is Dax Freed—"

"Dax Freed? Seriously? Did they make that up?"

Daphne laughed. "I know, right? Sounds like the name of your next hero. After you fix Damian's life of course."

"I don't know, Daph. It's a little ridiculous isn't it? It's like he's trying too hard. Seriously, that has to be a made-up name. Probably because you told this Ian guy that I need a bodyguard-boyfriend and they came up with something stupid to make fun of the assignment."

"I'm pretty sure Ian is more professional than that, Robbie. Please don't accuse the man of having a made up name when he arrives."

"I won't."

"It might really be his name. Dax could be short for something. And Freed…" The sounds of typing filtered through the line. "It's an old name, quite possibly Prussian and/or Jewish. There are almost ten-thousand people in the US with that name."

"Thank you, Madam Google," Robbie teased. "I could have done that myself."

"I know… Are you all right, Robbie?"

Robbie sighed. "I was scared when I realized someone had been inside, and I'm still pretty jumpy about it honestly. But I think I'm okay. Like I said, I have Lucy and a gun. Whoever broke in probably did so because the door didn't latch. They might have intended to leave the package on the porch, but if they saw me leave and saw the door…" She frowned. "Well, I guess they decided it would scare me more inside. At least they came in before it rained so they didn't track mud through my house."

She sounded clinical about it, but the truth was that she was still shaken up over it. Some unknown person had been *in her house*. With Ollie, though he seemed perfectly fine. Robbie had emptied the animals' food and water bowls and then washed them really well. She also planned to throw out anything in her fridge and pantry that was already opened. What if someone had put cyanide in her wine? Or in her leftover chicken soup?

Dammit, that had been a good pot of soup, too.

Nope, it all went out, which meant she would need to go to the grocery store tomorrow. She thought about ordering groceries, but what if the person who'd broken in worked at the grocery store or for the delivery company? There was no way of knowing, and she'd worry about it until she threw all that food away too.

"Maybe you should go to a hotel when Dax arrives. Just for the night."

Robbie gripped the phone in her hand. "No. Ollie wouldn't like it, and Lucy would howl at every sound. Assuming I could find somewhere that would let me bring them."

"You could. You're Roberta Sharpe for heaven's sake."

"I don't even know what that means," Robbie almost whispered as tears pricked her eyes.

"Honey, I know you've had a hard time of it with reader mail and reviews, but that's only a small fraction of what's out there. You know it as well as I do. Happy readers may or may not review, but they go on to the next book. Unhappy ones tell everyone how unhappy they are. I promise you there are a lot of happy readers out there, and they're willing to trust you to make things right. You'll redeem Velvet, or you'll write someone even better for Damian and they will eat it up. Trust me."

She didn't even trust herself anymore. When she'd sent Velvet into Neal Bolton's arms, she'd been sick to death of Damian LeBeaux and his moody ways. So what if Neal was a doctor and Damian was the king of the night? So what?

Not every handsome, dangerous, beautiful man was worth the pain. Not every man was a hero. In fact, she didn't think *any* of them were—or not like in her stories, anyway.

Romance novel heroes were fictional. She knew it better than most.

———

DAX PULLED up in front of a two-story white house with black shutters that looked as if it'd come out of the pages of one of his mom's *Southern Living* magazines. There were two single-story wings with huge windows on either side of the central structure, and lush flowering bushes along the front of the wings.

A long lane had passed beneath tall trees that stretched across it to create a canopy then ended in a circular drive in front of the picture-perfect house. There was also a garage to one side of the house and a barn with a fenced pasture. There were no animals in the pasture, but that didn't mean there weren't any in the barn.

The nearest town was about five miles away—a quaint, cute town that was probably packed with tourists in the high season. It wasn't far, but it felt a hundred miles from this place.

It was raining gently when Dax got out of his Ford F150 and shouldered his duffel bag, range bag, and laptop bag, locked his truck, and walked up the front steps of Roberta Sharpe's home. He rang the bell and waited.

A dog barked, but the door remained closed for long minutes. Annoyed, Dax rapped on it. He was tired and hungry and it was damp. He wanted to get inside and check the place out, then grab some shuteye.

The dog's barks increased in volume and pitch. He leaned over to peer through the window beside the door, but the glass was frosted and he couldn't see anything except the vague shape of a dog.

Finally, when he was ready to start shouting, he heard the twisting of the locks. The door dragged open an inch. Dark eyes gazed at him with barely disguised hostility.

"I'm from Black Defense International," he said, trying to keep the irritation from his tone. "Ian Black sent me. Are you Roberta Sharpe?"

Her brows drew down into hard slashes as she broke eye contact. Then she sighed and pulled the door wider. "Chill, Lucy," she said to the beagle, who stopped barking but didn't retreat. "That's me. Can I see some ID?"

He reached into his jeans pocket. "Sure. But maybe ask for that before opening the door next time. Make them hold it up to the peephole."

She nibbled her lip. It was a full lip. Pink. "You're right. But I still have Lucy, and she'd eat you up if I told her to."

He wasn't sure he believed that. He held out his driver's license. Her eyebrows lifted. "Dax Freed is really your name?"

"Is that a problem?"

"No." She waved her hands around then shoved

them into her jeans pockets as if thinking better of it. "Daphne and I were wondering if you and your boss were having a bit of fun with this assignment."

"How so?"

She stepped back. "It's nothing. Come in. I was just cleaning out the refrigerator."

He entered the house, and the dog sniffed his legs, tail wagging. Some killer. He stooped to pet her, and she licked his hand.

Roberta frowned. "Way to shore up the vicious guard dog reputation, Lucy."

Dax patted her head then rose again. "Can you show me around, Ms. Sharpe? I need to know where all the doors are and how many windows you've got."

She shrugged. "I can, but it's pretty obvious if you explore on your own. A door is a door is a door."

Her long brown hair was piled on her head in a loose bun. She wasn't very tall, probably about five-two, and she was a little on the thin side. He didn't think she'd always been that way because he'd seen publicity photos of her. She was made up and confident in those photos, and her cheeks were rounder. She looked like what you'd think an author was supposed to look like.

Smart. Studious. Vibrant.

This woman looked like she needed a good hot meal and some sleep. Sort of like him, though for different reasons. His was a temporary need brought on by flying to Europe and back in less than seventy-two hours. His sleep cycle was currently fucked. And the fast food burger he'd grabbed on the way hadn't sated his hunger for long.

"I can go through your house on my own if you like," he said coolly. "Thought you might want to know what I'm doing in your personal spaces, though."

She arched an eyebrow, but her gaze skittered away. He'd noticed that she made eye contact but not for long.

"Are you planning to go through my dresser drawers or peek in my nightstands?"

"I don't know. Is there anything interesting in there?"

Her eyes widened in shock, but again she looked away. Dax swore to himself. He didn't know what had made him say that, but it was probably the lack of sleep.

"Sorry. That was over the line."

"I've heard worse. If you write about murder, nobody asks where you get your inspiration. They don't waggle their eyebrows at you or call your work trashy. Write a romance, though, and suddenly people think you're some kind of nymphomaniac who must be writing about her life. They make comments and insinuations about you, and they think it's okay to ask personal questions." She lifted her gaze, her dark eyes flashing. "I'm used to it, but that doesn't make any of it okay."

Dax nodded, feeling slightly ashamed of himself. He'd read her books, and he could only imagine what people said to her. "You're right. You don't have to believe me, but I didn't say it because of your profession. I said it because I've been traveling for the past few days, I'm jet lagged and hungry, and I'd rather be at home in my own space. You sound like you're unwilling to cooperate, and it pissed me off."

She stooped to rub Lucy's ears. "I accept your apology. And I'm not unwilling to cooperate. I just… I don't know you, and I'm not very comfortable with people I don't know. I didn't want you here, but Daphne insisted. So I'm kind of pissed off too if you must know."

"Fair enough." Dax felt every bit of the past few days of weariness pushing down on him. "I won't get in your way, and you don't have to entertain me. I'm here to protect you. I'm good at my job, so you don't have to worry that someone's getting past me. But I need your cooperation or it's not going to work."

"I'll show you the house if it makes things go faster."

"It will. I can ask questions as we go instead of stopping to note them and asking later. I'll also tell you what I think needs to be done to make the place more secure."

"Let me show you to your room, and then we'll do the tour," she said, all business now. "I'm afraid I don't have much to eat, but there are a couple of frozen pizzas in the freezer. I could pop one in the oven."

"That's fine. I'd planned to order in until I got here and saw how far you are from town."

"Oh, it's not that bad," she said, leading him down a hallway off the entry. "There are a couple of restaurants who will deliver for me if that's what you want. It might take a while, plus how do we know someone won't poison the food before it gets here?"

He liked that she was suspicious. Meant she wasn't going to stupidly insist everything was okay. "Honestly, pizza works."

Roberta walked into a room off the hallway. "This is your room. There's an en suite bath over here," she added, walking over to an open door. "There are towels in the linen closet and toiletries under the sink if you need them."

Dax set his bags on the bed, weariness rolling through every cell of his body. "Where's your room?"

She swallowed. "Um, across the hall."

"Good. I need to be close by."

She looked a little disconcerted, but she nodded and hurried toward the door. "If you'd like to freshen up or anything, um, I'll put a pizza in the oven and then show you around when you're ready."

He wanted to do it now, but she was probably right that he needed to freshen up first. "Thank you, Ms. Sharpe. I'll be out in a few minutes."

She stood in the doorway, arms folded tight to her chest. "It's Robbie," she said softly. "Probably best you call me that if you're supposed to be my pretend boyfriend when I go on tour. Not my idea by the way."

"Robbie then," he said, watching her. She was interesting in a way he hadn't anticipated, though maybe it was the fact he'd read her books and felt like he'd been inside her head. It was an odd sensation, really. And probably complete bunk if what she'd said about people thinking they knew her was any indication.

She disappeared from view. Dax pushed a hand through his hair, yawning. Looked as if this mission was going to be a bit more challenging than he'd expected.

Chapter Three

"Well? Did Ian do as I asked and send a hunky bodyguard?" Daphne said.

Robbie lay in bed and pictured Dax Freed as she'd last seen him—eyes barely open and blinking slowly, dark hair mussed where he'd pushed a hand through it, lips glistening with oil from the pizza.

How she'd sat at the kitchen island with a man like him and eaten anything was still a mystery. She'd felt jumpy inside, like she was itching from the inside out and couldn't scratch. She'd wanted to run, and she'd wanted to stay. Lucy, the little traitor, had sat by his leg and looked at him with doe eyes. Even Ollie had emerged to cast a superior gaze on the man before sauntering off to one of his favorite sleeping spots.

"He could be a cover model," Robbie said. "No lie. The name is real, too."

Daphne gasped. "You did not ask him that!"

"No, I didn't." She kinda had, but Daphne didn't need to know. "He showed me his license for proof of identity when he came to the door. Unless it's fake," she added, wondering if this mysterious Ian Black and BDI could do something like that.

"Anything's possible, I guess. You should probably just assume that's his name though."

"Already with you on that."

"Might he inspire you to get some work done?" Daphne's voice was silky.

Robbie pinched the bridge of her nose. Her deadline was fast approaching, and she had nothing. Not a plot, not an idea, not even an opening line. She'd tried, but she failed every time. Nothing seemed to work.

"I doubt that. He's a stranger in my house, not a muse."

"Muses come from everywhere and anywhere. You told me that yourself."

"I like my muses imaginary. It's so much more enjoyable that way."

"Robbie," Daphne groaned. "You're only thirty-five, and yet you act like you're twice that sometimes."

"I feel twice that sometimes."

"If it weren't illegal, I'd have Trent shot."

"I've already thought about it, believe me. But it's not worth the risk."

Daphne snickered. "Sometimes I don't know whether you're pulling my leg or if you're serious."

Robbie shifted to make more room for Ollie, who was sacked out and pushing against her right side. Lucy was at the foot of the bed, snoring.

This was her life now. Going to bed with pets.

"I'm not serious. If I want to kill him, I will. *In a book*. In fact, I may kill him a few times."

"I think you should. Just don't kill Damian."

Robbie sighed. "I want to write something else, Daph. I have an idea about a romantic fantasy world with magic and—"

"Send me a proposal and we'll talk. But for God's sake, please get me the next Damian and Velvet story. Do you have a title yet?"

"No."

"How much have you written?"

"A bit." Robbie dug her toes into the sheets at the lie.

Daphne sighed. "You have a speech and a book tour coming up, and we both know you won't get any writing done while doing those things."

"I might. You never know."

"I *do* know. You're the kind of person who has to think a lot, and you need to be comfortable. You won't be comfortable on a book tour."

"Then don't send me."

"Sorry, toots, but it's what the finance people want. Your *King of the Night* series is big business around here, and even though your readers are angry, they're still buying the books. They want to see you, and we want them to keep buying."

Robbie knocked the back of her head against the headboard. Gently. "It's been difficult, Daphne. It's hard to write about romance when your life has imploded. Romance isn't real. At best, it's a wild ride that you'll laugh about someday when it's over. But not until the bones you broke when the relationship crashed and burned heal."

"I know, honey. But I need you to find your way and get back on track, okay? Damian and Velvet have given you a good life. They've given everyone at Spring Books a good life. Everyone here believes in you, babe. We all know you've got big plans for the vampire king and his mate, and we can't wait to see what you do next."

Robbie stared at the ceiling. "I know. I appreciate your faith in me. I'll get it done, and it'll be the best one yet. Then maybe we can talk about that romantic fantasy, okay?"

"Of course we can," Daphne said, sounding much cheerier than she had earlier. "Must run. I've got a date for cocktails in half an hour."

"It's nine p.m. You're going out now?"

"It's New York. Of course I am. So long as I'm in bed by one, I'll be at my desk by nine. Call me if you need anything."

"I will."

The call ended, and Robbie looked at Ollie. His tongue was sticking out the tiniest bit. Lucy was snoring.

Somewhere in the Pacific, Trent was ogling Kimberlee on the yacht he'd bought with Robbie's royalties. He was probably wearing a speedo—or nothing at all—and lying on the deck to sun himself. Or maybe he was fucking Kimberlee right now, her long tan legs wrapped around his slim hips as he pistoned into her.

"Stop it," Robbie growled to herself.

It wasn't that she still loved him, or even liked him

very much. It was just... Well, she'd thought their life together had been good. She'd thought he was content. She had been.

Lucy woofed in her sleep as if to say *liar*.

Robbie's thoughts drifted to the man in the next room. She could have put him upstairs in one of the rooms there, but she'd known he wouldn't allow it. A bodyguard had to be close, so she'd put him close. It hadn't been difficult since they wouldn't share a bathroom, but she was very aware of him being so near.

He was definitely something to look at. Taller than Trent, more muscular. He had an edge of danger to him that Trent didn't have. But Trent had been an architect, not a bodyguard. Trent sat in an office and designed buildings. He'd drawn the plans to renovate this house and to build the additions.

He hadn't stuck around for the completion, though. They'd been sleeping in one of the upstairs rooms while this wing had been built. Trent had never slept a night in the master bedroom, which was probably why she could do it now.

It'd been hard to stay in the house after he'd announced he was leaving, but it was her dream house, and she'd stubbornly refused to give it up.

Mostly, she was glad she'd stayed. Sometimes she felt her loneliness more keenly in this place.

She brought her thoughts firmly back to Dax Freed. He was something a girl could dream about if she hadn't lost the ability to dream.

He'd moved through her house with quiet command, his eyes constantly scanning the windows and doors. He'd checked all the locks, and he'd typed notes into an iPad he carried while they went room by room.

He'd taken pictures and sent them to his team, and he'd asked her to tell him what had happened when she'd returned home this afternoon and found the grisly memento.

She suspected he had a copy of the police report, but she told him anyway. He nodded along as she spoke. Then the oven dinged and it was time for pizza. She'd taken it out, sliced it, and got plates.

They'd served themselves at the island and sat on the counter-height stools to eat it. She hadn't been able to figure out how to get out of eating with him, so she'd stayed. Dax was polite, and the conversation wasn't too awkward. She hoped.

He hadn't stuck around, though. As soon as he finished, he said he had some things to do before he went to sleep. That was the last she'd seen of him. She'd gone to her office and tried to write, but nothing came. Eventually, she gave up and went to take a bath.

Now she turned off the light and closed her eyes, hoping she'd fall asleep soon. She didn't, though. Annoyingly, her mind kept drifting to Dax Freed the way it did when she was creating a new character.

Who was he? What drove him? What did he want from life?

"He's not a romance hero," she muttered in the darkness. "He's a man. Just a man."

How disappointing...

Chapter Four

DAX SLEPT THE SLEEP OF THE DEAD, THEN WOKE AROUND five a.m. feeling energized. He showered, dragged on jeans and a T-shirt, and emerged from his room to find Ollie the cat sitting in front of his door, tail flicking in feline judgment.

"Hey, buddy," Dax said, reaching down to pet the cat's silky fur. Ollie sniffed his hand then allowed a single pet before sauntering toward the kitchen.

Dax followed, hoping to find coffee. The kitchen was quiet, but the light under the range hood was on. It'd be another hour until sunrise, though the sky was beginning to lighten.

Roberta—Robbie, he reminded himself—had one of those coffee makers that used individual pods. He found the pods, but there was no cream in the fridge. In fact, there wasn't a lot in the fridge.

Robbie had told him a tad sheepishly that she'd thrown out everything that could have been tampered with by the person who'd entered her home. She planned to go to the grocery store today to replace it all.

He'd told her she'd done the right thing. In fact, he'd been a bit surprised that her mind had gone there—but maybe he shouldn't have been. The woman was very creative. She made up all kinds of shit, put it in a book, and made a lot of money for her efforts.

Dax brewed his coffee and set his laptop on the island where he'd had dinner with Robbie. He had a few things to do, information to research, but he took a moment to remember her sitting at an angle to him, her dark eyes wary but also curious. She'd wanted to ask him questions about himself, but she hadn't done it.

He figured that was part of being a writer. Insane curiosity about people and situations. How else did they make all that stuff up?

Ollie jumped on the island and glared at him. Then he meowed. Dax sighed. "Dude, I don't know where she keeps the food or if you're allowed to have any yet. For all I know, you're on a strict diet. What if I feed you and it's the wrong thing to do? Not to mention I bet you aren't supposed to be up here."

Ollie meowed again, louder this time. Dax sighed. "Fine. I'll see if I can find anything."

Ollie jumped down to follow. Dax found dry cat food in the pantry with a measuring cup and a note on the front of the bag. *Feed half a cup morning and night. No more. He's a scammer.*

Dax laughed as he filled the cup and went to pour it into Ollie's bowl. Ollie meowed and rubbed Dax's legs like they were besties. It made him think of his grandma's cat, Isabelle. She'd scammed for food too. And she'd always been *soooo* grateful when you gave it to her, but the second you did, she forgot you existed.

Dax dropped the food into the bowl, made a mental note to tell Robbie, and went back to his laptop. Nearly three hours later, after he'd studied the image of the photo and note Ian had sent, made a plan for putting in a wireless security system, ordered the equipment from BDI, drank three cups of coffee, and ate a plain bagel—because she'd thrown the butter out—Robbie emerged.

Lucy bounded over and he scratched her ears and told her she was a good dog. When he met Robbie's gaze, she was frowning at him. She wore a pink and gray flannel robe over what looked like a ratty T-shirt and yoga pants, fuzzy slippers, and her hair was a mess.

Her gaze skittered away when he looked at her for too long. He wondered about that since she did it every time, but he wasn't planning to ask. Too many other things he needed to know.

"Morning," he said.

Robbie yawned, covering her mouth with her hand, then threw him a bleary-eyed look. "Morning. You are *ridiculously* awake, by the way."

"Not a morning person?"

She shuffled to the coffee maker and took a mug from the cabinet above it. "No. Definitely not. Aw, hell." She was staring into the mug like something had gone awry.

"What? Is there a spider in there? Dried-on spinach?"

"No. I don't have any cream. Threw it away."

"I noticed."

"You like cream in your coffee, too?" She blinked at him.

"Yup. But I can do black when there's no other option. Trust me, this coffee is far better than the kind you run through a sock when you're downrange."

Her brow knit. "Is that English? I don't think I understood the important bits."

"It's English. Army speak. It means that when we deployed—went on a mission somewhere shitty, usually—we didn't have coffee machines and filters. We had sterno cans, questionable water, and clean socks if we were lucky."

"You were in the Army?"

"I was. For eight adventuresome years before I took a better offer."

"As a bodyguard?"

"Nope. As an analyst for the CIA."

She popped a coffee pod in and set her cup under it. "That sounds much more exciting than being a bodyguard."

"But not as lucrative."

He'd enjoyed the CIA, but he liked working for Ian better. Ian had recruited him when they'd been on a job together. Dax didn't regret leaving for a second. He wasn't exactly thrilled that he was here instead of working something more interesting than personal security, though.

They all did it from time to time, so he couldn't say he wasn't due. But it wasn't what he wanted, no matter how cute the famous author looked in her flannel robe and fuzzy slippers.

She let Lucy into the yard then retrieved her coffee and shuffled over to the window to watch the dog. Dax watched her. She was small and vulnerable, and a wave of protectiveness rolled through him. The idea of someone leaving her a photo of her in a coffin with a note that said she was going to die infuriated him.

He'd studied the photo. It was clearly done on a computer, and it wasn't even very good. But it was good enough to fool anyone who didn't know what to look for. Since he didn't have the digital file, he couldn't dissect the pieces of it. But he recognized a fake when he saw one, and he had an idea how they'd put the pieces together.

The note was done in a handwriting font, not actual handwriting. They'd have to wait to see if the police found any prints or DNA, but he didn't have high hopes for that.

He'd spent the morning, after getting the cameras and alarm equipment ordered, looking for photos of Robbie online that someone might have used and then exploring her reviews on the Good Books site and the retailer websites. There were a lot of angry and disillusioned readers out there, but he recognized it for what it was. Venting. People vented their frustrations when they expected something to be a certain way, paid their money, and didn't get what they wanted. It was normal.

There were a few that seemed a bit more invested in the world than might be healthy, but he didn't see any warning flags that indicated one of them meant to track Robbie down and threaten her.

She wasn't easy to find anyway. All fan mail and gifts went to a PO box in College Park, Maryland. Someone picked it up regularly, but he didn't know who yet.

Roberta Sharpe also had very active social media accounts, but they were too glossy and slick to be personal. There were pictures of her books, photos of half-naked men with quotes from her books, photos of what was ostensibly her office and shots of the interior of her house, but it wasn't anything he recognized.

"Whose house is in your Instagram photos?" he asked.

Robbie turned. "That's my assistant's house. She lives in College Park. She does my social media in tandem with my publisher."

"And picks up your fan mail?"

She nodded. "Yes. She comes out about once a month and gives me everything. She goes through it first, so if there's anything nasty, I don't know the specifics. I don't want to know."

Dax frowned. "If someone sent you threats in the mail, would you know?"

"Only if I really need to. Autumn keeps a list, and she can tell you who might have sent anything weird. She would also inform the police if there was anything truly threatening. I don't want to know unless I have to. It disrupts my ability to write."

"But you've gotten death threats over your latest book."

"People who are angry say things like *I hope you die*. It doesn't mean they plan to make it happen."

"True enough. But your publisher was worried enough to contact us a month ago. I assume that means you've gotten more threats than usual."

"Probably. But like I said, I don't look at the messages. I can't if I ever want to write again."

He thought he understood where she was coming from. "Your first book hit big, didn't it?"

She opened the door to let Lucy in. "I was lucky. Right place, right time, right story. I had to get an agent to negotiate the deal because I didn't have one when I got the first offer. She took the book to auction, and Spring Books won."

"Do you still have the agent?"

She started to open a can of dog food. "No. She passed away three years ago, unexpectedly. I haven't looked for anyone else. I still have two books to write on the contract she negotiated, so I guess I just haven't been motivated."

He could cross the agent off the list of people to talk to. "I'm sorry you lost her."

She upended the can and set the bowl down for the dog. "Me too. She was a shark. She helped make this career for me."

"Will you get someone else to negotiate the next contract?"

"Maybe. I don't know. They pretty much give me what I want."

"Why did you write feeding instructions on the cat food bag?"

She shot him a look. Then she laughed. "I put it there for me. Ollie can be quite pitiful, and I can be soft-hearted. I take it you fed him?"

"I did." The cat had disappeared a long while ago, presumably content.

"Thank you. He'll be back in another hour or two, asking for more. Best to ignore him."

"You weren't worried someone tampered with his food?"

"It's a new bag. I opened it last night after I threw the other one away."

He liked how much she cared for her pets. He'd read a lot about Roberta Sharpe and what kind of person she was presumed to be. People said many things about her, but not one of them had mentioned she loved animals.

Which told him they didn't really know her like they thought they did.

"Is someone staying in the house while you're on tour?"

She shook her head. "The only person I trust is my assistant, and she's going with me. I've booked Lucy and Ollie into a pet resort. I think they'll enjoy it. Or I should say that Lucy will. Oliver will be supremely irritated, I imagine. The pet resort is connected to the vet's office, though. If something happens, these two will be in the best place they can be."

"A good plan, then."

She finished her coffee and went back to the pot to prepare another one. "I didn't ask for anyone to be my pretend boyfriend. In case you were wondering."

"I know. The boss told me it was your publisher's

idea. I think she expects positive publicity over you having someone new in your life."

Robbie sighed. "She means well, but she didn't ask me before she told your boss. Anyway, I suppose we'll need a cover story."

She turned to face him, cup in hand. She didn't join him at the island, though.

"I'll leave that to you," he said. "You're the author."

"Have you ever thought about modeling?"

Dax startled at the sudden question. "No. Not interested."

"Too bad. I think you'd look good on a cover. Hmm, maybe that'll be the story. I met you at a cover shoot. Can you play a dumb jock?"

He wasn't sure if she was serious or making a joke. Before he could answer, she'd moved on.

"Strike that. Not dumb. Not implying all jocks are dumb. Or cover models either, by the way."

"That's good," he said mildly. "Wouldn't want to stereotype people based on how they look."

She didn't seem to be paying attention. "People would make fun of me or think I couldn't do better. *If* I were even interested in a man these days, which I'm not," she muttered to herself. "Smart and handsome is always a better combination."

"I'll be what you want me to be. But wouldn't it be easier to say we met and started dating? I'm an IT expert, so maybe I came out to fix your computer. The closer to the truth you keep it, the easier it is to remember the story."

"I suppose that could work. It's not exciting, but it

doesn't have to be. I hired you to fix my computer and fell madly in love. Obviously, you'd be madly in love with me, too."

"Obviously." He liked the way her imagination moved lightning quick from one scenario to the next. Must be hell in there when she was working on a book.

She managed to look at him for a full second longer than she ever had previously. Improvement maybe? But then she groaned and put a hand over her face.

"I hate this. Hate it. I don't want to go to the conference, and I don't want to go on a book tour. I also don't want to pretend we're happy. Daphne didn't think this through because she wasn't thinking about how pitiful I'll look when we inevitably split up. People will think it's me and Trent all over again."

He knew that Trent was the ex. Trent Sharpe, former architect, current playboy. He'd remarried within days of their divorce being finalized, and he'd walked away with half of Robbie's considerable estate. Because she'd first been published after they'd married, the judge had sided with Trent's theory that he'd been instrumental in making her into the author she'd become.

"We won't let them," Dax said. "However you want it done, that's what we'll do. I don't mind letting you dump me."

"Thank you. That's sweet." She set her cup on the counter and straightened. "I think I'm going to get dressed. Thanks for feeding Ollie. If Lucy wants out again, please let her go. She'll come back when she's done."

"I'll keep an eye on her."

"Thank you." She walked away then turned back. She still didn't make eye contact for more than a moment, looking past him instead of at him. "If I'd known what Daphne intended, I would have said no to the whole thing. It's a complication I don't need."

He didn't reply as she walked away. There was no point. He didn't like it any better than she did, but he wasn't going away.

Because whoever had walked into her house and delivered that death threat wasn't done yet.

Chapter Five

Robbie showered, dried her hair, and put on a little bit of makeup. She hated that she felt compelled to do so, but she needed some armor with a man like Dax in the house. Not to mention they were going to the grocery store today.

Tinted moisturizer, eyeliner, mascara, and lip gloss made her feel more confident when she looked in the mirror. She'd worn makeup all the time with Trent. She'd contoured, for heaven's sake!

When he left, she'd stopped caring. It had taken her a long while to realize that Trent had been very good at subtly tearing her down. He'd always asked her if she needed that extra helping of potatoes or if she wouldn't feel better if she made an effort to look pretty for him.

He'd asked the question after he'd been gone all day and she'd been at home, making sure the house was clean and dinner was on the table the way he liked it. She'd also been writing in the early days before she'd sold her book and changed their lives.

No matter what Trent had said in court, he'd had nothing to do with her writing. He hadn't encouraged it, and he certainly hadn't talked over story ideas with her. He'd wanted a stay-at-home wife because the firm he'd worked for had been very traditional, even if they couldn't dare openly say so.

The old men who'd founded the firm preferred a family man for advancement. They had a token woman or two, but Robbie knew what they were deep down. Men who believed they'd pulled themselves up by the bootstraps and deserved everything they had, and that it was men just like them who would really be the heart of the firm.

Robbie had been happy to stay home because she was an introvert and she wanted to write. Trent knew she wanted to be an author, but he always told her the chances of success were very slim for a new writer. He'd said that when the children came along, she'd be too busy for her little hobby anyway.

Then she'd sold *The Vampire Lover* and everything changed. Her little hobby became the thing that provided for them. The kids never came, though they tried for a while. After she'd had two miscarriages, Trent had said he wasn't sure they needed kids anyway.

By then, he'd realized the money wasn't a fluke and he'd quit work. Kids were no longer necessary for advancement, though at the time she'd thought he said it for her. That he loved her and was concerned for her well-being.

He'd told her he could help at home when he left his job. He'd helped a little bit, but he'd also played quite a lot. Literally. He golfed and went to the shooting range and worked out at the gym.

The only thing he'd done that meant anything to her was agreeing to move to this house and drawing up plans to renovate it. He'd seemed excited about everything to do with it, and he'd talked about how a new home would be a new beginning for them.

Instead, it had been the end.

Robbie sucked in a breath as she stared at her reflection. Tears shone in her eyes and her lip quivered, but she frowned hard and didn't let any of them fall. It wasn't *him*. Not anymore. It was the loss of her dream life with the man she'd thought was her other half.

"No such thing, Roberta," she muttered. "That's just the crap you make up."

It was good crap, though. She loved romance novels, and she loved writing them. She just didn't love Damian and Velvet anymore because, to her, they were a shadow of what she'd thought about her and Trent. What she'd wanted to be true rather than what was.

Her shadow king, willing to fight any evil for her. Willing to risk his immortal soul for her touch.

She'd always wanted to believe in romance, but it seemed as if romance didn't want to believe in her. The harder she'd fought for it, the harder it was to grasp.

Well, she was done fighting. Romance had proven it wasn't meant for her. She could write about it, but she couldn't have it.

She gave herself another hard look in the mirror. Insidious little comments floated through her mind, telling her that she looked too pale, too tired. That she needed to work harder on her appearance.

She picked up the makeup brush she'd put down, swiped it over her nose, then stopped in mid-motion. What the hell was she doing? That was Trent talking, tearing her down, making her feel small.

She dropped the brush and lifted her chin. It didn't matter what anyone thought, least of all the man living in her guest room. She'd spent too many years of her life caring about a man's opinion of everything she did.

No more.

———

"WHO KNOWS YOU LIVE HERE?" Dax asked as he drove through the small town of Mill Landing. The sun was peeking out from behind a cloud, and everything looked far cheerier than it had yesterday when he'd arrived.

The town didn't sit on the Chesapeake Bay, but on one of its tributaries. The Choptank River flowed past the town. There was a picturesque Main Street with a couple of restaurants and tourist shops along with a hair salon, an art gallery, three antique stores, and an ice cream parlor.

"A few people, I imagine. Aside from my family and friends, the townspeople know. I don't post about my personal life on social media, but it's possible someone else posted that I live in Mill Landing."

Dax nodded. He'd spoken with her assistant while she was showering. A quick text to Ian had resulted in the assistant's number appearing in his texts a few moments later. Dax hadn't asked Robbie because he'd wanted to speak to Autumn without Robbie first preparing her.

Fortunately, Autumn Pinkney was a complete professional. She kept good records about the kinds of mail Robbie got. There'd been a lot of hate mail, both email and snail, since the release of *The Vampire King*, which was why Daphne Linden had contacted Ian in the first place. But Robbie hadn't received any truly serious threats that had any of them calling the police.

Not until yesterday.

Dax had asked Autumn to forward everything she considered hateful and to scan in the written letters and send those along too. She'd done it efficiently and quickly. Dax had been reading and sorting the letters as Robbie emerged from her shower.

He hadn't told her that's what he was doing. He wouldn't unless he found something. She'd made it clear she didn't want to know about the hate mail her assistant received, and he wasn't going to cross that line unless he had to.

"Have you ever noticed anyone hanging around your house? Following you?"

She turned from where she'd been looking at the passing scenery. "No. I take Lucy for long walks on my property and I have never seen anything. Footprints sometimes, but I have thirty acres and not all of it is fenced. Hunters can stray onto the property. Hikers too. There's a trail a few yards from my property line in the back."

"These footprints aren't close to the house then?"

"Not really. In the woods usually, on the trail of an animal. If it's near the hiking trail, then it's most likely someone straying off the path. The woods are very pretty around here, and there's good fishing in the creek that runs through the property."

"Why don't you have a security system?"

She sighed. "I should, I know. The house is partially wired for it. My ex-husband had the wiring added to the addition and also to other parts of the house where we took down walls. It's not completely finished though, and getting the system never seemed urgent enough. Lucy is a great house alarm."

"Yes, but if you'd had security cameras, we could have seen who entered."

"I've lived in this house for almost five years and never had a problem." She sniffed, but it was an angry sniff, not a tearful one. "I moved to the middle of nowhere for peace and quiet. When we lived in Virginia, after my book blew up, people would knock on the door and want to talk to me. We moved to a gated subdivision, but it wasn't as private as we'd hoped. Then I found the farm online five years ago and it seemed perfect. It *has* been perfect. Until yesterday."

"No randoms knocking on your door at this house, then?"

"No."

Didn't mean someone hadn't found her anyway. He'd found her address online, but he'd had to dig pretty deep to do it. If someone knew she lived in Maryland and dug through property records, they could find her. It would be a laborious process, but it was possible.

There were other ways for a savvy stalker to find what they wanted, and that included getting to the people in Robbie's life. In his experience, people were often more trusting than they should be if they thought someone had a legit reason for information. All someone had to do was lie convincingly, and one of the people in Robbie's life would spill information like a leaky sieve.

She'd admitted she didn't know how many people knew her location, which meant any one of them could be the source of the info.

"Do you have any enemies?" he asked as he took the turn she indicated would take them to the Food Lion.

She didn't look at him. "I don't think so. I had a stalker a few years ago, but they went quiet and I haven't heard anything in about three years."

His senses perked up. "A stalker? You didn't mention that in the police report."

She bowed her head. "It didn't seem relevant. I haven't gotten anything in a long time, like I said. It was another writer. Pretty sure it was. I got a flurry of letters when the first book came out then more when the next three books dropped. Then it stopped. Like it never happened. I guess they got on with their life or something."

He didn't like it. She hadn't heard from her stalker in three years, and two more books had been published. But he couldn't rule out that this person had resurfaced.

"Why did you think it was another writer?"

"They talked about plots and word choices and berated me for writing the books a certain way. And they suggested I'd stolen the original idea from them, but they never said where I might have done this. They also threatened to tell the world." Her expression hardened. "I didn't steal it. I spent years dreaming about my stories before I wrote anything. It hurt for anyone to accuse me otherwise."

"I think if someone had proof, they'd have produced it by now. Do you still have the letters?"

She shook her head. "I burned them. They were so hateful. After the last one, that's when I told Autumn not to give me the mail anymore without going through it. I wanted her to read it and only send the good ones."

It made sense, but he hated that she'd gotten rid of the evidence.

"Did you report it to the police at the time?"

"Yes. They probably have copies. Or not, since they never arrested anyone."

"Okay." He'd ask Ian to look into it. If there were copies, he wanted to read them. "Anyone else we need to consider?"

Her hands clenched in her lap. "There are a great many people who don't like me much right now."

"Because of Damian and Velvet."

Her head swiveled toward him. "Yes, Damian and Velvet. What did Daphne tell you about that?"

"Nothing. I've read the books, and I can see why your readers are a little upset. Neal Bolton? Really?"

She groaned as she dropped her head in her hands. "You're supposed to be on *my* side."

"I am on your side. I read the books because I was told to in prep for this assignment. You had a good thing going and then, *blam*, you blew it out of the water. Didn't make a lot of sense."

"I'll fix it in the next book," she muttered, gazing out the window.

He pulled into the parking lot and found a space. Then he shut off the vehicle and turned toward her. "But you don't want to, do you?"

She hesitated a moment then shook her head. "I'm tired of Damian. Tired of Velvet. I'm not the same person I was when I first conceived them. I want to move on."

"So move on."

She snorted softly. "It's not that easy. I have a contract and I gave my word. I can't go back on it."

"Okay. Write the book they want you to write and then move on."

"Said like someone who's never written a book." She threw her hands in the air. "Don't you think I've tried that? I stare at a blank page every day and nothing happens."

"Sorry. You're right. I don't have a clue how it works."

She rubbed the heel of her hand against one temple. "I don't know why I'm telling you these things. You don't care."

"Maybe because you need to tell someone and I'm here? And I want to know. It helps me figure out what kind of person I might be looking for."

She was still frowning. "Maybe."

She seemed small and defeated. He didn't like it. He didn't know why he cared. This was a job and he had to stay objective, but he had an urge to soothe her anyway.

"I like the books," he told her. "I was surprised by the twist in the last one, but my life isn't ruined, okay? I think you have a lot of readers like that. Some are angry, sure. But it takes a twisted person to Photoshop you into a coffin and leave it in your house with a death threat. I'm going to find that person and put a stop to it."

She nodded but didn't look at him. "I don't know who would do something like that. I've thought it could be a local, someone who knows me in passing, knows my habits. Or it could be someone who's been watching me, right? Someone who found where I live and came to harass me. I suppose it could be my original stalker too. He or she could have resurfaced, angered anew by what I did."

The possibilities weren't endless, but they were many. He had to consider them.

"What about your ex-husband? Your family? Anyone there come to mind?"

Her mouth tightened at the corners. He didn't like having to ask these questions, but he needed to know if it was possible.

"Trent bought a sailing yacht. Last I heard, he was in the Pacific with Kimberlee, his new wife. I think he's got it pretty good out there, so I doubt it's him. My parents aren't the nicest people on the planet, but it's not really in their best interests to kill me. My estate is in trust, and they aren't the beneficiaries. Which they know.

I give them money from time to time, but if I die, they won't get any."

He really wanted to know more about her relationship with her parents. Another time, maybe. "Who is the beneficiary?"

"I started a charity to help women and children in need and another to help animals. All my money goes there, with a couple of bequests to friends. I doubt any of them are trying to off me for the money since only my attorney knows who gets what."

He didn't know what it was like to be in possession of a great deal of money, but he imagined that it changed people. Not always for the better. But Robbie seemed a lot more grounded and humble than he'd expected. He'd known she was reclusive, but she could've still been a snotty bitch. She wasn't though.

"That's good of you," he said. "The charities, I mean."

"I've been blessed. I want to give back." She unclipped the seatbelt. "Can the rest of this wait? I want to do the shopping before the store gets busy."

She didn't wait for an answer before she opened the car door. She was out and moving toward the store before he could stop her.

Exposing herself to unseen danger without a second thought. Dax threw open his door and bolted after her.

Chapter Six

SHE WAS A THIRD OF THE WAY ACROSS THE PARKING LOT when Dax caught up to her.

"Hang on a minute." He grabbed her arm when she didn't break stride.

She tried to shy away, but he held on and forced her between two parked SUVs that provided cover. She jerked out of his grip and he let her, but she didn't try to walk away.

"What?" she asked, her eyes fixed on the middle of his chest. Refusing to look at him of course.

A knot twisted tight inside him. He tilted her chin up with a finger until he could see her eyes. Dark eyes. Wounded eyes. Her lashes dropped after a long moment, shielding her gaze.

"Why won't you look at me?"

It wasn't what he'd intended to say, but her response bothered him. Was she afraid of him? He hadn't been a hard-ass with her. Hadn't gotten too close to her until now because he sensed it bothered her.

She lifted her lids again and their eyes locked. "I'm looking at you now."

"Yes, but you don't like making eye contact. Not for long."

As if to prove him right, her gaze skittered away. She forced it back, but he could tell it was an effort.

"It's not personal. It's just me. It makes me uncomfortable to look people in the eye. Always has."

"Okay," he said gently, unwilling to push for more just now. "I should have explained how this works better than I did, but you don't get out of the car until I tell you it's safe. You don't go anywhere without me, and you don't leave my side without my okay. It's for your safety."

She looked skeptical. "Do you really think someone would attack me in broad daylight in the middle of town?"

"I don't know what this person would do. It's my job to keep you safe, and that means I call the shots in public places where you're exposed."

Her eyes flashed hot. "Do you like bossing women around?"

"I boss everyone around when I'm responsible for their safety," he ground out. "I don't care *who* they are."

She didn't reply for a long moment. He got the impression she was turning over what he'd said. Her shoulders slumped in defeat. "I didn't mean to take off like that. I get uncomfortable when I have to talk about myself."

She didn't like to make eye contact and she didn't like talking about herself. He didn't know what had made both those things difficult for her, but he didn't think it was good. Some of it could be inherent shyness or introversion, but she didn't seem typically shy. She had grit, and she hadn't been cowering when he'd arrived yesterday. There was strength in her, but there was also uncertainty.

As if someone had tried to smother any self-confidence she might possess.

"I have to ask questions to try and understand who might want to hurt you. I'm sorry if it makes you uncomfortable."

She drew in a breath. "I'm not an idiot, I promise. I know you're doing your job. It's the other stuff that bothers me. The publicity stunt of you being my boyfriend. Having to pretend we're a couple. I don't want to do it."

He didn't like it either, but he understood why her publisher wanted it that way. He could still do his job while sticking close and pretending they were together.

"Gotta admit, I'm not used to that reaction from a woman. But if you're worried, I'll do most of the work. You just hold my hand and smile from time to time, and I'll play the part of protective boyfriend," he told her with a smile.

She returned the smile in what he thought was probably relief. His chest tightened. He'd only seen her smile in her author picture, but that hadn't been real. This one wasn't big, but it was genuine. It was also brief, and it winked out as quickly as it appeared.

"It's a bit humiliating, if I'm honest. The entire notion that I need a boyfriend or I'll look bitter and sad.

Nobody would think to tell a man he had to have a pretend girlfriend so he didn't look pitiful at a conference."

"They might. Depends on the man, right?"

"Maybe, but I doubt it. Still, Daphne ordered tall, dark, and handsome, and here you are."

"At your service."

He held out his hand. She stared at it like it might bite.

"Why don't we start practicing right now?" he said as gently as he could. "Hold my hand until we get into the store. I'll push the cart and you won't have to touch me again today."

It took her a moment, but she put her hand in his. A spark flared beneath his skin as he tightened his fingers around hers. She blinked and swallowed as if she'd felt something too.

Then they were inside the store and he was pushing a cart, following Robbie Sharpe around like a trained dog. Wondering the whole time if he'd imagined that spark or if it'd been real.

And just what the hell it meant.

ROBBIE DIDN'T LIKE grocery shopping on the best of days.

Today was not the best of days, but at least it was over fast. They got into the Food Lion when there weren't many people around, shopped for the rest of the week, and got the hell out.

There was a time when Robbie used to like grocery shopping.

Maybe that was a lie. Maybe she hadn't liked it so much as she hadn't loathed it. While Trent worked, she'd take her carefully made lists and go pick up things for the week.

Trent didn't like leftovers, so she'd had to plan meals to ensure there weren't any. Or weren't any he had to eat. He'd also liked his food hot and on the table when he got home. She hadn't minded back then because she'd loved the way he'd made her feel secure. She could stay home all day, take care of the house, cook, and dream about her stories.

Sometimes she missed the way she'd felt back then. Not the part where she'd worried about disappointing Trent. The part where she couldn't wait to dream about Damian LeBeaux. She *had* infused a bit of Trent into him. The good parts. What she'd thought were the good parts.

Velvet Asbury was the woman she'd wanted to be. Brave, strong, unafraid. Velvet stood up to an ancient vampire and intrigued him so much he let her live. Then he fell in love with her.

Perfection.

Except that no love was perfect, no relationship free from peril. She'd certainly learned that lesson over the years.

Robbie put away the last of the groceries, gave Lucy a chew bone for her teeth, and slipped Ollie a treat, despite knowing he'd hound her for the rest of the day for another one.

Dax had excused himself after helping her carry everything in. He'd asked if she needed help putting it away, but she'd said no. She'd needed a minute without him nearby so she could breathe.

He'd walked away and she'd watched him go, her gaze slipping from the broad swath of his shoulders to his fine ass encased in denim. Dax Freed was a walking wet dream if you were into that kind of thing.

Robbie sniffed. Her sex drive wasn't dead, but it was definitely in hibernation. She hadn't entertained anything but a vibrator in her lady parts in about four years now, sad to say.

That's the only thing that explained the shock of awareness that'd zapped through her when Dax took her hand outside the store. She'd felt a lightning bolt of heat arrow into parts of her that had made her want to gasp.

She'd managed not to, but her skin had burned every step of the way into the grocery store. She'd been relieved when he'd let her go and grabbed the cart. True to his word, he hadn't touched her again.

But she'd wanted him to. That was the most damnable thing about it. She'd *wanted* him to brush against her, even accidentally. Wanted him to take her hand or put a finger under her chin again.

She'd craved it, and that was definitely alarming. The man was here to protect her and find out who'd broken into her house, not romance her for real.

As if she wanted that anyway. Robbie sniffed again. She most certainly did *not*. Men were a hassle she no longer needed in her life. If all she did was get cozy with a vibrator from time to time, she could live a long and happy life free of relationship drama.

A fair trade, really.

She grabbed a Diet Coke and a box of crackers and went into her office. Surely, if she was feeling this jumpy inside—not to mention thinking about the way a man's jeans hugged his package, the soft denim cupping him like a lover—then it meant she must have something to give to the book. If she could just channel the energy into writing a few pages, she'd feel so much better.

Robbie powered up the laptop and opened the manuscript. The blank page stared back at her, the cursor blinking. Taunting her. She closed her eyes and thought of Dax Freed in his faded jeans and plaid button-down with the black T-shirt underneath.

Romance novel material.

He was, and he was in her house. If she could just *think*, she could make Damian talk to her again. She felt the whispers of Damian LeBeaux tickling her mind, but she couldn't grab hold of anything solid.

After an hour of trying to force it, Robbie snapped the laptop shut with a growl and flung herself from the desk. She needed to go for a walk. Needed to clear her head. Tears of frustration pricked her eyes as she stalked out of her office and went to the mudroom to grab Lucy's leash.

Lucy whirled excitedly as Robbie clipped the leash in place. She shoved her feet into her hiking boots and opened the door.

The sun was out today, but the ground was still wet and the humidity was high. She could choose the path that led to the road, but that would be hotter than walking through the woods. Lucy led the way along familiar paths, sniffing every blade of grass as she went, tail wagging.

Birds chirped in the trees and the woods smelled fresh and clean. Robbie breathed it in, her tension melting a bit more with every step she took. *This* was why she'd wanted to move to the country. To be in nature, where she didn't have to see a soul if she didn't want to, and to have her own space to walk and think.

She thought about the writers' conference next week and the book tour after, and she wanted to weep at the thought of leaving her home. She'd let Daphne talk her into it before *The Vampire King* released, and now she regretted it.

But Daphne and Spring Books had been too good to her over the years to let them down now. Without Daphne, Robbie might have written a first book that fizzled as soon as it hit the market. She might still be with Trent, still scribbling away in her spare time while he worked at the architecture firm.

Robbie shuddered at the thought. What would she be if she hadn't ever written down her dreams about Damian LeBeaux?

Lucy stopped sniffing and lifted her head, sampling the air around her with interest. Something crackled in the leaves, and Robbie spun to look, her heart jumping.

It was a squirrel. He lifted onto his hind legs to look at them both then scampered up a tree as Lucy lunged against the leash.

"No, Lucy. Leave the squirrel alone."

Lucy snorted and barked, and Robbie tugged her away from the tree. A few moments later, she was ranging out in front of Robbie again.

When she halted and sniffed the air a second time in a small clearing, Robbie indulged her. Probably another squirrel or a chipmunk searching for lunch.

A twig snapped as if someone had stepped on it and Robbie whirled.

A shotgun boomed.

Chapter Seven

Lucy barked and lunged against her leash as Robbie dropped to the forest floor, heart pounding madly. Someone had fired a weapon and it was close by. Too close.

She had to get out, but she couldn't run when she didn't know if someone was waiting for movement so they could fire again. She scanned the clearing, searching for a flash of clothing—and then she spotted the downed tree just outside the clearing.

If she could get there, she could hide behind it.

Unless they come from that direction.

Robbie closed her eyes as fear welled in her belly. *Just go!*

"Lucy," she hissed, tugging the dog toward her as she scrambled for the tree. It was a fat trunk lying on its side with vines and moss obscuring parts of it. Lucy didn't stop barking as Robbie hauled her behind it.

She couldn't hear anything now. The forest had gotten deathly quiet. Her blood pounded in her ears so hard that she couldn't make out any sounds beyond the whooshing in her veins.

Robbie wrapped her hand around Lucy's muzzle to quiet her, holding her against her body. She kissed the dog's head, trembling. Waiting.

Berating herself. Why had she left the house without telling Dax?

Another twig snapped. Muffled footsteps sounded against the leaves. She tried to make herself smaller, tried to meld with the tree trunk, but Lucy was wriggling and it was only a matter of time before they were discovered.

The footsteps came closer. They halted suddenly, as if someone was searching. *For her.*

Robbie held her breath, hugging Lucy tighter. The dog started to whine.

"Shh," Robbie whispered, throat tight.

A moment later a dark shape loomed over the tree and Robbie knew she was going to die. She'd ventured outside without telling Dax, and someone had found her.

Stupid, stupid, stupid!

Lucy broke free of Robbie's grip. It took a moment to realize the dog's tail wagged a mile a minute as she snorted happily. Robbie tilted her face up, blinking into the scowling features of Dax Freed.

She melted into the forest floor. Relief pounded through her as Dax offered a hand to help her up. She brushed leaves from her clothes. Tried not to think of the spiders that had surely crawled across her body while she'd lain in hiding.

"What the hell are you doing out here, Robbie?"

"I needed a break, so I took Lucy for a walk."

He was still scowling. "You're supposed to fucking tell me when you want to leave the house. I can't protect you if I don't know where you are."

She dropped her gaze, mortification rolling over her. "I'm sorry. I wasn't thinking. When I heard the gunshot, I realized I'd messed up. I panicked."

He took a step closer, until she could feel the heat and anger rolling from him. "And how do you think hearing gunfire made me feel when I knew you were out here alone?" He growled something unintelligible and stepped back. "You could have gotten killed, Robbie. Whoever broke into your house could have been waiting out here, watching for you. Did you even consider that?"

Her face flamed. She should have considered it, but she'd been frustrated about the book and doing what she usually did when she was blocked. She'd gone for a walk. Like an idiot.

"It didn't occur to me." Those words were hard to say.

Another gunshot blasted, farther away this time. Robbie spun at the sound, backing into Dax. He put his hands on her shoulders, steadying her.

"It's turkey season. Those are hunters."

"I thought…" She swallowed, unable to finish the sentence.

"I'm sorry you have to think that way at all, but it's safer for now. You have to consider every time you leave the house that someone is waiting for an opportunity. You can't go anywhere without me, Robbie."

His hands on her shoulders were gentle but firm. He'd bent his head to speak to her, his voice rasping close to her ear. It sent shivers down her spine.

"I won't do it again." She dropped her chin and forced out a breath. "Dammit, I hate TSTL characters. Looks like I am one."

"TSTL?"

"Too stupid to live."

Dax snorted. His grip on her eased, and she turned to face him. He really was something to look at, especially when he was laughing instead of growling.

Though there was always a time and place for growling. *Stop it.*

"I've never heard that term before," he told her.

"It's common in romance. It's usually the heroine who does something idiotic so the hero has to save her. She's too stupid to live and keeps proving it, but he saves her every time. It's frustrating because the only reason the character does stupid things is *so* he can save her. It's even worse when she's supposed to be smart in everything else."

"I don't think you're TSTL. I think you aren't accustomed to having anyone around, or asking permission to do what you usually do."

He certainly knew how to make her feel better, though she *was* an idiot for venturing out on her own. Even with Lucy, and even in her own backyard.

"You're being nice about it. Thank you."

He gave her one of those chin nods that guys did. "Last time though. Do it again, and I won't be nice at all. You've had two warnings. You shouldn't need a third."

She wanted to be annoyed with him, but he was right. If she didn't want to be TSTL for real, she'd had all the warnings she needed about not venturing away from his side.

"It feels like house arrest. But you won't have to tell me again. I promise."

"You can still go for walks. I need to go with you, and there's a perimeter we'll have to stay within. I've got a surveillance system arriving today from HQ. We'll get the cameras and equipment in place, then we'll have a better handle on who's coming and going. If this person tries to get close again, we'll catch them."

Lucy was pulling on the leash, the drama done for now as far as she was concerned. She had things to pee on. Dax noticed and nodded in the direction of the house.

"Let's head back. She can finish on the way."

They started to walk, Dax staying beside her except for the places where the trail squeezed down and he had to let her go first. He stayed close, though. She could feel his eyes on her, feel the heat of his stare on the back of her head.

She told herself it was silly. She didn't feel any such thing. She wrote that kind of thing so often that it seemed true, but it wasn't. There was no invisible thread connecting her and Dax. No spark of electricity when they touched. There was nothing but her overactive imagination and a lingering loneliness that urged her to see connections where there were none.

She refused to fall for that crap ever again. Look what had happened the last time she let herself be fanciful about a man.

When they reached the house, a black van sat beside Dax's truck. Robbie hesitated, but Dax put a hand against her back and urged her forward.

"It's my guys. Nothing to fear."

Robbie pulled in a breath. More strangers. More intrusion. The closer they got, the tighter her chest grew. She stopped and turned blindly to Dax. Lucy was looking at the van with interest.

"I'll, um, be in my office. Don't let me disturb your work."

"You don't want to meet the guys, do you?"

She shook her head. "It's not personal."

He scratched his chin. "Well, I understand that, darlin', but since you're headed to Vegas in a few days and have to sit on a panel with hundreds of people staring at you from the audience, think you might want to practice your people skills a little?"

Her gaze flew to his. There was humor in his hazel eyes, but there was concern too. It was the concern that nearly undid her. If he were pushing just to push, just to be a dick, that would be one thing.

"I, uh…." She dropped her chin and nodded. "Yes, of course. You're right. I'm going to have to pretend I like people when I'm in Vegas, so why not start now?"

Dax laughed. "Hey, at least you're honest. Promise they aren't so bad."

He took Lucy's leash and propelled Robbie forward. The van doors opened and two guys got out. Both tall, both handsome. One had shaggy dark hair that curled up at the ends and the other sported an almost military cut. They were smiling.

"Jared. Ty. This is Roberta Sharpe. Ms. Sharpe, these are my teammates. Two guys you can count on to get your security installed and working right with as little interruption as possible."

"Ms. Sharpe," Ty said. "Pleased to meet you."

"Call me Robbie. I'm pleased to meet you both."

"It's a pleasure," Jared added.

Dax whispered loud enough for everyone to hear, "Jared's a bookworm. I don't think he reads romance, but he likes big books."

"And I cannot lie," Jared replied, grinning.

Robbie recognized the joke. It was a song from the early 90s about big butts.

"It's not for everyone," Robbie said.

"I haven't had the pleasure of reading your work, but my mom was a huge romance fan when she was alive. She loved historical and paranormal, so I'm sure she would have loved you."

"I'm sorry she's no longer with you." Robbie knew the right things to say, but they always sounded hollow to her.

"Thank you. I appreciate that."

"I, um… I need to get back to work. It was nice to meet you both."

Both men nodded again, smiling. Robbie's heart thrummed as sweat pooled between her breasts.

"I'll walk you inside," Dax said, his hand on her

back again. Burning into her. "Be out in a few," he said to the guys.

They were already walking around to the back of the van to retrieve their equipment. "We'll be here," Ty said.

Robbie stepped up to the back door and turned the knob. Nothing happened. Dax reached past her to insert the key into the lock.

"Always lock the door."

She hadn't given him a spare key, but there was one hanging near Lucy's leash. Her house and car keys were together on the same ring in her purse, which made them bulky for pockets, so she kept a single key near the back door. He'd clearly found it on his way to search for her. It was no use to tell him she usually locked the door. She hadn't because he'd been there.

Robbie stared at the muscles of his arm as he twisted the lock. She could feel his heat where he curved around her, smell his scent as he bent close. A tremor vibrated through her. She had a dark urge to turn her head, tilt her face up, and see if he would kiss her.

How many times had she written scenes like this? How many times had she drawn out the sexual tension between the characters, pulling it taut, waiting for it to break?

Stop being fanciful. For God's sake, Robbie, channel this into THE BOOK.

The door opened and Robbie nearly stumbled through it in her haste to get away from Dax. She pretended it was Lucy's fault, but of course it wasn't.

The dog had burst through the door when it opened, but she hadn't tripped Robbie or tugged her off balance.

Dax put a steadying hand on her waist. And, oh damn, that was *soooo* much worse.

"Careful," he said.

Robbie stepped away and turned. "I'm fine. Thank you. How long will it take to install the equipment?"

"A couple of hours, probably. We're going to put trail cameras on the driveway and the path through the woods, and a few sensors and cameras closer to the house as well as on the barn. We'll also install window and door sensors and a security camera on each side of the house."

He didn't turn to go, and she couldn't seem to tear herself away. She'd unclipped Lucy, who'd taken off for the kitchen.

"You did good meeting Ty and Jared. It was good practice for next week."

Ridiculously, she glowed with his praise. She tucked a stray lock of hair behind her ear and ducked her head. "I've become a hermit out here. You were right that I needed to say hello. Thank you."

He winked at her then grinned big. "I love it when you tell me I'm right. You know not to leave the house without me, right?"

"Yes."

"Text me if you need anything. I'll be at your side in less than a minute. Lock the door behind me."

He stepped outside and she did as he said. Then she watched him stroll across the yard, her heart beating just a little too quickly after their exchange.

She liked him. It was a surprise because she'd thought more than anything that she would resent his presence.

But she really didn't. In fact, she liked it more than she should.

Chapter Eight

DAX AND THE GUYS WORKED THROUGH THE AFTERNOON to put up the cameras and rig the doors and windows with sensors. It wasn't hard work so much as tedious.

Of course the guys teased him about protecting a romance novelist who wrote about steamy sex, about how he needed to guard his virtue around her. He let them rib him for a while, but then he thought of her expression last night when she'd told him how people treated her for what she wrote.

"Dude, not cool," Dax said when he'd finally had enough. "Are you saying because she writes romance novels that it makes her a sex maniac? She deals with shit like that all the time because of what she writes."

His teammates shot each other a look. "Uh," Jared began. "Not really. We're just having fun."

"I know, but maybe think about it a little bit?"

Jared and Ty looked puzzled, so he continued.

"She writes about an ancient vampire and the woman he loves. Should I be worried she's going to turn me into a vampire? Or should I think she might murder me because she has dead bodies in her books?"

"Of course not," Ty replied.

"Then I don't need to worry about my virtue either, right? The woman writes about death and fantasy creatures, and nobody thinks she's going to kill anyone or turn them into a vampire. Why is sex different?"

"You're right," Jared said with a nod. "It's fiction. An author doesn't have to experience all the things in their books for it to sound authentic."

"Right. I'd have thought you of all people would know that since you read so much."

Jared held up both hands. "Got it, Dax. My apologies."

"Mine too," Ty said. "She seems nice if a bit awkward."

"She's reclusive, remember? I think people make her nervous, though I'm not quite sure why yet."

"She's an introvert," Jared said. "Success came very quickly for her. There have probably been a lot of people who tried to take advantage."

"Like the ex-husband," Dax replied. "He left her for a younger woman and got half her estate in the divorce settlement."

"Ouch. That would tend to make me not want to be around people either," Ty said. "She probably doesn't know who she can trust."

They continued to work and the conversation moved to other topics. Jared's wedding to Libby. Ty's wedding to Cassie. Both men were in the midst of planning events—or agreeing to plans their fiancées made—and both were eager to take that step.

Dax envied them their certainty. Long ago he'd had someone he cared about, but he'd screwed it all up with his inability to commit. He'd put off getting engaged while he joined the military and did his time so he could have money for college.

He'd thought she was on the same page, but Tara had fallen for someone else while he was gone. She'd sent him a Dear Dax letter after he'd been in the military for two years.

He'd spent a lot of time thinking that if he'd only told Tara he loved her, if he'd asked her to marry him—hell, if he'd married her and taken her with him—they'd still be together. But Tara was married to a good man who worked hard to take care of her and their two kids. Dax was happy for her. It'd taken him a long time to get there, but he was.

They'd been high school sweethearts, each other's firsts. Tara had been there for him through all the shit with his stepfather. She'd understood.

And he'd lost her because he'd taken her love for granted. In all the time they'd spent together, he'd never once said the words. He'd always said something stupid in return like "You too," or, "Ditto, babe."

He'd taken her for granted. The words hadn't come until it was too late. Until he'd called her and blurted them over the phone, feeling sick the whole time.

She'd sighed softly. *"Dax, I know you care. It's not enough. I need someone who won't hold back. I'm sorry."*

He'd deserved her gentle rebuke. Took him a long

time to realize it, but he had. He shouldn't have had so much trouble saying the words, but he'd been angry back then. Angry that his stepfather treated his little brother like gold while ignoring him, and angry that his mother let it happen.

"That's the last of it," Jared said, wiping his arm across his forehead. "Anybody tries to get to her now, we'll know about it."

Ty tossed the screwdriver he was holding into the toolbox. "Man, I'm starved. What about y'all?"

"I could eat," Jared said.

Dax was surprised to find he was hungry too. "Don't you have to get home to your women?"

"Nope," Ty said. "Cassie's filming videos and told me to fend for myself tonight."

"Libby's working on a big project for a client. She'll eat leftovers, but I don't have to."

"Think you could go pick something up and bring it back?" Dax asked. "I'll check with Robbie and see if she wants anything."

"Can do," Jared said.

Dax sent a text. He wanted to go and see what Robbie was up to, but he decided a text was better. Her reply was swift.

Robbie: I made dinner. There's enough for everyone.

Dax could feel his eyebrows climbing his forehead. *You want them to stay? To come inside and eat at your table?*

Robbie: <eyeroll emoji> I'm awkward, not inhuman. Besides, as you pointed out, the three of you are nothing like the numbers I'll face in Vegas and on tour. I need to start somewhere.

Dax looked up to find the other two waiting expectantly. He shrugged. "Looks like the reclusive Roberta Sharpe made dinner for us."

Ty's eyebrows rose. "No shit. Can she cook?"

Jared elbowed him. "Even if she can't, we aren't saying no."

"I honestly have no idea," Dax replied. "But like Jared said, we aren't saying no."

Ty grumbled. "Okay, but if it's bad I reserve the right to pick at my plate and stop at a drive-through on the way home."

"Fine. Just don't gag when she's looking, okay?"

Ty waggled his eyebrows. "No promises."

Jared elbowed him again. "Shut it, man. You wouldn't do any such thing."

"True." He grinned at Dax. "I just like teasing our serious friend here."

Dax rolled his eyes. "Let's go, douchebags. Be nice or I'll brick your phones so hard you'll think your name's Fred Flintstone."

ROBBIE SURVIVED dinner with three big, strapping men sitting at the table with her. Ty and Jared were polite, she relaxed in their company as the evening wore on, and they seemed to really appreciate what she'd cooked.

She hadn't planned to do it, but she kept thinking of Dax telling her she had to start somewhere. She wasn't the sort of person who did anything by half measures. When anyone challenged her, she threw herself into it.

Quietly, in her own way. But she definitely rose to the challenge. What was more challenging than cooking a nice meal for men she didn't really know but who looked like they could be half of a SEAL Team ready for action?

She'd stood in the pantry, sizing up her stock, and set about making a big pot of beef stroganoff. It was a meal she'd made for Trent that he'd loved. One that he didn't mind leftovers from. But only once. Never twice.

She'd whipped it together, cut up a fresh loaf of French bread she'd grabbed at the store, threw together a salad, and served it all up to three hungry men who'd finished everything on their plates and asked for more.

She didn't have to cook for anyone these days if she didn't want to, but she'd decided it was a good way to practice those people skills Dax had rightly said she was going to need to survive Vegas. She'd worked on her small talk, asking where they were from and if they enjoyed working for a personal security firm.

Once the meal was over, they thanked her profusely and Dax walked them out. Robbie stood in the empty space where they'd been and let out a long breath. It hadn't been bad, though. They were interesting, and they didn't make her uncomfortable. Not after the first awkward moments when she'd tried to force herself to make small talk.

Dax had taken up the charge for her, easing her into it, and it had worked. She'd relaxed without realizing it. When Dax returned, she was still in the kitchen, scraping plates and setting them in the sink.

"Let me help," he said as he came over to her side and picked up a plate.

Ty and Jared had offered to help. She'd refused because she'd been taught that guests never helped with clean up, but she didn't say no to Dax. He wasn't a guest anyway.

"Thank you."

"Are you putting them in the dishwasher?"

"No. They have a silver rim and I prefer to hand wash them."

He grinned. "You used the good plates on us?"

She felt a little bit of heat staining her cheeks. "I love pretty dishes, but I never get to use them. I thought, why not? It makes clean up harder, though."

"It'll go quicker with two of us. Do you want to wash or dry?"

"I'll dry since I know where they go."

They worked in silence for a few minutes. Robbie liked that he'd offered to help. He seemed to be the kind of man who did his share. He'd followed her around the grocery store earlier, pushing the cart and not bitching or complaining that he hated shopping. He was being paid to protect her, which meant he had to go where she went, but he could have acted like he had better things to do than shop for food.

Robbie thought of a million questions she wanted to ask, but she didn't voice any of them. Did she really need to know more about her bodyguard than she already knew? He wasn't going to be around forever, and she didn't need to get close to him.

"You didn't have to cook for us," he said after he

handed her a fork to dry. "But I'm glad you did. It was great."

"I used to cook all the time. I've gotten out of practice, but beef stroganoff is a meal I'm always confident about."

"Ty was worried when I told him you'd made dinner. He thought you might be a terrible cook."

Robbie laughed. "No wonder he looked a little dubious when he sat down. Since he ate two helpings, I'm going to assume he was pleasantly surprised."

"I think we all were."

She cocked her head. "Why?"

"I dunno, really. Guess we thought somebody like you would have a chef or something."

"I wasn't born with money. I was raised in an average middle class family. Like many Americans, my parents were in debt up to their eyeballs. Eating out was a luxury. I learned to cook from my mom, and I cooked every night for my husband before my first book took off."

Dax looked at her. "You cooked every night for him? Did he cook for you?"

She liked that his mind went there. Said a lot about him. "No. Trent didn't cook. Period."

"Shame. Cooking for your woman is one of the sexiest things you can do."

Robbie blinked. Somewhere down below, in a region she didn't want to name, a flame kindled. "Are you just saying that for my benefit because I'm a romance author?"

"Nope." He handed her a dish. "I mean it. If I go

out with the same woman a few times, one of the things I do is cook her dinner. It shows a level of concern that's more than superficial. Cooking for someone is one of the most intimate things you can do."

Robbie's heart thudded. Heat rolled through her. She was too young for a hot flash, but damn. This must be what they felt like. "That's... perceptive of you."

He snorted. "What, you think I can't be perceptive? Is it because I'm male or because I'm so pretty I must be shallow?"

Oh lord, he was too much.

"I don't really know you, so how can I say?" She sniffed. In fact, he *was* perceptive. Damned perceptive if the way he'd stepped in when she'd felt awkward tonight was any indication.

"Diplomatic answer," he said with a smile.

Robbie dried the last plate and stacked it on top of the others. Then she took a bowl from his wet hands. "Who taught you to cook then?" she asked, determined to move the conversation along.

"YouTube."

"Really?"

"Really. I didn't learn growing up, and I got tired of eating the same things all the time when I was on my own or the Army wasn't feeding me, so I figured I'd learn how to cook for myself."

"I watch a lot of YouTube videos when I want to know how to do something for my books. You can learn anything there."

"Yep. I'm not Bobby Flay, but I do all right."

"What's your signature dish when you're cooking for someone?"

"Steak on the grill with a baked potato and roasted broccolini or green beans. If the weather isn't right for grilling, then I like to make sausage and chicken jambalaya or shrimp and grits. In the winter, it's potato and corn chowder with Old Bay toast."

It took Robbie a moment to realize her jaw was hanging open. She snapped it shut again and dried a spatula. "That's quite a menu," she said. *Old Bay toast?*

"I like to have options."

"Don't suppose I could talk you into making any of that while you're here? Just because I want to eat it, not because we're dating for real or anything." She wanted to groan inside. Could she sound any more awkward?

Dax laughed. "Well, we *are* dating, even if it's not real. Tomorrow good?"

"Tomorrow is perfect considering you guys ate all the stroganoff."

He winked. "Then it's a date."

Robbie didn't want to like him, but he wasn't giving her a choice. Even when he growled at her for doing something stupid like leaving the house without him, it wasn't enough to make her dislike him for long. Especially when he was right to growl at her.

"I saw a grill on your covered patio," he said. "Do you have propane for it?"

"I don't know. Trent wanted an outdoor kitchen, so he put one out there. I've no idea if it works or not."

"I'll check it out in the morning."

"Sounds good. Guess that means steak then, huh?"

"Yup. Unless you prefer one of the other options?"

"Steak sounds wonderful."

He handed her the last dish and turned off the water, shaking his hands over the sink before grabbing a paper towel. "Important question though. How do you eat your steak?"

"The way God intended. Medium rare."

Dax offered her a high five. She slapped his hand, ridiculously pleased with herself.

"Amen, sister. Perfect."

They finished the dishes and went their separate ways. Dax to his computer and Robbie to her office where she got absolutely nothing done. After she climbed into bed later that night, her mind replayed every moment they'd shared throughout the day. Every interaction, every flicker of his gaze, every touch, every word. Even when he'd been pissed at her.

She liked him. Liked that he seemed to think deeply about things, such as how important it was to cook for someone. Liked the way he'd smoothed the path with his friends at dinner. He'd helped her find her bearings in the conversation without making it obvious that's what he was doing. He hadn't talked over her or excluded her the way her parents or Trent had.

She wasn't an idiot. She just had difficulty talking with people sometimes. Okay, most of the time. It wasn't her fault. She *tried*. She'd always tried, especially when her parents were embarrassed by her shyness or inability to say the right thing. She never did anything right according to them.

No wonder she'd married Trent when he'd asked.

Despite him being five years older, despite only knowing him for a few weeks, she'd jumped at his proposal, convinced everything was going to be perfect because a handsome man like him was interested in *her*.

But it wasn't perfect because nothing ever was. Robbie flipped over and punched the pillow. Lucy woofed in her sleep and Ollie stretched in protest.

Damn Daphne and her bright ideas anyway. Pretending that Dax Freed was her boyfriend was only going to mess with Robbie's peace of mind. She'd worked hard to get to a place of acceptance about her life, and now it was being upended again.

Damian LeBeaux had never felt farther away. Instead of thinking about her vampire king, she was thinking about a man she barely knew and wondering how it would feel to be with him, despite knowing that wasn't *ever* going to happen. Dax Freed was her pretend boyfriend, not her real one.

Nor did she want him to be. No matter how soulful his hazel eyes, how chiseled his jaw—or how perfect his ass in those faded jeans.

Chapter Nine

Dax was up early again, checking his computer and monitoring the feed from the surveillance cameras they'd placed around Robbie's property yesterday. There were a lot of animals, which was to be expected. Deer, raccoons, opossums, and a few coyotes. A bobcat sauntered on screen at one point, looking cool and unflappable. He stopped and raised his head, scenting the air. Then he ran, disappearing into the brush.

Dax frowned as a dark shape appeared at the edge of the camera's view. It took a few moments to move fully into frame, but the shape was definitely human. Whoever it was had worn a huge hoodie that covered their body and made it shapeless. They'd also worn a ski mask over their face, and they carried a large pistol in one hand.

Yeah, like that wasn't suspicious.

Dax watched as the person walked up the trail. He switched to the next camera and the person appeared there, coming closer to the house. At a certain point, they stopped and stared in the direction of the house for several minutes. The hairs on Dax's neck prickled. *What the fuck?*

He checked the other cameras, but the person wasn't on them. Only on the trail cameras and the one on that side of the house. Because of the sheer number of wildlife in the area, the cameras on the trail weren't set up to trigger an alarm. If they had been, they'd have gone off all night.

Dax thought it must be a man, but it could also be a tall woman who moved with a masculine gait. He returned to the point where the person was staring at the house. They were standing on the perimeter of the yard, about a hundred feet from the house itself. Then they turned and walked back the way they'd come. The cameras showed them pass by, and then nothing.

Whoever it was had braved a bobcat and coyotes, though maybe they hadn't known it. Or maybe that's why they'd carried the pistol. Whatever the case, the fact he or she had come so close to the house and stared at it in the dead of night was a little strange. If it'd been a hiker or a hunter, wouldn't they have stayed in the woods near the trail?

Dax gulped down the rest of his coffee, checked his weapons, and slipped outside to look for footprints. It'd been raining recently, so maybe he could find something and snap a pic of it. He took the key that Robbie kept by the door and locked it behind him. He also set the alarm with his phone.

He'd told Robbie not to open the door without using

the keypad to disarm the system. He hoped she remembered. Just in case, he sent her a text.

I'm outside. The security system is armed. Don't open any doors until I return.

She didn't answer, but he hadn't expected her to. Most people were smart enough to turn on the *Do Not Disturb* feature of their phone during the hours they slept, and Robbie was clearly no exception.

The morning air was crisp, and there was a light fog rising off the dewy fields across the creek. Birds chirped and flitted in the bushes, and a squirrel inched along a branch in one of the tall oaks.

Dax found the approximate location where the person had been standing last night. He approached carefully, scanning the area for any signs someone had been there. Depressions dotted the grass, but there were no definitive footprints.

He circled the area and then went parallel to the trail, sweeping his gaze across it as he walked. Though it was spring, the woods were still littered with autumn leaves that had fallen and become part of the forest floor. It was impossible to find a footprint in that.

He checked all the way to the edge of Robbie's property before going beyond it a few yards. There was a packed dirt road on that end of the acreage. With any luck, he'd find fresh tire tracks.

And, bingo, around a bend in the road, he did. Someone had pulled over to the side where the mud hadn't yet dried because it was in shade most of the day. Dax took out his phone and snapped a few pictures. Probably a common tire, which meant he wouldn't be able to pinpoint a vehicle, but he could get another camera and mount it close by. If the person returned to this spot, he could get a look at their plates and track them down that way.

Dax straightened and turned slowly, looking at the surrounding woods and fields for anything out of place. For anyone observing him from a distance. Not that he'd gotten a feeling in his gut like he usually did if there was danger, but neither did he take it for granted that he always would. One day it might not happen, and that would be the day he'd get gunned down because he hadn't been vigilant enough.

After he'd stood for long minutes, he headed for the house again, following the trail the person had taken last night. When he got back, he disarmed the system and opened the door. Lucy was waiting for him, tail pumping. She whined, jumping up and down and spinning, and he bent to pet her. Then he snapped on her leash and took her out.

He could have let her go in the yard the way Robbie often did, but he wondered if she might catch the trail of the intruder and follow it into the woods. He didn't want to be responsible for Robbie's dog running off, so he took her on a circuit of the yard. She did her business, snorting and scraping her feet in the grass before he took her back to the house.

Robbie was in the kitchen, in her robe, her lush brown hair piled in a messy bun on her head. Her dark gaze was bleary as she waggled her fingers at him. Her coffee finished brewing and she pulled the mug away before shuffling to the island and climbing on a stool.

"Thanks for taking her out, but you could have just opened the door for her. She won't go anywhere."

He shrugged. "It's okay. There was a bobcat out there last night. I thought she might catch the scent and go looking."

He wasn't telling her about the person because it would only rattle her. It was his job to keep her safe, and he would.

"A bobcat? Really?"

"Yep. There were some coyotes, raccoons, and 'possums too. Your woods are teeming with wildlife."

"I saw a bear once from my window. Scared the crap out of me. I didn't go outside for three days. That was over a year ago. Haven't seen one since."

"Sure it wasn't Bigfoot?"

She blinked up at him as if trying to figure out whether or not he was serious.

"I'm kidding, Robbie."

"Of course you are." She sipped her coffee primly. "But maybe don't kid until I've finished at least one cup, okay?"

He fixed another cup before joining her. "Were you up late working?"

She shook her head. "No, that train has left the station. Or maybe it hasn't pulled in yet. Whatever. No, I didn't write a word. I tossed and turned and thought about how my life is being upended with this conference and tour."

"And me."

"And you." She set the cup down. The skin under her eyes was dark, almost bruised with lack of sleep.

"You have to rest, Robbie. Maybe take something to help you relax at bedtime. Or drink a glass of wine."

She turned her cup back and forth on the granite. "I took a lot of Xanax after Trent left. Every night, and sometimes during the day too. It put me to sleep, but it also robbed me of the ability to create. I don't want that again."

"Then how about an over-the-counter sleep aid or even an allergy pill like Benadryl? I take one of those to stop sneezing and next thing you know, I need a nap."

"I haven't tried it."

"Maybe you should."

"I'll think about it." She sighed and picked up the cup again. "I haven't written a decent word in months now. I can't blame Xanax, really. It's me. Something's broken."

He hated how small she suddenly seemed. How frail and delicate. He reached for her hand and wrapped it in his. She didn't resist. She looked at him with liquid brown eyes, and he felt something shifting inside him again. Something hot and dark and needy.

He told himself to be careful. He couldn't get involved with her for real. Not that he intended to, but times like this, he fiercely wanted to keep her safe and chase those shadows away.

"You aren't broken, Robbie. You might be burned out, but you aren't broken. The woman who wrote those books is in there. Her talent isn't gone. It doesn't fizzle and die. It hibernates, maybe, in response to pressure. But it's not gone. You just have to trust it'll return when the time's right."

Her smile was wobbly. "That's the nicest thing anyone has said to me in a long time. Daphne always wants to know how the book is coming, and Autumn asks if I want to talk about it, if I need help with plotting, or if I just need a sounding board. Nobody ever says it's okay to take a break."

Dax squeezed her hand. "It's okay to take a break, Roberta Sharpe. You're famous, and people love you. They'll wait as long as it takes for the next Damian LeBeaux book. And if Velvet is really done with him, then he'll find someone even better. It'll happen when it happens."

Robbie stared at him, her eyes shining. A tear spilled down her cheek. She dashed it away. "Sorry," she gasped. "It's silly."

"It's not. You're operating on fumes, honey. And carrying the weight of too much expectation on your shoulders."

She nodded as the tears kept falling. Then she bent over at the waist, her head almost between her knees, her hand pressed to her mouth as if holding something back.

She couldn't though. She started to sob, nearly silent sobs that racked her body and made her tremble. It shocked him. He rubbed her back gently, not knowing what else to do.

It took a long while before the sobs lessened. "I'm sorry. Really. I have no idea what's wrong with me."

Dax stood and hauled her into his arms. His voice was gruff. "You're fucking exhausted, that's what."

He carried her toward her bedroom, her head

against his chest, her eyes closed as if she couldn't hold them open a moment longer. Her face was red and puffy, but she seemed done with tears for now. Dax pushed the door open with a foot and strode over to lay her down on the bed.

He pulled the covers over her body and she turned on her side, her liquid eyes staring up at him as if he were the only thing keeping her grounded. "Don't be so nice to me," she whispered. "I can't take it if you're nice to me."

"I'm not fucking nice. I'm taking care of my teammate. Can't operate with a soldier down."

"Okay."

His belly tightened. "Now go to sleep. I've got your back. No one's going to hurt you while I'm here. I promise."

He thought she might fight, but she nodded once as her eyes drifted closed. Five minutes later, her breathing evened out and she was asleep.

He stared down at her, the tension in his body easing a bit. Fucking hell, he couldn't afford any distractions. He had to keep her safe, find her tormentor, and get the hell out. Before Robbie Sharpe tunneled her way any deeper beneath his walls.

Chapter Ten

Robbie woke with a start. Where was she? What had happened?

She groaned as she remembered. She was in her own bed because Dax had carried her there.

After she'd sobbed her heart out in front of him. Embarrassment shuddered through her. What must he think of her?

The bedroom door was shut, and there was no Ollie or Lucy. The shutters were drawn closed but light streamed between the slats.

She was still in her robe, but she'd thrown the covers off. She pushed herself up and yawned. She was a little groggy, but it wasn't bad. It wasn't the exhaustion of barely sleeping for days on end. It was the kind of groggy that came with a lot of sleep. She groped for her phone. It wasn't there.

Dax must have taken it so no one could wake her.

She lay in bed and considered not getting out of it, but she wasn't wired to stay in bed all day. Instead,

Robbie got up to take a shower. She didn't know the time, but it had to be late morning by now.

After she put on a pair of leggings and a loose T-shirt, she shook her hair out and combed it before putting it in a ponytail. Then she took a deep breath and went to find Dax.

Lucy came bounding toward her, her butt wiggling as she panted excitedly. Robbie dropped down to pet her. "What have you been doing, pretty girl? Where's your brother? Is he sleeping in a sunbeam?"

Dax appeared in the cased opening that led to the kitchen. "Hey. How you feeling?"

Robbie felt the heat rising to her cheeks. "Better. Thank you." She stood and dropped her head a little, unable to look at him for very long. "I'm sorry I lost it on you earlier."

"It's okay. Everyone needs a shoulder to lean on sometimes."

"Well, thanks for being mine. But I shouldn't have involved you in my issues."

"What are pretend boyfriends for?"

He was trying to joke with her and she appreciated it, but it also pierced her deep inside. Because she'd wanted that moment between them to be real. She'd wanted his empathy and gentleness to be a true reaction, not part of his job. He'd called her his teammate, though. How much clearer could he get?

"I'd say you went above and beyond," she said, trying to sound nonchalant. She sniffed the air as her stomach rumbled. "Are you cooking?"

"Yep. It's not steak, sorry. Didn't think you'd be up

for that after sleeping all day—"

"Wait a minute—did you say *all day?*"

"It's almost five o'clock."

"I slept all day? Oh crap."

"You needed it. I figured it was better for you to get the sleep you need than to wake you so you could go back to bed tonight and risk not sleeping again."

"And if I'm up all night tonight?"

"Then you'll go to bed at dawn like a vampire. But I expect you'll have little trouble sleeping. You're running a pretty big sleep deficit, and your body knows what it needs."

Annoyance pricked her nerve endings. He was awfully certain of himself. Just like Trent had always been. "How can you possibly know that?"

"I was an Army Ranger and then a Green Beret—that's a special operations unit, if you don't know. Sleep deprivation comes with the territory. I recognize the signs. What's most needed to fix it is sleep and nutrition."

She was *so* going to google Green Berets later. She wasn't quite sure what it was, but she'd find out. Though she stubbornly wanted to insist he didn't know *her*, she suspected he was right. She could feel the exhaustion in her bones. Arguing with him would be a study in futility. Not to mention hypocritical.

"Speaking of nutrition, I'm starving."

"Come on, then. I'm fixing grilled cheeses and tomato soup."

He couldn't have said anything more perfect. "Comfort food."

"Exactly."

Robbie followed him into the kitchen. Ollie was stretched out on the cushioned bench that sat against the picture window. He yawned when he saw her. Robbie went over and scratched his head. He swiped a paw at her hand, but there were no claws. He tugged her finger toward him and licked it then let go.

"Brat," Robbie said with a laugh.

Dax looked up from where he was ladling soup into a bowl. He glanced at the cat and then back at her. "He's king of the castle, isn't he?"

Robbie sat at the island. "He is. I never had a cat before, and then one day there was a tiny kitten meowing at me in the parking lot of the Food Lion in town. I looked for other kittens or a mama cat, but there were none to be found. I brought him home, and he's been here since." She frowned. "Trent didn't want a cat and told me to take him to the animal shelter, but I couldn't do it. He clung to me as if I was his only hope, and I fell for him instantly. Lucy took to him immediately. Ollie didn't seem to mind her, so he stayed."

"How did you get Lucy?"

"The same way, really. She was a stray that wandered onto the property. I thought she might be someone's hunting dog. I put up fliers, but no one ever called. I also had her checked for a microchip, but she didn't have one. The vet said she was still just a puppy. Somebody probably dumped her."

Dax walked over and set a bowl of tomato soup in front of her. He returned a moment later with a grilled cheese sandwich and set that down too.

"They're lucky you found them."

"Or maybe I'm the lucky one. I don't know what I would have done without them when my ex walked out. They gave me a reason to get out of bed in the morning." She shook her head, mortified. Why couldn't she shut up around this man? "I'm sorry. That sounds pitiful as hell. But I wasn't expecting him to walk out. I knew we weren't perfect, but I thought that was normal. I was shocked."

Dax looked sympathetic. "I understand. I had a girl I thought I was going to marry. Not the same thing, I know. But I went into the military to earn money, and she married someone else instead of waiting. It hurt at the time, but it gets better."

She nodded. "It does. I'm over it now, but it was rough at first. I'm still angry at what he did, but not hurt anymore." Robbie looked at Lucy sitting beside her chair, staring up at her with doe eyes. "The thing I love about animals is that you don't have to worry they're pretending. When they love you, they love you. No questions and no agenda—other than treats of course. It'd be nice if humans worked the same way. But they don't. Heroes aren't real, and love stinks."

"You don't believe in love? Kind of cynical for a romance author, isn't it?"

She blew on a spoonful of soup. "I think it's out there, but I think it's rare. Not everyone gets a happy ending. In fact, most of us don't." She shrugged. "I've made my peace with that. It's better than getting hurt over and over because you keep flinging yourself at the flame."

Chapter Eleven

"What about you?" she asked. "Do you still believe in love after your girl married someone else?"

Dax got his food and sat diagonally across from her at the island. "I've seen people I know and admire who are in love. I believe their relationships are great, and there are deep feelings on both sides."

"But what about *you?* Do you believe you'll meet someone and, boom, lightning bolts? Or do you think that doesn't really happen and your friends just got lucky?"

"You aren't sounding very romance positive for a romance author," he teased.

She made a dismissive sound as she swirled her spoon around the soup. "Reality and fantasy are entirely different things. I stopped believing in the reality, but I still want the fantasy. I just know it won't happen."

He kinda hated to hear her sound so negative. But life could do that to you, and hers certainly had.

"Honestly, I don't know what I believe," he told her. "I don't think there are lightning bolts or love at first sight. I think love can grow, but I don't know how it happens."

"I think it's rare. Exceedingly rare. Daphne has never married and she's in her fifties. Autumn is twenty-six and doesn't have anyone either. I thought I had someone, but I was wrong. We didn't grow together at all. I think it was just smoke and mirrors, and I was too blind to see what was staring me in the face until he walked out."

"You aren't solving the mysteries of love tonight. Why don't you eat the soup instead of moving it around the bowl? We can talk about something else."

She nodded. "Probably best. What do you want to talk about?"

Lucy shifted to stare up at him since Robbie hadn't given her anything to eat yet. She was a cute dog and sweet. "Why don't you tell me about your first pet."

Robbie reached down and scratched Lucy's head absently. "I never had any pets until I got Lucy. My mom thought they were too messy."

Her mom sounded like his stepfather. Dax had wanted a dog so bad when he was a kid, but Ken said no way. When his little brother wanted a dog a few years later, he'd been allowed to have one. Dax was old enough not to care by then. Or not much, anyway.

"This soup is pretty good," Robbie said. "Is it one of the things you learned on YouTube?"

"It's out of a can." His voice was a little rough. Over

an old memory? Shit, he was going soft. "I ordered some groceries while you slept. Like I said, I didn't think steak was gonna work today. Got some for tomorrow."

She smiled. He liked her smile. "Thanks for taking care of me. And I really am sorry I melted down like that. It's not typical, I promise. I'm usually stronger."

He held her gaze for as long as she allowed it. There was something arresting in those dark eyes of hers. "Everybody reaches a breaking point. No need to apologize."

Her lashes dropped over her eyes. "You're more understanding than my ex-husband ever was. I'm not sure if it's because you're being paid to be here or if you're just that way naturally."

He heard the apprehension in her voice. The fear she didn't matter. He wanted to make it go away. "I've seen a lot of shitty things in my life. I don't feel an obligation to fake understanding, no matter how much someone pays me."

"Fair enough. But if you aren't really as nice as you're pretending to be right now, I'd prefer you act the way you really are. It'll save me liking you too much and being disappointed later."

He understood why she bristled. She wasn't accustomed to people caring about the pressure she was under. All they cared about was the payday that came from her talent.

"I don't pretend to be something I'm not. I don't have time for that shit. I'm too busy making sure I do my job right and keeping the people under my protection safe. It's harder to keep you safe if you're not taking care of yourself. So maybe it's selfish of me to feed you and tell you that you're entitled to lose your shit every once in a while, but I'm okay with that if it gets you the rest you need. And if that makes me not nice in your book, I'm okay with that too."

"That's an honest answer. I appreciate it."

"I won't lie to you. I'll keep things from you if you don't need to know, but I won't lie."

Silence fell between them as they ate.

"Thank you for fixing dinner," Robbie said a bit later. "It's just what I needed."

"You're welcome."

"Did you learn grilled cheese from YouTube as well?"

"Sure did. Do you like it?"

She took another bite. "It's good. But it's not American cheese."

"Nope, I don't like that processed shit. Not good for the body. It's mild cheddar."

"I like it."

"I got ice cream for dessert."

She perked up. "Chocolate?"

"And vanilla. Have both if you like."

"I might just do that." When she finished eating, she pushed her dishes away and leaned back on the chair. "I think that's the best grilled cheese I've ever had."

Dax shook his head, grinning. "Laying it on a little thick, aren't you?"

She laughed. "Maybe so. But I could get used to having someone cook for me."

He already knew her ex never had. "You could hire a chef."

"I could, but then they'd have to hang out in my house for hours while they prepared everything. No thanks." She frowned. "Guess it's going to be difficult to get someone to cook for me then, huh?"

"True. But I'm hanging out, and you're doing all right with it."

"You're here for a different reason. But if I'd had my way, you wouldn't be here at all. I have to admit it hasn't been all bad. You're pretty useful."

"Tell me what you need, Robbie. I'll get it done."

When she colored slightly, he knew she was thinking of things she probably wished she wasn't. He was thinking of them too. It annoyed him, though he'd known when he'd said the words how they sounded. Deep down, he wanted more of her than he had a right to. More of her than was safe.

Robbie Sharpe was a job. He'd read her novels, and he'd been more than a little aroused at the picture she painted of her hero and heroine when they were intimate, but she'd told him pretty plainly that life and imagination were two separate things.

For instance, her hero was a dirty talker at times, but he thought it'd probably be a mistake to talk to her like that. She was reserved. Some guys might think that meant she would be a total wildcat in bed, but he thought she'd be like she was in life. Reserved, unable to make eye contact for very long.

Dude, stop thinking about taking her to bed. It's not happening.

No, it wasn't happening. He was feeling the effects of deprivation. It'd been too long since he'd been seeing anyone, and he wasn't the kind of guy who liked one-night stands. He indulged on occasion, but it hadn't been recently.

Meanwhile, all his teammates were pairing up and acting ridiculously happy about it. Ty frigging Scott of all people. Never would have thought Ty would fall so quickly, but he'd taken one look at Cassie Dixon doing her thing on her YouTube channel, and that was it. He'd been mentally planning a wedding since.

Dax didn't want a wedding, but he'd take some hot sex. Just not with a client. Definitely not with someone as vulnerable as Robbie. He didn't think she was capable of sex with no strings and no feelings. Hell, feelings—writing about them—was what had made her famous. It was clear she felt things more deeply than many people did.

"So why a vampire?" he asked, changing the subject entirely. Trying to scrub his mind of the image of her legs wrapped around his hips. "Why not a CEO or a cowboy?"

"I don't really know." She shrugged. "Damian walked into my mind fully formed, and he was the most dangerous thing I'd ever seen. I liked that about him."

"And where did Velvet come from?"

"Velvet is everywoman. That's what romance novel heroines are, really. You want women with busy lives to identify with your heroine. To want her to succeed, to want to spend time with her. Velvet isn't perfect. She's flawed, and the odds are almost always stacked against her."

He thought he understood. "She's an orphan, and she's lost her job and her apartment before Damian shows up. He takes one look at her as she's walking down a dark street in New Orleans, and he wants to possess her rather than kill her."

"That's the magic of it. The one woman who's different. Who's special. Who brings a dark warrior to his knees with only the power of her presence. It's heady stuff, and romance readers like me love it. Always have."

He thought that explained a lot. Robbie had written a hero who was dangerous but fell for an ordinary woman. A woman he would protect and worship despite her imperfection. It was the ultimate fantasy for anyone, really. To be loved for who you were. To be special to *someone.*

"Except you blew the magic up in the last book. Velvet is with Neal. Damian is alone."

"It felt right at the time. Life isn't perfect, and neither are relationships. But I'll fix it."

He leaned back in his seat and studied her. She didn't look at him of course. "I believe you will."

She smiled. "Thank you. I think you're the only one, though."

"Nah. Lots of people do."

She tucked a lock of hair behind her ear and gazed past him. He'd noticed it was a trick of hers. Her way of pretending to look at you.

"Can you tell me why you don't want to look at me?"

Her gaze snapped to his for a moment then skittered away again. "What makes you think that?"

"Perceptive, remember?"

She looked at her empty bowl. Shook her head. "It's a defense mechanism. I was very shy growing up. Painfully so. My parents are both extroverts, and loud, and they didn't understand me at all. They were constantly telling me to speak up, to look people in the eye, to walk up to their guests and make small talk. They loved to entertain and had people over all the time. It was torture, and I was terrible at it. I cried. I hid in my room. They made me do it anyway." She drew in a breath and slowly let it out again. "You're confident. It radiates off you. You could walk into a room and have everyone eating out of your hand. I can't do that. And if I don't look at you, I don't have to pretend that I can. I hope that makes sense."

Dax's belly twisted at the thought of a shy young girl being forced to talk to strangers when all she wanted was to be left alone. He didn't know her parents, but he thought he might not like them very much.

He leaned toward her and put a hand on her cheek, made her look at him. He knew he shouldn't, but he couldn't stop himself. The look in her eyes was apprehensive, and it killed him. He dropped his gaze first, let it wander down her arm. Then he took her hand, gently, and twined their fingers. She didn't fight him, and he was glad.

"Roberta Sharpe, you *can* walk into a room and have everyone eating out of your hand."

He turned her hand over, traced his fingers over the thin line running across her palm. He could feel the shiver ripple over her, but she didn't pull away. Need pooled in his groin, hot and heavy. He wouldn't give in to it, but damn how he wanted to.

"This hand does things no one else can do. It translates the words from your head to the page, and *nobody* can do it like you do. You don't have to say a word, but I promise you, darlin', that you *can* command a room simply by walking into it."

She was staring at him when he looked at her again. Her eyes were wide and liquid. Her pulse thrummed in her throat. He wanted to bite that pulse. And then he wanted to kiss it.

Shit.

"You say the most incredible things."

"I'm only telling the truth. You're Roberta fucking Sharpe, the vampire queen herself, and people adore you. All you gotta do is be yourself, Robbie. Those writers at the conference? They want to be you. But there's only one you, so go out there and own it."

"I'm not sure I know how," she whispered.

"Then it's a good thing you've got me to help you, isn't it? Trust me, honey, you're going to walk onto that stage in Vegas and awe everyone."

She pulled her hand away, but she was still staring at him. He stared back as desire thrummed in his veins. Her gaze dropped as he knew it would. Disappointment ate at him as she pushed her chair backward and stood.

"I, um, I have some work to do. Thanks for dinner."

He watched her walk away, his cock aching, his heart hammering. Lightning bolts? Love at first sight? They weren't real, but lust was.

He was definitely in lust with Roberta Sharpe. And there was no relief in sight.

Chapter Twelve

Robbie woke early the next morning, feeling more refreshed than she had in ages. Lucy lifted her head and wagged her tail. Ollie had left as soon as the sun peeked over the horizon. She knew because she'd had to let him out, silly cat.

Robbie stretched and reached for her phone, patting Lucy before she picked it up. The time said 7:30.

Wow. Early, but not ridiculously so. She thought about going back to sleep, but she didn't really feel like it so she sat up and scrolled through her email. There was one from Autumn about the itinerary for next week, and one from Daphne asking when she could see pages from the new book.

Robbie ignored them both for the moment. She'd answer later. Dax had been right that she'd be tired last night after sleeping all day. By eleven, her eyes had been drooping.

Normally, she'd stay up until one or two, sometimes

later, but last night it'd been impossible. She'd had to put down the book she was reading and turn off the light.

Lucy stretched and jumped down, and Robbie knew that was her cue. She went to the bathroom, brushed her teeth and took care of morning business, then put on a light sweatshirt and yoga pants before following Lucy to the kitchen to let her out.

Dax was already there, looking handsome and wide awake, and her heart flipped at the same time that her stomach lurched. When he'd touched her last night and told her she was Roberta fucking Sharpe, she'd thought that if she was another woman entirely she would have jumped him.

Arousal had flooded her system in that moment, making parts of her ache that hadn't ached in years. Not that she didn't take care of business on her own sometimes, but there was something about getting aroused over a flesh-and-blood man touching her that felt different. Sharper somehow.

That sharp ache was still there, still unquenched. It shocked her, really. Alarmed her too. Dax Freed wasn't there for her. He was there to do a job. Hell, she didn't even know if he had someone waiting at home. She hadn't asked.

"Morning," he said, his gravelly voice strumming her senses like a maestro.

"Morning," she said, trying to sound bright and cheery.

"Want some coffee?" he asked as she went over to the door to let Lucy out.

"I can get it," she said, turning as she closed the

door.

He was already on his feet. "No problem. I'm getting another cup anyway. I'll fix yours first. Cream, right?"

Robbie forced herself to breathe evenly, trying to will the ridiculous pounding of her heart to subside. "Yes. A good splash, please."

She watched him prepare the coffee, opening the machine and inserting a pod, then closing it with a snap and pressing the ON button. When it was done, he strolled over and put the cup in her hands.

"Thank you," she murmured, glancing up at him because she couldn't prevent herself. Her heart thumped.

He grinned. "You're welcome."

When he walked away again, Robbie couldn't help but stare at his ass. It was a very fine ass that filled out his jeans to perfection. No doubt about it, he was sexy enough to grace a book cover. She hadn't lied about that.

Put a cowboy hat on him, or a baseball cap, and he'd look right at home. Make him a billionaire in a suit, or a Regency rake in a frock coat and a cravat, and women would swoon.

Hell, give him fangs and a dark scowl, and he could be Damian LeBeaux.

No. Robbie gripped her cup. No way. She was *not* turning Dax Freed into her vampire king.

"I probably should have asked before," she blurted. "But do you have a girlfriend?"

He shot her an amused look. "No. Why?"

Oh lord. Way to be awkward, Roberta.

"Because it's hard to imagine how a man who cooks you dinner at night and fixes you coffee in the mornings can be single."

There. That sounded perfectly reasonable. Not a word said about his good looks, either.

He finished preparing his own cup and turned to lean against the counter, one leg crossed over the other, biceps flexing as he put one hand behind him on the flat surface and the other lifted the cup to his lips.

Lucky cup.

Robbie wanted to smack some sense into herself. *Pretend boyfriend, not real.*

"Haven't found anyone I want to spend that kind of time with. Plus the job makes it difficult. Most women don't like the idea of their man taking off for a job with little if any notice."

"Ty and Jared are getting married, aren't they?" She seemed to remember that from the conversation when they'd stayed for dinner.

Dax sipped coffee. Belatedly, she sipped her own. She'd spent way too much time staring at his ass to do it before now.

"They are. Several of the other guys are married or getting married. Even the boss is married now, though his wife tried to kill him before they figured it all out and realized they were in love."

Robbie blinked, knocked out of her Dax Freed fantasyland. Thank God.

"Literally tried to kill him? Surely not."

He laughed. "Literally. Fortunately, she failed. I

probably shouldn't be telling you any of this, but I'm sure you've thought of crazier things with your imagination. You won't be shocked if I tell you she was once an international assassin."

"But not now?"

"Not now. Though I still wouldn't want to get on her bad side."

Robbie opened the door to let Lucy in and gave her a treat. Ollie materialized from nowhere and wanted his treat too. "Rotten cat," Robbie said as she gave him a tiny piece of a kitty treat.

When she was done, she joined Dax at the table. "I can hardly credit what you're saying is real. It sounds like a brainstorming meeting of a writers' group."

"It's real." He looked thoughtful. "I can arrange for you to meet Natasha. In fact, it might be a good idea for you to meet everyone. It can be practice for Las Vegas."

"I don't know," Robbie began.

"I think you'd like these people. You already know Ty and Jared, and you can meet their fiancées, Cassie and Libby. There's also Maddie, Angie, and Tallie. They'd all love you."

Robbie felt a curl of apprehension, but there was also curiosity. Lots of curiosity. "You do realize that all those women's names end in a *y* or *ie* sound, right?"

"Including yours," Dax said with a grin. "You'll get along fine."

"I can figure out what their names must actually be. Except for Libby and Tallie. What are those short for?"

"Liberty and Tallulah."

"Hmm, good heroine names. Assuming I ever get to

write about anyone but Velvet."

"Why did you name her Velvet?"

"It's what she said her name was." Robbie felt a little self-conscious saying that when it was clear everything came from her imagination. But it was true. Her characters arrived with names and personalities, and it was her job to uncover what she could of them while telling their story. Velvet Asbury hadn't been as fully formed as Damian, but she'd had definite ideas about herself.

Dax didn't laugh or roll his eyes the way Trent had when she'd told him about her book. He'd stopped laughing when her agent sold the first one at auction, but she'd never forgotten that he hadn't taken her seriously at first.

"Does it always happen that way?" Dax asked.

"No. I have to search for names sometimes. That's why I like those two."

"What about Dax? Think that'd be a good character name?" He winked at her.

"Nah, too fake," she teased.

"Want some breakfast?"

"Are you trying to make me swoon, Mr. Freed, or is this how you really are?"

That sexy grin appeared again as he got to his feet and spread his arms. "It's all me, baby. What do you want? Eggs? French toast? An omelet?"

"What kind of omelet?"

"Ham and cheese. Sound good?"

"Sounds amazing. Can I help?"

"If you want. Crack two eggs into a bowl for me."

Robbie got up and went to do as he asked while he

took ham and cheese from the fridge, got out a pan, and dropped some butter into it before turning it on low.

"Where did you get your name?" she asked. "It's a little unusual."

"My dad. Dax is French in origin and it's often given to first born sons. He wasn't French or a Dax, but he liked the name, especially since he and my mother tried a long time to have me." He sliced ham into little bits then started to beat the eggs. "He died when I was three."

"Oh. I'm sorry."

"It was a long time ago, but thanks. Mom remarried and had another son. So I have a little brother. His name is Sean."

He said everything like it was perfectly ordinary, and yet she imagined him as a little boy being told his dad wasn't coming home again. It must have been awful for him. Not that he would have understood much at three, but he would have noticed the absence.

"My dad is Robert, and his dad was Robert, and his dad was Robert, and so on. I guess you can figure out how I ended up being a Roberta. My parents wanted a son, but never had one. I came later in life for them both. Dad is eighty now. Mom is seventy-five. I really wish he'd been an Eric. That would have been sooooo much better."

Dax poured the eggs into the pan. "But then you wouldn't be Robbie, and that's pretty cool, right?"

"My mom hates that name. She always calls me Roberta."

He finished the omelet and slid it onto a plate, then

started the next one. "That one's yours."

"Thanks." She picked up the plate and cut off a bite right there at the counter instead of going to the island or table to sit. She liked standing near him, talking like it was something they did all the time. She wasn't uncomfortable, and that was a novel feeling. "Do you think names affect who you become? Like if I'd been an Erica or a Jasmine or a McKenna, I'd be more outgoing and less shy?"

"I dunno. Maybe. Or maybe who we are is just encoded in the DNA. There's nothing wrong with being shy and introverted. If you weren't who you are, maybe Damian and Velvet wouldn't exist either. That would be a bad thing for a lot of people who love your characters."

Robbie chewed a bite of omelet. "Maybe so. Still, I think I'd have been more confident growing up if I weren't Roberta. I always thought it was a granny's name, and I hated it. Plus the other kids made fun of me. It was difficult when there were Madisons and Kayleighs everywhere and they were the pretty, popular ones."

Dax finished his omelet and slid it onto the plate. Then he stood there and cut into it like she had. "Yeah, but where are the Madisons and Kayleighs from your school now? Do you know?"

She shook her head. "I didn't keep up with them."

He ate a bite and so did she. It was companionable to stand close together and eat, though she supposed they could go sit down. But neither of them moved.

"You didn't keep up with them, but I promise you

they know where you are. *Who* you are. Don't regret not being one of them, Robbie. You're you."

Now, why did that make her eyes sting? "You are one smooth talker, Dax Freed. I might have to hire you just to pay me compliments every day."

There was a knock on the front door. Robbie stilled. Lucy stood up, hackles rising, and barked. Dax put his plate down and reached around to the small of his back. A moment later, he had a weapon at his side. She shouldn't have been surprised, and yet the sight of it gave her a start. It was a wicked looking 9mm pistol. She only knew because she'd researched them for her books.

"Expecting anyone?" Dax asked.

"No."

A moment later, the creak of the door sounded and Robbie's heart shot into her throat. She wouldn't have believed the look of complete calm and utter violence that came over Dax's face if she hadn't seen it.

Lucy took off for the front of the house, still barking. Dax followed, motioning for Robbie to stay where she was. As if she intended to confront anyone breaking into her house.

"Goddammit, Robbie, call off your idiot dog!" a man yelled.

Robbie dropped her plate on the counter with a *thunk* and went storming toward the front hallway.

"Holy shit! Who the hell are you?" Trent said as Robbie rounded the corner and discovered Dax with his pistol aimed straight at Trent's cheating, lying carcass.

"Who are *you*?" Dax growled.

"It's my ex-husband. Don't shoot him. Yet."

Chapter Thirteen

Dax lowered his Sig P320 and then tucked it into the Kydex holster at his back. Trent Sharpe stood blinking in the sun-warmed entry to Robbie's home, his face pale beneath the tan he must have gotten sailing around the Pacific with his new wife.

That thought made Dax want to growl at him, see if he could make the dude go even paler. He didn't, though. He stood like a trained guard dog and let Robbie handle it.

She snapped her fingers and Lucy returned to her side, tail wagging. "What are you doing here, Trent? And what makes you think you can just walk in like you belong?"

Trent's gaze snapped to Dax and back to Robbie. "You didn't change the locks. I took a chance."

"Why would I change the locks? You got what you wanted. I didn't think you'd be back again. What is it you want now?"

Trent jerked his chin toward Dax. "Who's the muscle? And why is he in my house, pointing a gun at me?"

Robbie stiffened.

Ah hell, no. Fucker wasn't getting away with that shit. *His* fucking house? After he'd dumped her and taken half her earnings.

Dax put an arm around Robbie and tugged her toward him. She stayed stiff as a board for about half a second, but then she went with it. Thankfully. Robbie wasn't stupid, and she knew what he was doing. She put a palm on his abdomen, over his T-shirt, and his skin blazed hot.

Fucking hell.

"Don't think it's your house anymore, boss," Dax drawled. "You let the lady go, and now she's mine."

Robbie curled her fingers just enough to let him know she didn't like being claimed like she was something to be owned. But dammit, this asshole thought he could walk back in like nothing had happened and say it was his house? Ask her what she was doing?

No. Hell no.

"Dax is a professional bodyguard," Robbie said coolly. "He's also my boyfriend. Lucky me, right?"

Trent frowned. Hard. "Where did you get this guy? And why do you need a bodyguard? Is this Daphne's idea? You realize he's only with you for the money, right?"

Dax wanted to choke the sonofabitch. He started to move, but Robbie's grip tightened.

"Oh, you mean like you were? Don't worry. My next husband will sign a prenup. Or maybe I'll just settle for fucking his brains out instead. All the fun, none of the expense."

This time Dax thought he was going to choke on his tongue. Okay, so maybe Robbie wasn't as shy as he'd thought. He had a picture of her legs wrapped around his hips as he drove into her wet heat. *Fucking beautiful.*

"Babe," Dax said, trying very hard to keep his mind from throwing those mental images at him, "Let's find out what Terrance wants and then he can go."

"It's Trent, asshole." Trent's nostrils flared and the corners of his mouth went white. Dax noted that he was tall, five-eleven or six-foot, which meant he could have been the person on the video.

"Trent. Sorry. I'm not sure your name has ever come up before." He kissed the top of Robbie's head. She didn't try to get away from him, which was a good sign. "Afraid we've been so busy we haven't discussed you at all."

Robbie patted him awkwardly. "Uh, babe, let's not tell him everything."

He kissed her head again. "You're right. Sorry. You make me crazy though. Figured he'd understand."

Robbie met his gaze for once, her dark eyes wide and maybe a little shocked. He wondered if he'd gone too far, but she turned back to Trent, her spine stiffening with determination.

That's my girl.

"I'll repeat, Trent, why are you here? Does your wife

know you're breaking into my house? And how is the lithe and limber Kimberlee by the way?"

Trent had the grace to look sheepish. "It's not breaking in if your key still fits the lock. And I guess Kimberlee is fine. I haven't seen her in a few months."

"Trouble in paradise?" Dax drawled.

Trent shot him a look. "Can we talk in private? Without your muscle-head boyfriend taking up space?"

Robbie sighed. Dax thought she was about to give in, so he gave her shoulder a squeeze.

"We can talk, but only if Dax searches you for weapons first. And we have to stay in his sight the entire time."

Trent's eyes bugged out. "What? Why? Do you really think I'd hurt you?"

"Doesn't matter what she thinks, my man. It's what I think. Either you submit to being searched or you walk your ass back out that door."

Trent looked disgusted. "Fine. Search me. But I have a pistol in an ankle holster. Personal protection."

Dax set Robbie behind him and took his pistol out again, keeping it at his side for now. "Take it out slowly, eject the magazine, and slide everything toward me."

Trent started to drop to one knee.

"Let me warn you," Dax said before the man could reach for the gun, "I did eight years in the Army. I've eaten guys like you for breakfast. So don't fucking try anything."

Trent paled again. He lifted one hand in the air and then pulled up his pant leg with the other. Dax nearly laughed. The asshole had a pocket .22 caliber in a little holster. Not that it wouldn't do damage in the right hands, but a .22 was the kind of bullet that only made a determined attacker angry if your aim wasn't perfect. Not to mention the ankle holster wasn't exactly within easy reach, which sort of negated the personal protection aspect.

Not his problem.

Trent removed the .22 and ejected the magazine before sliding both toward Dax. It wasn't the weapon the mystery person in the woods had carried, but that didn't mean Trent wasn't a suspect anyway.

Dax strode forward as the other man got to his feet again. He patted Trent down while the dude looked more and more pissed at the whole thing. Once he was done, he turned to Robbie. "He's clean. Where do you want to talk to him?"

"Is outside okay?"

Dax nodded. He'd checked the cameras recently. The only creatures on any of the trails were deer, so he wasn't worried someone was lurking in the woods with a rifle.

"You heard the lady. Outside. And give her your key before you start talking, or I'll remove it forcibly."

ROBBIE DIDN'T WANT to spend a single moment alone with Trent, but she also knew it was the only way to get rid of him. If she refused, or if she insisted that Dax stay, he'd never tell her what he came to say.

She wanted to know. If he wanted more money, she

wanted to know it now. She hadn't missed what he'd said about Kimberlee, and she was curious about that too.

Once, if Trent had walked back into her life and told her Kimberlee was gone, she'd have been relieved and hopeful. Now, she felt nothing. Numbness, maybe. No relief. No happiness.

Nothing but an empty space where Trent had once resided.

There were other feelings swirling inside her right now, but they had nothing to do with Trent and everything to do with her dark, beautiful protector who stood just out of earshot, leaning against a tree, watching her and Trent with eyes that missed nothing.

Dax had put his arm around her. Kissed her head. Insinuated they were intimate. She knew he'd done it for Trent's sake, but there'd been a jolt of awareness deep inside when he'd said the words. She was still quaking inside from his touch, and it had been nothing in the scheme of things.

What would it be like if he touched her skin to skin? If he slid his cock inside her and fucked her slowly and thoroughly so that she came unglued beneath him?

"Why do you have a bodyguard?" Trent asked.

Robbie dragged herself back to the present moment. She held out her hand. "Key."

Trent dropped it in her palm with a look of disgust. "The bodyguard?"

"Just look at him. Why wouldn't I?" Daphne didn't want Dax to look obvious at the conference or on tour, but she'd said nothing about telling Trent. Good thing because Robbie wanted to rub his face in how hot and competent Dax was.

Trent rolled his eyes. "A guy like that's with you for the money. You have to know that."

"A guy like what?" She knew what he meant, but she wanted him to go there. To say she wasn't attractive enough for someone who looked like Dax Freed.

Trent shrugged. "A meathead. Hired muscle."

Robbie hated the knot of tension in her gut. He hadn't said it aloud, but she heard it anyway. The implication that there was no way any man would ever be interested in her for her sake. Like she was only attractive because she had money. Even if it were true, he had no right.

"It doesn't matter, Trent. I'm not marrying him. So long as he keeps me satisfied, I don't much care."

Trent's mouth tightened in anger. Too fucking bad.

"This isn't like you, Robbie."

"How would you know? You walked out four years ago after you'd been cheating on me for all of two months. It took me a long time to get over that, but I've decided it's time to see what *I've* been missing. If Dax is any indication, I was missing *a lot.*"

Let him digest *that*.

He ignored the taunt. "I've been thinking about you. Wondering how you were. I saw the reviews for the new book, and I was concerned. I thought about you alone out here, preparing for that big conference in Las Vegas, and I thought you might want some support."

She shouldn't have been surprised he knew about the conference, but she was. He was supposed to be in

Fiji or something. She folded her arms over her chest. "As you can see, I have support."

Trent's forehead glistened with sweat. He was nervous. She could thank Dax for that.

"I made a mistake, Robbie. I let myself be manipulated. I should never have fallen for Kimberlee's bullshit. I was vulnerable because you were so often writing, ignoring me, and she offered the attention I thought was lacking. But she never loved me. She wanted the money. She's the one who told me to go after half the estate."

Robbie's belly roiled with anger. "And you did it, didn't you? I wasn't aware you did what you were told. You certainly never did anything I wanted you to do."

Trent reached for her hand. She jerked it away. Out of the corner of her eye, she could see Dax straighten. If she needed him to intervene, he would. It was comforting to know he was there. Even if he was getting paid, he was on her side. That felt good.

"I wasn't in my right mind. I've been miserable without you, Robbie. I *miss* you. Kimberlee was a mistake."

Robbie pinched the bridge of her nose. "Trent. Good God, why are you doing this? It's too late for us. You made your choice. Dragged us through the courts, took away my ability to write for a long fucking time, and now you want me to let you back in like it never happened?"

He shook his head. "Not like it never happened. I just—I want another chance. I want to do it right. Romance you. Treat you the way you deserve. I want *us* back. I don't believe for a minute that guy means anything to you. Or that you mean anything to him. I loved you before you were famous, and I still love you. I want to prove it to you."

"Where is Kimberlee?"

"Gone. I told her I was still in love with you, and she left."

There was a time when Robbie had dreamed about this scene. When she'd dreamed of Trent returning to her, begging her, telling her he'd been so very wrong. She'd made him grovel, of course. But in the end she'd believed him and taken him back.

This moment was hollow, though. It wasn't real. He might believe what he was saying, but she didn't. Not anymore. If Kimberlee was gone, it wasn't because Trent had told her he was still in love with his ex-wife.

Fresh anger bloomed in her soul.

Dammit, she deserved better. Maybe she'd never get it, but knowing she deserved it was a major step forward. It gave her courage.

"I don't think it'll work, Trent. You hurt me too badly. It took a very long time to get over you, but I *am* over you. I won't go back to that place where you can hurt me ever again. I'm sorry it didn't work out with Kimberlee, but I'd suggest maybe you try again with her instead of me. I'm done."

He stared at her in stunned disbelief before an ugly sneer formed on his face. Predictable.

"You fucking cunt," he growled at her. "I supported you while you wrote that first book. I was the one who made it possible for you to be Roberta Sharpe. Hell, you kept my name! I helped make you, Robbie. Don't you ever forget that."

"Time for you to go, bud," Dax said in a voice laced with violence.

Robbie hadn't heard him approach, but she was glad he was there now. She turned toward him, her eyes blurring with angry tears. If she didn't get away from Trent, she'd commit a felony on his ass. Dax wrapped an arm around her and tugged her against his side.

"This isn't over," Trent said, hands clenching into fists at his side. "You need me, Robbie. I'm the only one who understands what it's like to be with you, the only one who ever will. Without me, you'll keep writing shitty books that piss people off. Your career will tank and we'll both be without a fucking dime. Is that what you really want?"

Robbie felt his words like darts piercing her heart. Trent always knew how to wound her. How to play on her fears of inadequacy and her belief that she wasn't as good as people thought. One day, they'd see it was all smoke and mirrors and that she didn't have an ounce of talent. Daphne would kick her to the curb. Her readers would move on and not look back.

"Dude, I cannot stress this enough," Dax said evenly, "but if you don't get the fuck out of here *now*, I'm going to break every tooth in your head and make you swallow them one by one."

"I need my pistol."

"Sorry, but you don't have a permit for it. I checked. The police will pick it up later. If you'd like to go explain to them why you're carrying an unlicensed firearm, more power to you."

"Swear to God, Robbie, you're going to regret this," Trent said, backing away.

Dax started to move, but she held on tight. "Let him go. He isn't worth it."

Chapter Fourteen

Dax did as she asked. He kept his arm around Robbie while Trent stalked to his Maserati and slammed the door. The asshole revved the engine and gunned it, throwing gravel from the driveway in their direction as he sped toward the road. They were too far away to get hit, but it pissed Dax off anyway.

He'd already noted the fucker's license plate. When he got back inside, he'd log in and run it. The tires weren't the same as the tracks in the woods. The Maserati had twenty-inch tires, and the tracks he'd found were made by a sixteen-inch tire, quite possibly a Michelin based on the tread pattern. Sixteen-inch Michelins were very common, so narrowing it down to a specific car would be impossible.

But at least it was another data point. Just because Trent was driving a Maserati didn't mean he hadn't driven something else two nights ago, same as his .22 caliber pistol didn't rule him out either.

The other thing Dax planned to do was get someone

out to change the locks. Trent had handed over his key, but that didn't mean he didn't have another one.

"You okay?" he asked Robbie.

She took a step away from him as if realizing she was still clinging to him and nodded.

He wanted to drag her back again, but refrained. "Do you want to talk about it?"

"Not really." She frowned in the direction Trent had gone. "He wanted me to take him back."

"And you told him no, which is when he raised his voice."

She nodded. "I told him to go back to Kimberlee, and he called me a fucking cunt. I guess you heard the rest of it."

"I heard him. First of all, no man who respects you or claims to care about you would ever call you a name like that. And second, I hope you don't buy his bullshit. You're the one who made Roberta Sharpe, not him."

"I know. He used to tell me that I needed to stop dreaming about characters and plots because it was childish. People like me didn't become famous writers. He's right that he made it possible, though. Because I stayed home to cook and clean and be a housewife, I had time to daydream when I was alone. I wrote in snatches when I could. It would have been harder with a regular job."

"I suspect you'd have found a way."

Her gaze met his. She didn't look away, and he found himself caught by what he saw in her dark eyes. There was a world of pain in Roberta Sharpe's soul. He had an urge to make it go away. Not that he could, but he wanted to. Too bad he had issues of his own to deal with.

"Maybe I would have. I wish I'd used my maiden name for my books. Now I'll always be Roberta Sharpe."

"It's a pen name. Same as if you'd called yourself Kayleigh instead of Roberta. What if you'd gone with Kayleigh Sharpe? Or what if you used your pets' names? Lucy Oliver—hey, that's good."

A smile turned up the corners of her mouth. "Cute. Maybe I'll write the romantic fantasy I want to write and use that name instead. Daphne would have a cow." Her smile faded. "She wants to know where I am with the new book. I'm nowhere. I keep trying to force it, but nothing happens."

"Guess you aren't ready yet."

It was all he knew to say. He didn't know what it was like to be a writer, but he imagined it was the same as painting or composing music. First you needed inspiration, and then you created. His thing was computer code, and that just came to him. Coding was creative, but in a technical way, not an artistic way like writing books.

He got lost in writing programs when he wanted to stop thinking about the real world for a while. It was his form of escape. If there was such a thing.

She folded her arms and looked over at the creek and the field beyond. "What if I'm never ready? What if it's over, and I can't do it again?"

"If you never wrote another word, would you be happy?"

She shook her head.

"Then you'll figure out a way."

She turned to him with a watery smile. "I've known you for three days now, and you've said more nice things about my creative ability than Trent ever did. Is that crazy or what?"

"He's an asshole. I'm glad you told him to get lost."

"There was a time when I wouldn't have told him to leave. I used to dream of what just happened, minus him getting angry. He'd come back and tell me he'd made a mistake. He'd grovel, and I'd finally relent. Then we'd be happy." Her expression hardened. "Not at all how it works in real life. If I took him back, he'd cheat on me again."

"I think you're probably right, and I'm sorry about that."

"Thank you, but I'm okay with it. Not the cheating, but the knowing. Because I won't let him hurt me again."

"Hey, you want some ice cream?" He didn't know what else to say. Plus, women liked ice cream when they were sad. Or angry. Either way.

"It's a little early, isn't it? We were still eating breakfast."

"Oh, yeah." They'd had to leave the food behind when Trent arrived, but he could fix that.

"Thank you, Dax. For all the stuff you did and said. It made Trent angry, which I enjoyed very much."

"My pleasure. Want to go inside and reheat breakfast?"

"Sounds good."

He was glad she hadn't let Trent ruin her appetite. It hadn't been difficult to hold her close and tell her ex that she made him crazy. The funny thing was, now that he'd touched her, held her by his side, thought about what it'd be like to take her to bed, he wanted to see if it was true.

He wanted to strip her naked and make her gasp his name, and then he wanted to hold her close and make her feel safe. He couldn't, because it wasn't professional or wise, but he damned sure wanted to.

ROBBIE SIGHED when her phone rang, but she picked it up and swiped to answer. "Hello, Daphne."

"Sweetheart! I'm just so excited about the conference, and I wanted to see how the speech is coming along."

"Are you in a cab?" Robbie could hear traffic noise. Honking horns, screeching brakes, the sounds of city life that fascinated and repelled her at the same time.

"Yes, darling. I've got a meeting, but I wanted to check in and see how it's going. How is the bodyguard? Has he inspired any new words?"

Robbie's attention was caught by the movement of the zero-turn mower rolling into view. When she'd mentioned she needed to find someone to mow her lawn since the teenage boy she'd been using quit so he could concentrate on bringing his grades up, Dax said he'd do it.

He wasn't wearing a shirt. She hadn't expected that.

Her mouth dropped open and butterflies swirled in her belly. Since he'd hugged her possessively earlier, she'd been having trouble thinking of much else other than the way his solid body felt against hers.

Of the way it *would* feel if they were both naked.

"The bodyguard is singularly gorgeous, if you must know. He might inspire some words soon. We'll see."

Daphne laughed. "That's wonderful to hear! Guess I wasn't so dumb to insist on a beautiful man after all."

"I don't know, Daph. He's very distracting. For instance, he's mowing my lawn right now. Shirtless. I can't tear my eyes away."

"Take a picture for me. I want to see."

Robbie laughed. "He's too far away. I'll try to get one when he comes closer."

"I must say that you sound in a good mood. I haven't heard you like this in a long time."

"I don't know that it's a good mood. Trent was here this morning, and that definitely didn't put me in a happy frame of mind."

Nor did the idea someone who wished her harm was still out there. Nothing had happened since Dax arrived, but that didn't mean the person had given up. She thought about it every time she walked through the living room and saw the piano. It made her stomach twist with fear to think someone had been inside her home.

"You're kidding! What did he want?"

"To get back together, or so he said. I threw him out." She told Daphne the shortened version, though she left out the bit where Dax put his arm around her and kissed her head.

"Good for you, Robbie," Daphne said when she was done. "Good. For. You. Now tell me, are you working on your speech? Do you have a book title yet?"

Robbie's throat tightened. "The speech isn't done, but it'll be easy. This is a writers' conference, and they mostly want to know about my writing process and how I got a book deal. I don't have a title for the book. It'll come to me when it comes."

"Fine, fine. Just asking. So long as you're writing, I won't push too hard. I'd love to see some chapters though."

"It's still too rough," Robbie lied. "I'm not sure I won't change a lot of it, so I'm not ready for questions yet."

"Okay, just send me something soon. I'm dying to know what happens! Must dash. We're pulling up to the building."

They said goodbye, and Robbie put down her phone with a trembling hand. One of these days, if the words stubbornly kept refusing to come, she was going to have to tell Daphne the truth. But not yet. She still had time. She'd need a miracle at this point, but there was time.

Dax rolled across the lawn, his tanned torso glistening with sweat. He had on sunglasses and a ball cap, and he was the sexiest thing she'd seen outside of her imagination in eons. Ollie jumped onto her desk and stared out the window. Robbie reached up to pet him, and he pushed his head into her hand.

"He's easy on the eyes, isn't he?" she asked the cat.

"Bet he's terrible in bed though. Because no man who's that pretty in real life can do everything right, which is why I need to stop thinking about it, agreed?"

Pretending to date him was completely different from actually dating him. A man like that might be possessive as hell, an alpha caveman when you crossed the line from professional to personal. She shivered. That was the sort of man she wrote in her books, but she didn't want it in real life.

And yet...

"Still, what if he isn't bad in bed?" she murmured. Ollie purred and kept looking at Dax as he went from one end of the yard to the other. "What if he knows his way around the lady bits like a pro, huh? Not that we need to go there, because it would be way too complicated."

Not to mention it wouldn't be real. The way Dax Freed looked, he could definitely do better than a reclusive romance novelist who couldn't even look him in the eye for more than ten seconds. He'd said he didn't have a girlfriend at home, but that didn't mean he wasn't in the early stages of dating someone. Or didn't have plans to date someone as soon as he was free of this job with her.

Stubbornly, Robbie woke her computer and opened the blank pages of her next book.

"Come on, Damian. Talk to me."

Nothing happened, and her gaze fluttered upward. Dax was still there, still mowing, still looking like a wet dream come to life. She stared at him for a long time, at the ripple of muscle playing in his back and arms, at the sweat rolling down his torso, and felt desire flickering hot and strong inside.

But there was something else, too. Something...

She sat up straight and blinked. Damian whispered in her head. She closed her eyes, and he appeared. He was dark and beautiful, dangerous as always. He was also different somehow. But he was talking to her and she wasn't about to question it.

Robbie put her fingers over the keyboard and started to type.

Chapter Fifteen

DAX FINISHED THE YARD AND PUT THE MOWER BACK IN the garage. He'd turned on perimeter alarms for the trail cameras so he could keep tabs on any suspicious activity while he was busy. It was mostly animals, but there was the occasional hiker or two who strayed off the trail. They usually found their way back to it again.

Nothing had been unexplained or menacing, so Dax had kept mowing. Whoever had entered Robbie's house four days ago had done so when it was unoccupied, which suggested they weren't going to waltz in when there was activity.

Ian had called to say the police had lifted no fingerprints or DNA from the photo or box. Whoever had done it had likely worn gloves while creating and delivering their message, which meant they'd put thought into what they were doing.

Not the message he'd been hoping for. Random angry person was a lot better than person with a plan.

If the intruder turned out to be any of the angry

readers who sent random *I hate you* messages in response to Robbie's new book, Dax would eat his computer. No, this was someone with a plan, and that didn't sit well in his gut.

He was nowhere on the tire tracks, but he hadn't expected to be. Jared and Ty had returned and put up a camera near where the mystery person stopped and entered the woods, but the only traffic out there so far was random hunters in trucks that didn't typically have sixteen-inch tires.

As for Robbie's stalker, Ian was sending over what they'd gotten from the police reports. Basically, someone had sent her unhinged letters and emails around the publication of her first four books before going completely silent a few years ago. It wasn't impossible they'd resurfaced after all this time. Maybe Damian and Velvet's split angered them enough to break their silence.

The house was quiet when Dax stepped inside. Lucy was in the kitchen. Her tail thumped when she saw him. Ollie wasn't there, though. Dax went to pet Lucy then straightened and listened for the clicking sound he'd heard. Computer keys. Coming from the direction of Robbie's office.

He stopped in front of the door. Her back was to him, her desk facing the view. Ollie lay on her desk, off to one side, and Robbie typed like a woman possessed. Maybe she was writing a book, or maybe she was writing a scathing email. Either way, he wasn't interrupting her.

After he showered, he checked his inbox. He'd done

some digging on Trent earlier, and he was hoping for answers. He already knew the Maserati was borrowed, so that was no surprise.

"Well, shit," he murmured as he scanned the new info. He fired off a copy to Ian.

He'd have to tell Robbie what he'd learned, but first he was putting steaks on the grill and buttering her up with food. She'd eaten the reheated omelet this morning, but she'd refused lunch. Dax was making sure she ate dinner.

When Ian had given him this assignment, he hadn't wanted it. He couldn't say that now.

Not since witnessing her ex-husband call her names and suggest the only reason Dax could be interested in her was for the money, which had pissed him the fuck off. He'd felt her stiffen with hurt at the implication, and he'd wanted to dropkick Trent Sharpe into next week.

Then he'd wanted to take Robbie inside, strip her naked, and fuck her with all the passion and attention she deserved. Hell, maybe she was shy and maybe she wouldn't look him in the eye while he did it, but he damned sure knew he could make her moan.

But before she moaned, she had to eat. Dax went to the kitchen, took out the steaks and salted them on both sides, then prepared the potatoes and green beans for cooking before going out to start the grill. Robbie had an amazing outdoor kitchen, and the propane was good to go. He'd discovered she had an underground tank for the house, and the grill tapped into that. The tank was full, which he'd expected because Robbie had the money to keep it that way.

Unlike his parents when he'd been growing up in Florida. People had this idea that Florida was tropical, but it wasn't that way everywhere. The panhandle could get cold in winter, though not necessarily freezing. But when your house had no propane then it was fucking freezing to you as a kid. He remembered cold showers in summer, huddling under blankets in winter because his stepdad was a loser and his mom was too tired to start over. Sean would come cuddle with him and they'd pretend they were on a mission in space, because space was cold, but eventually they'd had to get out of bed and rush through dressing.

His mom had called just last week, asking when he thought he'd get back to Pensacola. Sean was in jail again, and Ken—Dax's stepdad—was out of work. He was a carpenter, and a damned good one, but he drank a little too much sometimes and had trouble making it to jobs when he was in the bottle. Mom still gave piano lessons, but it wasn't enough to make up the difference when Ken wasn't working.

Dax had said he didn't know when he'd make it down, but he'd send some money to help them get through. He always sent money, and Ken never thanked him. Mom did, but she was ashamed so Dax didn't ask questions. At this point in his life, he didn't expect anything. He sent money because it was his mom, and he did what he could for Sean—but there wasn't a lot he could do.

His brother had been indulged too much, and he expected everything to be handed to him. While Dax worked for his first car, his stepdad presented Sean with his own wheels—an old car, but still a car—as soon as he turned sixteen. That was only part of it. Sean was just handsome enough, and charming enough, to weasel his way out of trouble in high school.

But it all changed when he graduated and joined the military. He'd joined the US Navy, which should have been perfect for him, but then he'd done the boneheaded thing and started smoking weed. Didn't take the Navy long to find that in a piss test.

Buh-bye, Sean.

Dax's little brother had been bitter since. He took jobs, lost jobs, fucked too many women without condoms and had three little kids to support, and still couldn't get it together. This time he was in jail for stealing a bottle of Jack from a gas station liquor store. Of all the fucking things.

Dax went back inside to get the potatoes and green beans, which were wrapped in foil and ready for the grill. He'd put those on first, let them cook for a while before he added the steaks. Those only needed about four minutes per side, give or take.

He grabbed a beer and kicked back in a chair under the pergola near the outdoor kitchen.

It was peaceful out here. The yard was filled with birds and butterflies, and the views were incredible. He could see the faded red barn from where he sat—an old tobacco barn—and the creek that divided the yard from the field beyond.

He took a sip of his beer and opened his laptop to go over the information about Robbie's stalker. The reports contained all the messages and letters. They were definitely unhinged, going on and on about the stories and how she should have done them differently. One mentioned a writers' group that met once a month at a library in Arlington. That was interesting.

Dax pulled up the website for the group and looked over the current members. There were about fifty of them. Some were published authors with links to their own sites, and some had blogs that said they were working on publication. Nothing leaped out at him. The site didn't indicate how long someone had been a member, so that didn't help him determine who might have been there when Robbie was getting the letters.

The vegetables were almost done when she emerged from the house with Lucy. The dog bounded into the yard, and Robbie walked over to where he sat. He closed the laptop. Her hands were shoved into the pockets of her jeans, and she wore a fitted knit top that hugged her breasts. She was a little on the thin side, as he'd noted before, but her breasts were full for a small woman. He itched to get his hands on them. His cock started swelling at the thought.

He dragged his eyes from her tits and forced himself to think of other things. Dick deflating things. Unsexy things.

"There's a beer for you in the fridge if you want one," he said, nudging his chin toward the counter-height refrigerator built into the outdoor kitchen.

She opened the door, taking the beer out and using the bottle opener he'd left there. The top flipped off and she strolled over to take the chair beside him. "Smells good. I take it we're having steak tonight?"

"Yep. Just waiting for the veggies to get a little closer, then I'll pop the steaks on the grill."

"Want to eat outside or in?"

"How about outside?"

"Okay. I'll go get plates and silverware then."

He got to his feet before she could. "I'll do it. You sit and enjoy that beer."

She hesitated then sank against the cushion. "I guess I will since you put it that way."

He returned in a few minutes with what he thought they'd need. He'd had to search for steak knives, but he'd found them. He set everything on the table then checked the potatoes and green beans. They were done, so he moved them to the top shelf before dropping the steaks onto the grill to sear.

"Thank you for making dinner," Robbie said.

"You're welcome. Seemed as if you were working when I went inside to shower earlier. I thought I'd take care of dinner if you were still at it."

He heard her sigh. "I was writing."

He closed the lid of the grill and turned. "A book or an email?"

She laughed. "A book. *The* book. Damian is talking to me again."

"He talks to you?"

She sipped her beer. "Don't look so shocked. I don't mean he literally talks to me. I just hear his voice in my head." She closed her eyes. "Strike that. It sounds even worse that way."

He chuckled. "I get it. And I'm glad."

"Me too. I don't know how long it'll last, but I wrote five thousand words. That's a lot, if you don't know."

He checked the steaks. Still needed a little more sear before he flipped them. "It sounds like a lot. Are you happy with what you wrote?"

She kind of scrunched up in her seat. Then she smiled. "Maybe. I don't know. I might decide tomorrow that the whole thing is crap."

He hated like hell to intrude on her good mood, but he had to give her the option to know what he'd learned. He'd save the questions about the writers' group until later.

"I ran a background check on Trent. You want to know what I found? If not, I won't tell you until you're ready. Might explain why he was here today, though."

Robbie sat up a little straighter, determination in the set of her chin. "I want to know."

Best way to deliver bad news was to say it. Like ripping off a bandage. "He's broke. There's nothing left of his half of the divorce settlement."

Chapter Sixteen

Robbie was numb. Then she was angry.

"He spent twenty million dollars? In two years? Is he fucking crazy?" Her voice rose as she spoke so that she finished almost on a shout.

Dax looked grave. "It's a lot of money, but not if you have rich tastes. He spent six million on the yacht. He bought luxury cars, jewelry, an apartment in Paris and one in Venice. He took private jets everywhere, even if it was the next state or country over. He bought his own plane when that wasn't good enough, which was another six million gone. His wife spent a fortune, too. Did you know you can pay a hundred grand for a handbag?"

Robbie shook her head.

"Me neither. Buy ten of those and you've pissed away a million. They also gambled at casinos in Monaco and Las Vegas. Then there were the taxes they failed to pay."

Robbie couldn't believe it. "Wow. I mean *wow*. I guess I know why he wanted me to take him back."

It made her angry, and it made her feel that same inadequacy she'd always felt about herself. Trent had come to beg, but only because he was out of money. Not because he loved her and thought he'd made a mistake like he claimed.

Robbie took a swig of beer. "That lying son of a bitch. He said *you* wanted my money when it's him!"

She wished he'd drive back and try again. She'd *really* give him a piece of her mind. She'd been too polite when she'd told him she wasn't interested.

"You gonna be okay?"

"I'm fine. Pissed, but fine. I'm really glad I told him to get lost, you know? If I'd believed him, given him another chance, what would he have done to get his hands on more money?"

"I can't answer that," Dax said. "But I'm glad you told him no, too. You ready for steak?"

"Yes. Definitely."

Dax took the plates from the table and fixed them with steaks, baked potatoes, and green beans. He got butter and sour cream from the fridge and set those on the table. Then he took the seat across from her and nodded to her plate.

"Cut it and tell me if it's the way you like."

Robbie sliced into her steak, revealing a warm red center with pink juice. Her mouth watered. "It's perfect. Thank you."

Dax nodded and they began to eat. Everything was delicious and she discovered she was hungrier than she'd thought. The news about Trent made her angry but not so upset she couldn't eat. That was a good sign. When

Trent had announced he was leaving her, the stress caused her to lose almost thirty pounds. She'd put some of it back on, and then she'd lost weight again over the past few months. Not being able to write, plus worrying how people were going to react to *The Vampire King*, had taken a toll.

Now, however, she was hungry. She ate everything on her plate as they talked about unimportant things. The weather, the view, how she'd found her farm in the first place, her plans for building a new barn and getting a couple of horses someday.

It was small talk, but it was pleasant and surprisingly effortless. Maybe she was getting used to Dax being around. Or maybe he was just easy to be with. He didn't make her talk about Trent or her feelings, and she appreciated that. She needed time to process everything.

"Tell me about you," she said after they'd been talking about the farm and her plans.

His easy manner didn't change, but there was something about the way he looked at her that said there was a limit to what he'd say. "What do you want to know?"

"Where did you grow up?"

"In the Florida panhandle, near Pensacola."

"Aaand?" she prodded when he didn't say anything else. "Do your mom and stepdad still live there? What about your brother?"

"They do."

"What's it like? Do you go home very often?"

He seemed to hesitate, or maybe she imagined it. "It's muggy as fuck in summer, but it can get cold in winter. Sometimes—rarely—freezing. And no, I don't go back very often. The job keeps me busy."

"How did you end up living in DC?"

"I took a job with the CIA after I left the military."

"Were you a spy?"

His grin gave nothing away. "You have one hell of an imagination, don't you?"

"Sorry," she said a little sheepishly. "I like to know things. But you aren't a character in a book, so I should probably stop pelting you with questions about who you are. I can get carried away."

"It's fine. But I'm done talking about me. It's not all that interesting anyway."

She begged to differ but didn't say so. She couldn't figure out how without sounding like she was flirting with him. She didn't need him thinking that.

"You want dessert?"

"You made dessert?"

"We still have ice cream."

"Sounds good to me." She reached for his plate to stack it on hers.

"I'll take the plates in and get the ice cream," he told her, easily pushing her hand aside and grabbing her plate instead.

"You don't have to wait on me," she protested.

"You wrote today. That's cause for celebration, don't you think?"

Robbie couldn't quite stop the smile that formed as she watched Dax and his hot ass stride over to the back door. He'd been there *three days*. Three days, and he seemed to understand more than Trent ever had about how important her work was to her. Didn't make him a prince or anything. He could just be better at pretending interest than Trent ever was.

The smile faded. She despised her ex, but that didn't mean he was wrong about Dax being interested in her money. She'd be a fool not to consider it. It angered her that Trent could still crush her spirit after all this time. That he could make her question her judgment with a few emotionally charged words.

But he could. Her happiness evaporated as she waited for Dax. He returned with the ice cream a few minutes later. She waited for him to sit across from her, dipped her spoon in the bowl and licked it. Stewed over her thoughts. He didn't seem to notice, which pricked her a little.

"What else did you learn about Trent from your report?"

He looked up. "He split with Kimberlee about three months ago. He's also been in the area for a week. Just got that message when I was inside."

Her belly twisted. Trent had still had a key to the house until this morning. "He wouldn't threaten me, if that's what you're thinking. Not like that."

"I didn't say he did."

"But you *were* thinking it."

"I have to think about everyone, Robbie. It's my job."

She dropped her spoon. "It doesn't make sense. He's broke and wants to get back together, not kill me. He's not in the will, which he'd be a fool not to realize." She picked up the spoon again, shoved ice cream in her mouth.

"I agree it makes no sense. Neither does blowing twenty million in two years."

Her heart thumped as she swallowed a big spoonful of ice cream. He was right about that. And Trent was definitely an asshole. But she still didn't think he'd have a good reason to threaten her. Unless it was for show? To make her feel vulnerable enough to want him to stay in the house with her so he could work on her emotions and worm his way into her life again?

It was devious, but he might just do it. He wouldn't have anticipated Dax being there to stop him from staying.

"Tell me about the Capitol City Writers. Were you a member?"

Robbie's thoughts crashed to a stop. "Why do you want to know about them?"

"I got a copy of the stalker letters you gave the police. The group was mentioned."

She nodded, trying to get her mind off her ex's motives and onto the right track. "I thought it might be someone from the group at one time, but I didn't really know anyone very well. I went to a few meetings before I sold my first book, but that was ten years ago. We used to critique five pages of a work in progress. I took pages of an early version of my first book. I stopped going when I realized that all they did was workshop the first five pages over and over again."

"How many people were at the meetings?"

"Ten to fifteen, usually. They did writing exercises

and read pages for each other. There wasn't anything about the business or how to query editors. I had to look that up online myself. They were nice people, but it wasn't what I needed."

"They have a website. Looks like several of them are published."

"Really?" She hadn't kept up with them over the years. Maybe she should have checked back once in a while. "Good for them. Perhaps someone else took over and started moving the group in that direction. When I was there, it was two women in charge. One was an English professor, and I'm not sure what the other did. Anyway, they were the ones behind the writing exercises and critique sessions. They never emphasized the business end of writing and got upset if anyone tried to talk about that instead of what *they* wanted to talk about."

"Do you remember their names?"

"Michelle was the professor. The other one was… Laura? Lori?" Robbie shrugged apologetically. "It's been a long time. Are you suggesting one of them was stalking me?"

"I don't know, but I'd like to find out."

"But why? The letters stopped three years ago. And they weren't death threats."

"'*Liar. Thief. You won't get away with it. I'll tell the world what you did.*' That's in the last letter you got."

Robbie's heart pounded in that way it used to when she'd opened the letters in the first place. She hated being dragged back to that place again, but she understood he had a job to do.

"That's not a death threat."

"No, but one of the letters in the batch your assistant sent, the ones that came after the release of *The Vampire King*, used the same words in the same order. Except this one had some new words added. '*You deserve to die for what you did.*'"

Robbie's belly tightened. "You think she's back."

"She?"

"I don't know if it's a woman or not," she forced past the knot in her throat. "I just always assumed."

He nodded. "I'm sorry, Robbie. But, yes, I think this person is back."

Chapter Seventeen

Dax lay in bed with his laptop, looking over the trail cameras one more time, thinking about the Capitol City Writers. He'd looked them up again, but the website was something that'd happened in the past eight years. There was no member named Michelle, though there was one named Laurel.

She had a website and wrote thrillers. There was a picture. He'd show Robbie in the morning and see if it was the same woman.

As for Trent Sharpe, there was no evidence he'd been the one to leave the threat. Yet Dax had to consider the possibility. Robbie didn't want to believe he could have done it, but the man had a key and there'd been no signs of forced entry. The door not latching was feasible, but that still didn't let Trent off the hook. He might not have an obvious motive, but he *could* have one. Being twenty mil in the hole was a pretty big reason to make someone desperate.

Dax surfed over to Facebook and logged in with one

of his alternate profiles. Then he searched for Trent Sharpe. Once he'd gotten the info from Ian that Sharpe had been in the area for a week, he'd known he was going to have to dig deeper. It was too much of a coincidence that the man turned up at the same time a deranged person found Robbie's home address.

There were several Trent Sharpes, but Dax found the one he wanted easily enough. It wasn't locked down, and everything he posted seemed to be public. There were pictures of him on his sailing yacht in nothing but a speedo with a lithe, tanned woman lying on the aft deck, a waterfall of pale golden hair hanging over her shoulder as she propped herself on an elbow and smiled at him.

The photo was six months old and clearly taken with a selfie stick. There were a lot of photos like that, including photos of a naked Kimberlee—with her boobs and pussy hidden by adding solid bars over those areas—smiling into the camera.

She was a pretty woman, and obviously didn't mind being nude on camera. Unlike Robbie, he imagined. Robbie was beautiful, but probably not the type to allow anyone to take nude photos and post them on the internet.

There were more photos of the two of them as well as videos Trent had shared from TikTok. Lounging on the Riviera, standing beside a baccarat table in Monaco, boarding a private plane, skiing in the Alps. Trent had burned through a fucking fortune living the high life.

Dax opened one of his programs and copied the link to a script he'd created. He sent Trent a private message, ostensibly from one of his friend's accounts—fake, of course—hoping the asshole was dumb enough to click the link. If he did, Dax could scan his phone or computer and look for the Photoshopped image of Robbie in the coffin. If he found that, he'd go ninja warrior on the motherfucker's ass.

He checked out Trent's TikTok, but the man was more active on Facebook and Twitter. Kimberlee was the one on TikTok. And, look at that, she'd found herself a new man who appeared to have even more money than Trent used to have. He was older than Trent as well, judging by the head of iron gray hair.

Dax didn't give a fuck about her. She was clearly a fortune hunter, and she'd moved on to richer grounds. It was the least Trent deserved after what he'd done to Robbie.

Dax's phone buzzed a few minutes later. It was Ian.

"Got some news on Sharpe. Three days ago, he was at a bank in Rockville at the same time someone was leaving that mystery gift for Robbie. Couldn't have been him who delivered it."

Not what Dax had wanted to hear, but that didn't clear the man entirely. He thought of the way Sharpe had turned vicious on Robbie earlier, calling her a fucking cunt. It'd taken everything Dax had not to flatten Trent then and there. Robbie hadn't deserved that, but the way she withstood it told him it hadn't been the first time her ex had spoken to her that way.

Which only made him madder. Respect was key in any relationship, and Dax didn't think Trent had ever respected his wife if the way she'd talked about him refusing to cook for her or take care of basic chores—even when she was making millions—was any indication.

He'd also called Lucy an idiot dog this morning, insulting a creature Robbie loved before he'd asked her to take him back. Total fuckhead.

"He could have an accomplice. Someone he gave the key to who delivered it for him," Dax said. He wanted it to be true because he didn't like the guy, but that didn't mean it was.

"Seems a serious risk to take, but when the riches turn into rags, who knows what people will do? He was at the bank looking for a loan, but they haven't given him an answer yet. I'm inclined to think he won't get it. He still has the yacht, but he's borrowed against it too many times already. He's about a month away from repossession, maybe less."

"Day-um. How can anybody spend that kind of money in two years and have nothing left?"

"You do know a third of lottery winners tend to go bankrupt, right? They ignore the tax implications and spend too much on frivolous shit. Trent Sharpe treated his divorce settlement like lottery winnings. It's biting him in the ass now. Meanwhile, Robbie is flush and only getting flusher with her new book, despite the uproar."

"Which is why he showed up today to ask for another chance. Doesn't make sense he'd have left that threat, but maybe he wanted to scare her. Make her think about being in this house alone. He knew about the stalker because they were still together then. Maybe he wanted to frighten her into thinking that person had found her so he could swoop in and protect her."

It was a long shot, but possible. It was also possible her stalker really had found her and the whole thing with Trent was an unlucky coincidence.

"If it's true, then he's an even bigger idiot than he appears. You hacking his computer?"

"Yep. On it now. If he clicks the link I sent, I'm in. If not, I'll approach another way. If that photo is there, I'll find it."

And then he'd make sure Trent Sharpe got picked up by the police as soon as possible.

"Let me know if it turns up."

"Copy. Got another line of inquiry on the original stalker."

Dax told Ian about the Capitol City Writers and the two women who used to run it, as well as the similarity in language from the last letter Robbie had gotten three years ago and one of the current ones. The current one wasn't a diatribe, though. Just those same words, albeit with a death wish thrown in.

"Could be he or she has resurfaced," Ian said. "You think it's one of those women?"

"Robbie thinks the stalker was female, and a writer. Doesn't mean it's either of them, or that it's even related to the intruder, but it's something else to look at."

"Agreed. Jesus, other than that, all we've got so far are a bunch of emails and letters from a lot of cranks who're pissed off about her new book. Even then, the majority of them want her to hurry up and release the next one so they can find out what happens. You can add Natasha to that list. Libby got her reading the books, and she just finished the last one. She's pissed off about it, too."

"Oh, shit. I better not tell Robbie. I wanna take her to Brett and Tallie's tomorrow to meet everyone before we go to Vegas. She needs practice with a small crowd. Better nix the idea."

"Nah, Tasha won't say anything. I'll threaten her."

Dax snorted. "Yeah, right. She'll eat you for breakfast and spit out the bones."

Ian chuckled. "Trust me, Dax, I've got leverage. She'll toe the line."

"Your funeral, boss."

"Daddy, are you coming to read me a story?" It was Daria, Natasha's recently turned seven-year-old daughter. Ian and Natasha hadn't been married long, but Daria had taken to calling Ian Daddy like she'd been born to it. Ian was crazy about her, too.

"Oops, gotta run. The princess had a bad dream, and Natasha let her stay up. Must be bedtime now. Just a minute, sweetheart. I'm talking to Dax."

"Hi, Dax!" Daria yelled. "You have to come over and watch cartoons with me again!"

Dax laughed. "Tell her hi back, and tell her I'll come watch when I can."

Ian repeated the information. Daria called out, "Thank you!"

"She's watching something called *Bluey* these days in addition to the German language stuff. It's cute. Maybe give one a peek so you know what you're in for. She's going to hold you to it now."

"That's okay. She's a sweet kid. And smart as hell." He didn't have a lot of experience with children, but Daria was something extra.

"She *is* smart. I think we're going to have to get her into some gifted programs ASAP, or we'll have a cunning little rebel on our hands."

"You may end up with that anyway," Dax said with a laugh.

"Lord, give me strength," Ian muttered. "Gotta go read that book or she'll be back to give me hell. Holler at you later."

Dax did his rounds of the internet. He checked Facebook again, but Trent hadn't clicked the link. He'd give it until morning before he tried something else.

He closed the lid and tugged off his T-shirt when he heard the creak of Robbie's door. There was a footstep, then nothing. He waited, straining to hear Robbie or Lucy, and then he heard Lucy's toenails clicking on the wood floor.

Robbie called after her in a soft voice. He couldn't hear what she said, but it sounded like she was right outside his door. Dax slipped out of bed and went over to tug it open before she could retreat.

Robbie yelped, and he immediately felt like an ass. "Sorry. I thought I heard something."

She pressed a hand to her heart. She was wearing a tight-fitting tank top and loose pajama pants with a drawstring at the waist. He imagined easing the drawstring open and slipping his hands inside to cup her ass in his palms.

Shit. Abort, abort, abort. He did not need a raging woody when all he had on was a pair of athletic shorts.

"It was me. I was trying to decide—" She closed her eyes for a moment, then looked straight at him. He wondered how long that would last. "Trent has been texting me. I thought you might like to see it."

Every protective instinct he had flared to life. "Yeah, I would."

She slipped her phone from the little pocket made for it on the front of her pants. Cute.

"You want to come in?" he asked, taking the phone from her fingers.

Her gaze dropped to his chest and her throat moved. "I... um... Sure."

He pulled the door open and went over to the bed. He could have tugged on his shirt, but he didn't. He liked seeing Robbie flustered as she tried not to notice his skin. Maybe he wasn't the only one suffering from deprivation.

There was a chair in one corner of the room, and she took that while he perched on the bench at the end of the bed. He read her texts, laughing inside at the name she'd assigned to her ex-husband.

Asshole: Hey, sweet girl. I'm really sorry about earlier. I lost my temper. It was seeing that guy there, looking so fucking smug. Like he owns you. I got pissed. Please forgive me.

Robbie: Thanks for the apology. Dax isn't smug. He's doing his job to protect me. You may not realize it, but I've gotten threats. It's Dax's job to keep me from getting hurt.

He gave her a smile. He liked that she said that. He wasn't supposed to be obvious at the conference and on tour, but he didn't care if Trent knew he was her protector. Hell, he didn't care if the world knew, but it wasn't his call.

Asshole: I would never hurt you. Not like that. I mean I know I hurt you, but I'm so fucking sorry. I was stupid and blind and I just miss you so much. Give me a chance, Robbie. We were good together. You're my other half. I need you.

That was the end of the string. "You haven't answered him."

She spread her hands. "I know when I do, when I reject him again, he'll say something shitty. I just don't want to deal with it."

He handed her the phone. "Why don't you say what you want to say then block him? Or tell him if he replies with anything other than a polite response, you're blocking his ass permanently? Tell him you need time if it makes you feel better."

She nibbled her lip.

"Do you need time, Robbie?"

"No. There is no way on earth I'm taking him back after what he did, and I don't just mean cheating. He tried to erase me, Dax. For years, he tried to erase me—and I didn't want to see it. I kept thinking he was right. I did need to try harder, do better, be more engaging. I needed to watch what I ate so I didn't get fat, and I needed to be a good wife so he could succeed at his job. I internalized all of that, and it was so much like the things my parents said to me that I thought it was true. Even when I started out-earning him, I thought it was true."

Dax's gut twisted. He took her hand and tugged her

from the chair to the bench. Then he wrapped his arms around her and held her against him. All the while knowing he was playing with fire. That his cock was taking notice of her sweet scent and her soft curves and that he was going to need to work to keep her from discovering it.

He put his chin on her bowed head, rubbed it across the silk of her hair. "Your parents and Trent are wrong. Nothing they said makes any sense, Robbie. You're perfect the way you are. You don't need to fit anyone else's idea of perfection to matter. They're all jealous of you for not needing them to be content, and they want to tear you down. Don't you fucking let them."

She relaxed into him, her body subsiding by degrees, and he kept holding her. She had her phone in her hands and she started to type. He didn't intend to read it, but he could see it too easily.

I need time, Trent. This isn't going to happen overnight, if ever, and you need to understand that. Now please don't text me again tonight. And if you reply with anything other than goodnight or I understand, I'm blocking you permanently. Your move.

"I know you saw that," she said after she hit Send. "I'm not entertaining the idea of letting him come back. I just don't want to fight with him about it. If he thinks there's a chance, then he might be on his best behavior."

"Good thinking."

A moment later, her screen lit up. *Goodnight, honey.*

Robbie sighed. "I guess I could have figured that out for myself. I'm sorry I disturbed you."

He eased away from her, though he didn't want to. Her cheeks were a little flushed, which he hadn't noticed while he'd held her. "You didn't disturb me. I'm here for you, remember?"

She leaned back against the end of the bed and closed her eyes. "I know, but there are some things I should be able to do for myself. Telling my ex-husband to get lost is one of them."

"Seems to me you already tried and he didn't listen. He's not going to stop, Robbie. He's out of options and broke. You're not."

"Maybe I should just give him money. Then he'd go away."

"It's your money to do with as you want, but I've been in this business long enough to know it won't happen that way. You give him anything, he'll be back once he's spent it. He'll never stop trying to bleed you dry if you let him. Your business, but I don't recommend it."

She was quiet for a long moment. "I don't give my parents money very often for the same reason, so I know you aren't wrong. Why is it when people ignore and belittle you for your entire life, they still feel entitled to your success when you get some?"

He hated the hurt in her voice. Made him want to share things he usually kept inside. "I don't know. I send money to my mom. If I didn't, she and my stepdad would lose their home. I don't care about him, but I do care about her. Even if she did pretend like he wasn't a dick to me growing up."

Well, fuck. That last bit had slipped out. Not at all what he'd intended to reveal. Made him feel like an idiot. He usually tried to keep things surface level. So much easier than letting people in. They couldn't disappoint you if you didn't let them in.

"Oh, Dax. I'm sorry." Her small hand reached out and curled into his. Made it easier to tell her the rest since he'd started. The shit he kept behind armor-plated walls but couldn't seem to hold inside a second longer.

"It's okay. He didn't beat me or anything. Nothing like that. He just visibly preferred his own son—my younger brother—to me. He'd take Sean to McDonald's for burgers, only the two of them, and he'd buy Sean gifts when he had money, which wasn't very often, just for breathing. He never got me anything like that, and never took me for burgers. I mean, I knew he wasn't my dad, but it still hurt because I was a kid and he was supposed to love me too. I knew Sean was his, but I would have liked just a little of that attention for myself."

She squeezed his fingers. Her voice when it came was choked and angry. "How can people be so cruel to kids? I've never understood. How the fuck do you hurt kids like that?"

"It's okay. It was a long time ago. Doesn't matter anymore." It didn't, but it clearly still had the power to wound. Probably always would somewhere deep down. "To answer your question, I'm no longer surprised by what people do."

He'd seen enough shit in the Army and CIA and then with Ian's team. Holy shit, the crap people did—to each other and to children. Sometimes he woke up in a cold sweat thinking about the horrors he'd seen. The things he'd had to do to stop bad people from doing more of the same. It haunted him, even when he knew it was right. That he was on the side of morality and making people safe to live without fear.

Made his stepdad's petty shit seem like nothing. And it was nothing, but not when he'd been six or eight or twelve. Then, it had been everything wrong with his world.

"I shouldn't be surprised, but I am," she said, head bent. "My parents weren't mean, not intentionally, but what they did was abusive. I've mostly cut them off, but I still see them on occasion. I bought them a retirement condo in Myrtle Beach, and they still whine about how they need a new car or new golf clubs or whatever. If I bought them a Mercedes, they'd want a Rolls. If I got them a Rolls, they'd want a Ferrari. It never ends. So I don't listen to it."

He brought their clasped hands to his mouth and kissed the back of hers. "I think you're pretty amazing, Robbie. Fuck anyone who doesn't agree with me."

She gave him a watery smile before looking away again. "Guess you didn't know you were also going to be a therapist when you took this job. I hope you're getting extra pay for putting up with my crap."

He put his fingers under her chin and gently turned her head so she had to look up at him. He could see her pulse thrumming in her throat, but she didn't look away. He took that as a good sign.

"I like you, Robbie. I didn't expect to, especially after the way you told me a house was a house was a house when I wanted a tour the first night. Damn if you aren't interesting as hell, though. The way your mind works fascinates me, and the fact anyone ever made you feel less than amazing pisses me off in ways I can't begin to describe. I'm not getting extra pay for listening to you talk about yourself, and I wouldn't want it anyway. I'm paid to protect you, and that's what I'm going to do. Everything else is because I like you."

Her gaze dropped. Disappointment flared that she still wouldn't look at him for very long. But it quickly subsided when he realized she was staring at his mouth. His dick started to harden again. Her lashes lifted, dark eyes meeting his. Her pulse seemed to quicken, fluttering in the hollow of her throat.

Dax let his gaze drop to her mouth the way she'd done to him. He studied her lips. The lower one was fuller than the top, and the top had a little dip in the center. They were a dusky pink, and he wondered if they were as soft as they looked.

He told himself that kissing Robbie was the wrong thing to do, and yet he wanted it so fucking bad his balls ached with the need to press his mouth to hers. Just to see.

He wouldn't do it, though. He wouldn't take advantage of her trust. She was vulnerable. It'd be wrong to kiss her when her guard was down.

"It's okay," she whispered, and his eyes snapped to hers. "I want you to kiss me."

Chapter Eighteen

He stared at her for so long she started to wonder if she'd read the situation wrong. Embarrassment flared inside. Her body tensed, ready to propel her back to her room.

Before she could act, he cupped her cheeks and leaned toward her. Her eyes fluttered closed—and his mouth pressed to hers. So softly that Robbie thought she might melt into a puddle right there on the cushioned bench.

Her heart hammered wildly, and the blood beat in her ears so that she couldn't hear anything except her own pulse. She didn't know what had possessed her to take the leap and tell him she wanted him to kiss her, but she was glad she had.

Maybe it was the way he'd looked at her mouth or the way her skin had tingled beneath his gaze. Whatever it was, she'd found herself speaking before she could stop. And then she'd had to endure what felt like endless moments, but was probably only a few seconds, before his mouth touched hers.

His arm went around her hips, dragging her closer. She skimmed her palms up his arms and around his neck, trying not to think too hard about all that smooth muscle and nude skin on the way. From the moment he'd dragged his door open and she'd beheld him without a shirt, her body had been preparing for the sexual tension to snap. Her nipples tingled and budded, her pussy ached with dampness. Her clit throbbed.

She'd been telling herself it was only her. Even when he'd held her close to reassure her. Even when he'd kissed the back of her hand. Even when he'd put his fingers under her chin and said he liked her.

She'd been looking at his mouth, thinking how beautiful it was, and then he'd looked at her the same way and she'd told him to kiss her.

Thank God she had.

Their tongues touched and tangled, their lips tasting and teasing. It went on and on. Robbie's body was a mass of raw nerves. She wanted him to touch her. Wanted him to slide his hand over her breast, cup its weight, thumb her nipple.

But she couldn't will him to do it, and she couldn't tell him either. That *really* would be going too far. It was her body that wanted more, but her brain wasn't so sure. Yes, it'd been a long damned time. Too long. But she'd known Dax Freed for approximately three days. He might be the most skilled player to ever coax the panties off a woman he hardly knew, and she might be falling for every bit of it.

She knew it, and still she kept kissing him. He didn't make any moves. He kissed her, nothing more. Kissed her so long and expertly that *she* was the one who wanted to beg.

She couldn't, though. Couldn't get past the idea that begging a man she'd just met to have sex with her was too pitiful. The last thing she wanted to be was pitiful. A mercy fuck because he had some empathy for her.

Or maybe not even a mercy fuck. Maybe it'd be a *mercenary* fuck since she had a lot of money. He might be doing this for no other reason than her bank account was pretty fucking big, and she was alone. A lonely, rich, pitiful woman.

Robbie squeezed her eyes shut tighter and pushed him away before she lost the last shred of her dignity. He seemed to be breathing as hard as she was if the rise and fall of his chest was any indication.

"I shouldn't have done that," he said roughly.

"I wanted you to." No matter her insecurities, she couldn't let him take the blame when she'd asked him for it.

"Yeah, but I should know better."

She didn't know why hearing him say that hurt, but it did. He got to his feet and shrugged into his shirt.

Robbie stood. "I should go."

He raked a hand through his hair. "Probably a good idea."

She turned away, hurt, frustration, and confusion warring inside her. She was almost to the door when he caught her wrist and stopped her. Then he turned her and pushed her against the wall, caging her in with his muscular body. It ought to have frightened her, but it didn't.

If anything, it thrilled her.

"Listen to me, Robbie. I shouldn't have kissed you, but I fucking *wanted* to. So damned bad. I want more than that. I want to strip that tank top off your sweet body and suck your nipples until you see stars. Then I want to drag those maddening pajama pants off and suck your clit before I fuck you into the best orgasm you've ever had. I *want* to do those things, but not because you're feeling vulnerable or lonely or because I'm convenient. Or even because you're rich and I'm not—though I have money, and I don't need yours." He leaned in, ran his nose along the column of her throat, then lifted his head to spear her in place with his gaze. "That's not why I'm here. I'm not supposed to want you. I'm supposed to protect you, and I'm trying really fucking hard to do that. Even from me. Understand?"

Robbie swallowed. The heat and strength of him surrounded her, but he didn't scare her. "Yes," she whispered, her body on fire with the desire to be touched.

He took a step back, his eyes pinned to hers. She couldn't tear her gaze away. Strangely, she didn't want to.

"Go to bed, Robbie."

She stood with her palms to the wall, breathing him in, wanting to breach the distance between them and go back to that place of want. But it wasn't possible. Not tonight. Maybe not ever.

"Please," he said roughly. "Go. We'll talk in the morning."

"O-okay." When she was in the hall, she turned around. He was still standing there, still looking impossibly sexy and broody. "I'm sorry, Dax. I shouldn't have asked you to kiss me."

"I'm not sorry you did. Better not ask again though. For both our sakes."

Robbie nodded before slipping into her room with Lucy and closing the door. She stood with her forehead on the wood, breathing evenly, trying to calm her racing heart and aching body.

He said not to ask again. But she wanted to so much it hurt.

Chapter Nineteen

Nerves fluttered in Robbie's belly like trapped butterflies. She swallowed as she checked her reflection in the mirror. She'd put on a blue maxi dress with white Keds and a thin white sweater to cover her arms.

Why had she agreed to go to a cookout with a bunch of strangers? She'd spent the morning working—avoiding Dax, really—and when she'd emerged from her office and seen him in his athletic shorts and form-fitting tee, her stomach knotted so tight she'd caved in as soon as he told her what he wanted to do.

She could still tell him no. It wasn't too late. She was the client, and Dax couldn't make her do anything she didn't want to do. Except boss her around about her personal safety, which was completely different from forcing her to attend a random event with people she didn't know.

Her phone buzzed with an incoming text. She groaned when she saw the name.

Asshole: Hey, beautiful. How are you today?

How was she? She'd gone to bed sexually frustrated. She was falling for a man who might not be any good for her, despite saying she was done with men, and someone had broken into her house and threatened to kill her. Oh, and her stalker was almost certainly back in the business of writing hateful things to her.

Yeah, so not all that great really.

Robbie snatched up the phone, frustration humming deep inside. *Fine, thanks. I'm working right now. Can't text.*

It was a lie, but she had no problem lying to Trent. He certainly hadn't had a problem lying to her.

Asshole: Okay. I want to see you soon. Can we figure something out?

Robbie: I'll text you later.

Asshole: Tonight?

Robbie groaned. *Yes. Bye.*

He didn't text back. She thought he might be learning. Now if only she could find the balls to block him permanently, she'd be doing great. But she didn't like confrontations, and he would damned sure get confrontational if she blocked him.

She grabbed her handbag and went to meet Dax. He was waiting in the kitchen, at the island, and her heart skipped a beat. Good lord, he was handsome. He wore jeans, a navy T-shirt with three buttons at the neck —undone—and a pair of black Nikes.

He looked her over with heated eyes. Her skin prickled.

"Do we really have to go?" she asked.

"You don't have to do anything you don't want to

do. Like I told you, it's good practice. But if you'd rather not, say the word and I'll text excuses."

Robbie grumbled. She knew he was only trying to prepare her. Vegas was going to be a thousand times more intense and busy. She couldn't run away when she had a contract to fulfill. Her assistant was an extrovert who had no problem talking to people, but she could only do so much. The organizers had paid Roberta Sharpe for a speech, not Autumn. She was stuck.

When this was all over, Robbie was flying to New York and choking Daphne. She should have never let her outgoing, extroverted, never-met-a-stranger editor/friend talk her into any of it. Not even the book tour.

"I'll go."

"Thought you'd see it my way."

Robbie glared. "Don't be smug."

He laughed. "I'll try." He turned his computer toward her. A smiling blond lady of indeterminate age stared back at her. "Do you recognize this woman?"

Robbie went closer, peering at the screen. "Should I?"

"Her name's Laurel Johnson. She writes thrillers, and she's a member of the Capitol City Writers, though nothing on her site or theirs tells me how long she's been a member."

"Laurel? I guess that could have been the name, but she doesn't look familiar. It could be the photo throwing me, though."

It was airbrushed and glamorized, which was why the woman looked of indeterminate age. Dax canted the laptop toward him so he could type and she could still see the screen. A website came up.

Laurel Johnson - Bestselling Author of Books that Go Bump in the Night

"Cute tagline," Robbie said.

"She published her first book six years ago, actively writing for twelve. She's on the planning committee for the conference in Vegas and she's speaking on a thriller panel there."

Robbie's heart thumped. "You think she wrote the letters?"

"I don't know. It's possible. She lives in Waldorf, Maryland. It's a couple hours' drive to Mill Landing."

"How would she have found out where I live?"

Dax clicked one of the tabs on Laurel's site. Her booklist came up. He pointed to the publisher name. *Spring Books.* "Maybe she found out through your mutual publisher?"

"Daphne would never share my address."

"She's not the only person working at Spring Books. Someone else might not be so careful."

Robbie nodded slowly. Dax spun the computer around to face him and clicked it shut. "It seems unlikely it's her, I'll grant you that. Ms. Johnson has a professional writing career and her books are about detectives, not vampires."

Frustration and fear hammered her. "It's been five days since someone broke in. I'm not saying I want them to come back, but the fact they haven't done anything since—couldn't that mean it was just a nasty, opportunistic prank?"

He seemed to be studying her. Finally, he spoke. "The night after we put the cameras in, there was someone who parked on the road on the north side of your property. At approximately 3:12 a.m., they walked through the woods holding a pistol. Their face and body were obscured by a mask and bulky clothing. They walked to the edge of the woods and stopped about a hundred feet away. They looked at the house for several minutes before turning and disappearing into the trees again."

Robbie's insides turned to liquid. She grasped the back of a chair, held it tight. "That was the day after the break-in."

He nodded. "There's been nothing since. Still doesn't mean it was just a prank, or the person isn't looking for an opportunity to try again. They're still out there."

"Was it a man or woman?"

"Couldn't tell. Tall enough to be a man, a somewhat masculine gait, but nothing definitive."

Fear tightened her throat. "They saw the cameras. That's why they covered up."

"Maybe. But they already came prepared because their face was never visible. That doesn't mean they knew about the cameras, though. I'd hide my face too if I was up to no good."

A masked person with a pistol, staring at her house in the middle of the night. It was creepy as hell. "I don't want to leave Lucy and Ollie alone. You have to cancel for us."

He got up and came over to put his hands on her

shoulders. "The house alarms will be set, the police know to patrol more frequently since the break-in, and I'll be getting perimeter alarms while we're gone. If anyone approaches the house, I'll know. So will the police. Ollie and Lucy will be safe inside. I think we should go because I think you need to get out, but if you're too scared to leave them, we can stay."

Robbie bit her lip nervously. She knew herself. She didn't want to go at all. But was she using the break-in and threatening person on her property as an excuse, or did she really think her pets were in danger?

Her house had an alarm system now. The police patrolled the area regularly. The cameras would capture anyone approaching the house and send an alert. It didn't get much safer. And she couldn't stay holed up in her house forever. Staying would mean she was letting her enemy win, letting them scare her so badly she couldn't function like a normal person. She already had enough problems acting normally.

"Okay. I'll go."

"Good." He smiled at her. "You look beautiful by the way."

"Thank you. I'm not just scared about the house," she admitted. "I'm scared about meeting your friends."

"Don't be. You're fascinating, and they're going to love you."

"I get tongue-tied. I never know what to say."

"Which is why we're practicing. They'll understand. You're a quiet person, which is fine. Hell, some of them are introverts and some aren't. Warning though. Libby will talk your damn ear off. Maddie too. You don't even have to say anything. Just nod or give short answers from time to time, and they'll do all the work."

Could it really be that easy? "I might."

"It's going to be fine. You can also stick by my side if you're more comfortable. I won't leave you except to fetch drinks, okay?"

"You don't have to stick to me like glue. But don't leave me alone for long."

He squeezed her shoulders. "I won't. You ready to go?"

Robbie drew in a breath. "Ready as I'll ever be."

Chapter Twenty

THEY PULLED UP TO A HOUSE IN A LUSH GREEN SETTING that backed up to water and had a small dock of its own. There were several cars in the drive. Robbie huffed in a breath.

"You got this," Dax said. "Follow my lead."

She nodded. He came around to her side and opened the door. She was surprised when he wrapped her hand in his and led her toward the house. Her heart throbbed as he knocked. A moment later, the door flew open and a small woman with curly blond hair stood there, a big smile on her face.

"You came!"

"You invited us," Dax said. "Of course we came. Tallie, this is Roberta, though I think she prefers Robbie. Robbie, Tallulah, who most definitely prefers Tallie."

"I do indeed. Come on in, you two. I'm so excited to meet you, Robbie. Dax says you're a writer."

"Um, yes. I am."

"That sounds exciting."

"It can be," she said, feeling a little warm. Robbie noticed that the other woman had one hazel eye and one blue. She'd never seen that before. It was arresting, and it made Tallie seem a little like a mythical creature.

Tallie smiled again and pointed at her face. "Heterochromia. In case you were wondering. It's hereditary."

Robbie looked away. "Oh, I didn't mean—"

Tallie hooked an arm in hers and dragged her inside. "Nonsense. You'd have to be very unobservant not to stare. I'm used to it."

"I don't really, um, stare at people," Robbie protested.

Tallie patted her hand. "It's okay. Promise. Brett!" she hollered. "They're here!"

A tall man emerged from the kitchen with a platter in his hands. "Hey, dude, glad you could make it. And you must be Roberta Sharpe."

"Robbie."

"Robbie, then. Glad to meet you. Come on outside and meet the rest of the gang. Dax, grab a couple of drinks for you and Robbie. Wine and beer in the kitchen. Sodas and water in the cooler outside."

Robbie thought she was about to panic at the sheer exuberance going on, but it didn't actually happen. Tallie kept chattering as she led Robbie outside, arm still wrapped in hers. They made the rounds with Tallie introducing Robbie to everyone. Then she deposited Robbie at a table with Libby, Maddie, and Angie. Dax appeared with a glass of wine, and she took it gratefully.

She needed a drink to calm her nerves. She was worried about Ollie and Lucy, though Dax had promised he'd tell her if he got any perimeter alerts she needed to know about. If someone approached the house, the police would be on the way.

She was also overwhelmed with all the chatter and activity going on.

Dax didn't stray far. He stood behind her, touching her shoulder from time to time to reassure her, and talked with one of the men. She felt his touch like a brand. It both unnerved her and reassured her. Of all the people here, he was hers.

Her advocate. Her friend? She thought he might be, though maybe he was just doing his job. He'd told her that everyone at the party would know he was on assignment. They didn't have to pretend to be a couple like they would in Vegas. The disappointment she'd felt had surprised her.

"I promised Jared I wouldn't say anything," Libby said, dragging Robbie's attention from her own tortured thoughts. She was a pretty blond with glasses. She leaned forward conspiratorially. "But I think Damian had it coming. He needs to realize he can't take Velvet for granted." She pretended to pull a zipper across her mouth. "That's it. All I wanted to say. But brilliantly done, you. Can't wait for the next one."

She lifted her wine glass, waiting for Robbie to clink it. Robbie did, a bit stunned but also grateful.

"How are you getting along with Mr. Tall, Dark, and Nerdy?" Libby asked.

Maddie, the dark-haired one, laughed. "Dax is the least nerdy computer guy I've ever met. I mean he knows his code and everything, but he doesn't live in his mom's basement with a bank of ten computer monitors and every video game known to humankind."

Robbie thought of Dax's naked chest. No, definitely not the kind of guy who sat at a computer all day.

"We're getting along fine," Robbie said. "He leaves me to work and cooks dinner. I can't complain."

Maddie and Angie both looked interested. "Cooks dinner, huh?" Angie said. She was a redhead, pretty. Dax had told her that Angie worked at BDI too. In forensic accounting. There was also a lead pipe with her name on it in a bar they had in the basement of BDI. Robbie was going to need more detail about that at some point.

Maddie was an art appraiser, Tallie was an interior designer—it showed because her house was gorgeous— Libby worked as a virtual assistant, Cassie was a fashion and makeup YouTuber, and Natasha was a former international assassin turned combat and arms trainer at BDI. Except that she was currently heavily pregnant so not doing too much combat these days.

Robbie couldn't wait to lay eyes on Natasha, but she and Ian weren't there yet. Neither were Cassie and Ty.

"Dax is a good cook," Robbie said, dragging her thoughts back to the conversation. "It's been nice not to have to think about dinner while I'm working."

Libby's eyes gleamed. "Guess you can't talk about that, huh?"

Robbie laughed. "No. Sorry."

Libby sighed. "It's fine. I'm fine. I swore I would *not* talk about this. Jared made me. But I really am so excited to meet you. *Really* meet you, not just at a book signing or something. Jared said you cooked them dinner when they installed your security system. Thank you for that. He was very happy when he got home that evening."

Robbie glowed with the praise. Sometimes flattery felt wrong, but this didn't. Libby genuinely wanted to thank her for taking care of her man. "I'm very happy to hear he enjoyed it. My cooking skills are a little rusty."

"Not according to Jared."

"I can give you the recipe if you'd like."

Libby's eyes lit up. "Yes, please. I love trying new dishes, and since I know he likes it, it would be great to surprise him."

"I'll email it when I get home if you'll give me your address."

"Happy to," Libby said. "I can text it to you, or type it into your notes app. Whatever works. Or I'll text Dax and he can tell you. I absolutely do *not* want you to think I'm trying to get your personal info. I know it's been hard since the latest book came out."

Robbie swallowed as the three women looked at her. Tallie had gone back inside to check on food. Still, Robbie didn't feel uncomfortable. Maybe it was Dax's presence nearby, or maybe it was that these people had his trust.

"It has been a little difficult. People get invested. They, um, don't like it when you shatter their expectations."

"It's just a book," Angie said. Her eyes widened after

she said it. "I mean, sorry, it's not just a book to you and I wasn't implying—"

"It's okay," Robbie interrupted with a laugh. "I know what you mean. It's not real life and no one is really being harmed, so why do people get so angry, right?" She shrugged. "I don't know. I *am* grateful to them for caring about my characters so much, and most of them are truly great people. There are some, though… Anyway, it *is* just a book, and life can be much worse. But I think for some of them it's an escape and that's why they get upset. They wanted to be happy, not sad, and I made them that way."

"I didn't see it coming," Libby said. "I was upset that I'd reached the end, but I'll one-click that next sucker so fast my e-reader will be smoking for a week. I need to find out what happens."

"And what if it's permanent?" Robbie asked. "What if Velvet was never right for Damian, and he needs to find his true mate instead?"

Libby pulled in a breath and let it out, her cheeks puffing almost comically. "Then I guess I'll get over it. I'll have to, right?"

Robbie smiled. "Yes, I guess so. But don't despair yet. I'm still writing, and anything can happen."

Tallie emerged from the house with two women. It was clear which one was Natasha as she had a big belly and looked beautiful. The other must be Cassie. Tallie brought them over to where the women were sitting and introduced Robbie.

Libby cut a look at Natasha, who arched an eyebrow as she maneuvered herself into a chair. After everyone asked Natasha how she was feeling and they'd discussed that for a while, Natasha looked directly at Robbie.

She was lovely, with blond hair and blue eyes and a tiny gap in her front teeth. She also had a gorgeous mermaid tattoo that covered the inside of her forearm beneath the diaphanous material of her sleeve. Robbie was trying to reconcile the fact she'd been an assassin with the sweet, expectant-mother look she had going.

"I have been threatened under pain of death by my husband not to ask you about your plans for Damian and Velvet," Natasha said. "And I won't. But thank you for the hours of entertainment. I have discovered romance novels, thanks to Libby, but yours were the first I read."

Robbie felt the sting of tears forming. She loved what she did, and it always made her happy when she knew someone found enjoyment in her stories. "Thank you. I'm truly honored."

"Oh fine," Angie said, rolling her eyes as she picked up her phone. "Somebody give me a link. I need to read these books."

"Me too," Maddie and Cassie said at the same time.

"And me!" Tallie called out from where she was holding a platter while Brett took something from the grill.

"Maybe wait," Robbie blurted. "I kind of did something bad in the last book, and you won't find out what happens for another year."

"No," Libby said, shaking her head. "Don't warn them. They can suffer like Natasha and I have to. We can form a support group or something."

Angie laughed. "I'm not afraid. Here." She handed her phone to Libby. "Find it and buy it for me. I'm logged in."

"Done," Libby said a few moments later. "That's only the first book in the series, but once you finish that, it's easy to go to the next." She picked up her phone and typed with her thumbs. "Sending the link to everyone so you can get it yourselves."

Robbie was surprised at the warmth flaring inside. She'd only just met these women, some of them clearly didn't read romance, and they were all buying her book because two of them said they'd enjoyed the series.

"You really don't have to," Robbie said. "It's not necessary."

"It's not necessary," Tallie said, coming over to join them. "But we've been talking about starting a book club anyway, so why not let your book be the first? Maybe you could join us when we discuss it."

Robbie was still trying to figure out how to respond when Dax spoke. He put a hand on her shoulder as he did so. Every nerve in her body seemed to coalesce in that particular spot. Her mouth went dry, arousal zinging inside her.

"Robbie is not coming to your meeting to discuss her book. She has writing to do. Hearing your opinions, especially if you don't like something, interferes with the creative process."

It stunned her that he knew, but she was also touched. She put her hand on his and every pair of eyes focused on that action. She squeezed quickly and let go.

"It's true," she said, feeling awkward again but

determined to plunge through. "Weird maybe, but true. Besides, if you felt like you could only say nice things because I was there, that wouldn't be right. You should feel free to hate everything about it—but don't tell me, please."

"I never thought of that," Tallie said. "And I should have. I designed a room for a designer's showcase once then had to listen to a bunch of people tell me everything they hated about it in a 'meet the designer' session. It was very uncomfortable. I went home and cried. I mean, it was early in my career and I was still learning, but it crushed me. No matter how many positive things people said, it was the negative things that stuck with me."

Robbie nodded. "That's pretty much how it goes. I'm sorry that happened."

Tallie smiled. "It's okay, I got over it. But I totally understand what Dax is saying. Sorry I asked."

"It's fine. Thank you for inviting me. Maybe if it's someone else's book," she said, and then couldn't believe she had. But really, she didn't think she'd mind discussing books with these women. Just not her own.

"Then we'll do that," Tallie said firmly.

"Food's ready," Brett called as he set something down on the trestle table on one end of the patio. "Come fix a plate and don't be afraid to pile it up. We've got plenty."

Dax gave her a plate then proceeded to ask what she wanted as they went down the line. He filled the plate for her while also filling his. She didn't know if he understood how much it helped that he did that for her. It was a stupid part of her anxiety that she would have rushed through the line and only grabbed a small amount without really thinking about it. With him asking and helping, she ended up with a full plate of things she genuinely wanted to try.

They spent the next couple of hours eating, laughing, and talking before Dax leaned over and said, "Should we go let Lucy out?"

Robbie nodded, surprised to discover three hours had passed. She'd actually relaxed and had fun. With people. She'd even stopped feeling awkward after a while.

After the goodbyes were done, and the invitations to come again were issued, Dax walked her to his truck and opened the passenger door. Before she got in, she impulsively turned and put a hand on his chest. "Thank you, Dax. I had fun. I didn't expect to, but you were right. They were easy to be around."

"I'm glad." He ran a finger over her cheek. "You're beautiful when you're happy, you know that?"

She wished he'd do more than skim her cheek. Wished he'd put his arms around her and kiss her again, but she knew he wasn't going to. "Thank you. You make it easy for me to relax. I appreciate it."

He looked as if wanted to say something more, but then he nodded. "You're welcome."

He waited for her to get inside and belted in, then went around to his side and backed out of the driveway. The twenty miles back to Mill Landing seemed to pass much quicker than it had when they'd been going the opposite direction. They made small talk, though she kept wishing he'd tell her she was beautiful again.

Finally, Dax slowed before the long driveway that led to her farm. The headlights swept across the trees as he turned. Something in the trees caught Robbie's eye. Before she could make out what it was, Dax swore.

A second later, it hit her why he was so pissed. Swinging from one of the branches was a body.

Chapter Twenty-One

"It's not real," Dax growled.

Robbie's eyes were wide, her face pale. He hated that someone had taken what had been a good day for her and ruined it. If he got his hands on the sonofabitch, he'd fucking snap their neck.

Robbie spun to look behind them as he kept driving, but he knew it was too dark for her to see the body hanging from the tree. "How can you be sure?" she gasped. "What if someone committed suicide? What if…" She gulped, and he knew she was swallowing tears. "What if my book upset someone so much they took their life over it?"

He squeezed the wheel, anger a tornado inside. "I've seen hanging bodies. That isn't real, it's a dummy. It's swinging in the breeze, which means it's light. There was a hood over the head, and the body was too formless. Someone created it from stuffing jeans and a sweater with filling, like a Halloween prop. I'll check it out after I've gotten you safely inside and cleared the house. Also, if someone did kill themselves over your book—which is *not* the case here—that's their choice. Not your fault, Robbie. Never your fault."

She wrapped her arms around herself. He could hear her breathing. Dragging in air, trying to keep herself calm. "Right. Of course. Who would do such a thing though?"

"Someone who wants to scare you."

"There was a sign on the body."

Shit. He'd hoped she'd been too shocked to notice.

"Yeah. No doubt a message. I'll see what it's about."

She turned liquid eyes on him. "You didn't get a notice when they did that?"

"No. The first trail cam is a little farther along the drive. The cellular signal is better there."

"Do you think they were watching for us to leave?"

"It's possible. I don't know."

Dax parked beside the garage then disarmed the house alarms with his phone. They entered through the side door. Lucy was barking like mad as he slid the key in the lock. She bounded out the door and ran around them, bouncing up and down. Ollie sat inside the door and meowed when they walked in.

Dax was reasonably certain no one had entered the house, but he left Robbie standing in the entry with her pets while he removed his weapon from the holster and cleared the house. When he returned, she was sitting on the bench in the entry, Ollie in one arm and her hand on Lucy's head.

His heart squeezed at the sight of her looking small and scared. She'd done well with everyone today, but that wasn't what she would remember. "The house is clear. Nobody here. I need to go back down there and see what I can find out from the dummy."

Her spine stiffened as she sat up straighter. Her expression made him want to tear someone's throat out.

"Please don't leave us here alone. If someone's out there, waiting—" Her eyes squeezed shut. "I don't want someone to hurt you."

He would have laughed if she wasn't serious. He went over and knelt in front of her, putting his hands on her knees. Ollie was purring. Lucy licked his hand.

"Babe, I wasn't going to drive. If someone's there, they won't know I'm coming. I've done a lot of recon missions. I'll be all right."

She put a hand on one of his and squeezed. Her fingers were icy. "Can't you call the police? Or one of your friends?"

He searched her face. She didn't look away from him for once, and it chipped away at his determination. Whoever'd put the dummy there could be waiting, but he wasn't afraid they'd get the jump on him. Still, he took his phone out and texted Ian. Most of the guys were still at Brett and Tallie's, which was only twenty miles away. Someone could be there in a half hour or so. He could call the police, but they had enough to do without helping retrieve a dummy from a tree.

Ian texted back within moments. *Jared and Colt are on the way.*

Dax showed her the phone. "Not going anywhere. They'll secure the area and remove the dummy."

Robbie nodded as she leaned against the wall and closed her eyes. "Thank you."

When Jared and Colt arrived forty-five minutes later, Robbie was sitting at the kitchen island with a glass of wine she'd hardly touched. Dax already knew what they'd found because he'd been texting with them. They didn't have the dummy when they walked in. They'd put it in a trash bag to take back to BDI HQ where they'd go over it for prints or fragments of DNA, along with the sign that said what he'd begun to expect it would say before Colt texted the photo.

Liar. Thief! You deserve to die for what you did. You won't get away with it.

"We've checked the perimeter. Couldn't find anything. No cars parked nearby either."

And the only notifications he'd gotten from the trail cams were animals.

"Okay, thanks. Appreciate you coming out."

"Would you like a drink or something before you go?" Robbie asked. "Coffee?"

Dax was almost surprised to hear her voice. She'd been quiet for a long time now, and he hadn't tried to force conversation out of her. He knew she was processing it in her own way.

"Thanks, but I'm good," Colt said.

"Same," Jared added.

"I'm sorry to drag you away from the party," she said. "It was fun."

"It was, and you didn't," Colt told her. "This is what we do. Not happy someone did this to you, but happy to help. Always. We're all here for you, not just Dax."

Robbie bowed her head. "Thank you."

Colt shot him a look that said *we need to find this fucker.* Dax couldn't agree more. He walked them outside where they talked a bit about what happened next. It would take at least a couple of days before the lab had anything, and by then Dax and Robbie would be in Vegas. But maybe they'd get lucky and find who'd done this so Robbie could live without fear once she got home again.

"I've checked the trail cams," Dax said. "Nothing but a few deer. Need you to check the GPS location on Laurel Johnson, though."

He'd informed the team earlier about the author who might have been in the Capitol City Writers when Robbie was there. Considering the woman was on the committee for the conference that was about to start in Vegas, he'd be awfully surprised if she had time to harass Robbie. But he had to check.

"On it," Jared said, tapping his phone. Dax was usually the one to go searching for someone's digital trail, but he didn't mind handing it over this time.

When he went back inside, Robbie was still at the island. Still turning the wine in her hand rather than drinking it. She looked up with glassy eyes. "I'm scared, Dax."

He walked to the island and wrapped his arms around her, thoughts of keeping his distance evaporating in the face of her fear. "I know. It's gonna be okay."

She closed her fists in his shirt, let go again. "I'm

pissed as hell, too. What kind of person does that? It's sick."

"Someone who wants to scare you." He stepped back, brushing her hair from her face. He ached to kiss her but didn't. "The note pinned to the dummy said the same thing your stalker used to say." He repeated the phrase. Her eyes squeezed shut.

"I don't know what that means. I've never known what it means. Damian and Velvet are *mine*. They always have been. I didn't *do* anything."

"I know." He didn't know, not really, but he believed her.

She put her head in her hands. "I don't think I'm going to sleep tonight."

"I'm here. I won't let anyone get to you. You need to try. It's about to get crazy with the trip and your assistant arriving."

Autumn Pinkney was coming tomorrow to help her prepare, and they were flying to Vegas the next day. Everything was ramping up, and he still didn't have the answers he wanted.

She nodded. "I know… But I don't think I can sleep. I… Do you think you could sleep in my room? The bed is huge, and Lucy will get between us. I know it's a big ask, I really do, b-but I'd feel safer if you were there."

Dax's gut tightened. The last thing on this earth he wanted to do was spend the night in Roberta Sharpe's bed like they were besties having a sleepover. But he couldn't say no. Not when he knew she wouldn't sleep otherwise. Maybe, once she drifted off, he could go back to his own room.

Even as he thought it, he knew he wouldn't. He wouldn't leave her in the middle of the night like he was sneaking out after a one-night stand. He'd lay there all fucking night, miserable, aching for her, so long as she slept.

Dammit, this assignment sucked hard, just not in the ways he'd thought it would.

"Yeah. I'll do it."

———

ROBBIE FELT SOMEWHAT foolish for asking Dax to go to bed with her, but when she walked out of her bathroom in pajamas and saw him sitting on one side of the bed in his athletic shorts and a T-shirt, legs crossed at the ankles, she wasn't all that sorry anymore. He glanced up at her and smiled reassuringly. He had his laptop open and Lucy snuggled beside him. Ollie was sitting at the foot of the bed, tail flicking, staring at the scene like something was completely wrong.

Robbie approached her side, feeling self-conscious. She pushed the covers back and got in, then leaned back against the headboard, her blood humming.

"You still want me here? I can go if you've changed your mind." His voice was a low, sexy rumble that arrowed straight to her lady bits.

She thought about it. Thought about him walking out the door, shutting it behind him. A kernel of uneasiness flared inside. "I haven't changed my mind. And I'm sorry, I know it's stupid."

"It's not stupid. Somebody did something shitty that

scared you, and you don't know who they are or where they are. Wanting company is completely understandable."

"I'll be better tomorrow. I swear."

"I know you will. You've been living out here for years by yourself. This is something new, though. You just have to wrap your head around it."

Her phone buzzed. She must have groaned because Dax looked over at her.

"Problems?"

"It's Trent. I promised I'd text him back tonight, but I never did."

Asshole: I thought you were going to text me. It's after 10.

Robbie: Sorry. Been busy. What's up?

Asshole: I said I wanted to talk to you, remember?

She was conscious of Dax just a few inches away. He wasn't looking at her, but he knew she was answering Trent. He didn't ask what they were saying. Her thumbs hesitated over the keyboard. What was there to say? Really? She already knew she didn't want Trent in her life again. She'd just been avoiding telling him. Avoiding the confrontation.

She thought of the women she'd met earlier. How happy and self-confident each of them seemed. How brave they'd been when faced with adversity.

She'd gotten the story of Angie and the lead pipe. The woman had been locked in a pitch black warehouse, and she'd defended herself with a rusty pipe she'd found on the floor. Even when she couldn't see a thing, she hadn't let it stop her. She'd walked that warehouse, mapping it in her mind using nothing more than her hands on the walls. She'd ventured into nothingness as she'd moved into the middle, but she'd kept going. That's how she'd found the pipe and been ready.

Tallie had been kidnapped and held captive by a sick doctor who did human experiments. Libby had survived a woman-hunt and being kicked and beaten when she'd been hiding information from her boss. Maddie and Angie had survived being locked in a cage with a bomb —which, apparently, Natasha had done to them when she'd been working for the other side. Cassie had been held in Ty's apartment for hours by a cop-turned-stalker. And Natasha—well, she hadn't talked about much, but Robbie suspected she'd survived far more than any of them had.

If they could get through all that, Robbie could get through this. Starting with telling Trent it was over between them for good.

I know, and I'm sorry. But it's not going to work between us. I can't forget what you did to me. To us. I don't want to talk, and I don't want to get back together. I've moved on. I suggest you do the same.

She hit Send, her insides swirling.

She didn't have to wait long for a reply. She read it because that's what those badass women would do.

Asshole: Fine, but don't say I didn't warn you. Hope you're prepared for what happens next. It's your funeral, Roberta.

Anger spiked. Robbie tapped the keyboard furiously. *Are you kidding me right now? Do you think this is a joke? Are you the one who broke into my house and left a death threat? Did you show up at three a.m. with a pistol and stare at my house? And what about that fucking dummy with the note?*

She threw the phone down, disgusted and furious. Lucy whined. Ollie lifted his head from where he'd finally settled down. Dax frowned at her.

"What's wrong?"

"I told him it wasn't ever going to happen. Then he threatened me."

Dax shifted instantly onto high alert. She could see it in the set of his jaw, the seriousness of his expression. He'd scented danger, and he was prepared to protect her. The knowledge warmed her, made her feel less alone.

"What threat?" he growled.

She picked up her phone and thrust it at him. He read the exchange, his expression clouding. "Motherfucker."

Remorse set in. "I shouldn't have told him those things about what happened, should I?"

He handed the phone back. "It's okay. It doesn't change anything."

Their fingers brushed, and her skin tingled with heat and want. She was losing her mind. That was the only explanation for why she'd asked him to come to bed with her, and why she wasn't asking for anything else.

He'd told her it couldn't happen between them. That it *shouldn't* happen. Because he was supposed to protect her, not get involved with her. But they *were* involved. She was. And she wasn't so sure it was a bad thing.

Maybe he wasn't any good for her, and maybe her money was tempting, but didn't she know herself better now? She wasn't going to fall in love with a man just because she lusted after him. She could want him, and she could have sex with him if the opportunity arose. Didn't mean she had to marry him.

Like Daphne had said, she needed to act thirty-five instead of twice her age. Though she had seventy-year-old readers who were more adventurous than she was. She knew because she'd read their letters.

Robbie decided she was really going to give Daphne hell when this was over. Why did the damned woman have to ask for a tall, dark, and handsome bodyguard as if she were placing an order for takeout or getting her hair colored? The whole boyfriend thing was over the top and completely unnecessary. Daphne should have gotten a female bodyguard because Robbie wouldn't lust after a woman and wouldn't be arguing with herself about her feelings right now.

Her phone buzzed and she stifled a groan.

Asshole: What the fuck are you talking about? I don't know about any of those things, though you're probably making it all up for attention. How else you getting that big dickhead to stay with you and give you his cock? If he really is, which I fucking doubt. Pitiful, shy thing like you? What I meant is you aren't going to like what happens next because I was married to you before you got famous. I know everything about you, and I've got no reason to keep it to myself now.

She was blinded by fury. And hurt. She typed an answer and hit Send. Then she blocked him so he couldn't respond.

I know you're broke, you stupid asshole. I know that's the only reason you want me back. Well, fuck you. I don't care if you're broke. You never supported my dreams, and you aren't getting another dime of my money. Go to hell!

"Everything okay?"

"Perfectly fine," she sniffed. She wasn't telling him what Trent had said about her being too pitiful to be interested in. It hurt too much, and a tiny part of her feared it was true. "I told him to go to hell and blocked him."

"You're shaking."

"I'm mad."

"I'm sorry, honey. I know it's not easy to have this conversation with him."

"It's not, but it's necessary. I hate confrontations, but sometimes you have to stand up for yourself. I let him push me around far too much in the past."

At the cookout, she'd met a group of women who didn't let anyone push them around. Not only that, but their men also supported them in whatever they wanted to do. She wanted to be like them.

"Did he threaten you again?"

Heat rolled through her. "No. He was being a dick, trying to push my buttons."

"You gonna be able to sleep?"

She huffed a sigh. "Eventually. Maybe. I don't know."

He snapped his laptop closed and reached up to turn the lamp off. She did the same then slid farther beneath the covers. Lucy moved over to her side. Ollie walked onto Dax's chest and started to purr. She realized as her eyes adjusted to the dark that Dax was rubbing Ollie's chin, and her heart melted a little bit more. Trent had never petted Ollie. He hadn't wanted the animals in the bedroom at all. She'd gone along with it, which pissed her off even more when she thought about it.

Her mind wouldn't stop spinning through everything that'd happened that day. Trent, the cookout, the nasty surprise at the end of her driveway. She couldn't get the image of the dummy swinging in the trees from her head, though she was grateful it hadn't been a real person. Still, that initial moment when she'd first seen it, she'd feared that it was.

"Dax…"

"Yeah?"

"You said you'd seen hanging bodies before."

He didn't speak at first, and then he sighed. "I was in the Army, babe. I saw a lot of shit that most people don't see."

She hesitated. "How did you…? How *do* you…?"

"Deal with it?"

"Yes."

"One day at a time. You never forget that shit, but you can't let it rule you. You figure it out, and you deal with it. There are shitty people in this world—evil people, greedy people, people who don't respect any lives but their own. But there are also good people who care, who make sacrifices, who make the world a better place by contributing to it in some way. You think about the good people, and you think about how they're worth fighting for, and you keep going."

She thought about what he said. Pictured him in a uniform, weapons hot from use, face streaked with blood, dirt and sweat. There would be dust swirling everywhere, people with bombs strapped to their bodies, and innocents caught in the cross fire.

It wasn't simply her imagination. It happened to men and women in the service all the time. She reached across Lucy's warm body and touched his arm, slid her way to his hand so she could grasp it. His hand was warm, the perfect complement to her freezing one.

"Thank you for your service," she whispered. "I should have said that before now."

He squeezed softly. "It was an honor to serve. Now go to sleep, babe. Tomorrow's gonna be busy."

She didn't think she would, but so long as he held her hand, she drifted into a sleep that was punctuated with dreams she wouldn't remember in the morning. Dreams that disquieted her and made her whimper so that Dax turned on his side and stroked her hair, whispering soft words.

She wouldn't remember those either.

Chapter Twenty-Two

"It was a threat," Dax growled. "Trent Sharpe told Robbie it would be her funeral. Exact words."

Ian frowned and shook his head. Dax could see because they were on a secure video call.

"Not disagreeing, but it's not specific enough to detain him. He had a heated text conversation with his ex-wife when she told him she wouldn't give him another chance. Words were exchanged."

Dax wanted to punch something. Preferably Trent's face. "I know, boss."

"We've got GPS info on his location. If he makes a move toward the farm, we'll pick him up. But he left Mill Landing an hour ago, and he appears to be driving back to the city. His phone was near Robbie's place yesterday, but the sun was still up. Not likely he placed the dummy then."

Dax didn't like it. Trent had specifically used the word *funeral*. It was suspect as hell considering the photo of Robbie in a coffin, but that didn't necessarily mean the two were connected. Especially since Dax hadn't found any evidence on Trent's computer when the asshole finally clicked the link he'd sent.

There was no photo of Robbie sleeping, and no composite photo in a coffin. There were photos of her, but they were all publicity photos. If he'd had any personal ones, they'd either been wiped or they were resident on a different computer.

It was likely Trent's new wife hadn't wanted him to keep photos of his old one. Especially if any of them were intimate. Dax didn't like to think of Robbie making compromising photos with Trent, but maybe she had. He didn't think it was her style, but that didn't mean Trent hadn't bullied her into it.

If he had, Dax thought he might like to track the guy down and make him regret it. Hell, there were a lot of things about the way Trent treated Robbie that Dax would like to make him regret if he got a chance.

"He could have reconnoitered the place earlier then came back without his phone to hoist the dummy."

"He could have," Ian agreed. "But why not leave the phone behind both times? If he's smart enough to do it the second time, he'd have done it the first."

"He might have forgotten the first time."

"Valid point, though it's certainly sloppy as hell. But he's not an operator and never has been. Somebody without mission experience could make a mistake like that. I'm not convinced, though."

Dax wasn't either, but it was all he had at the moment. His gaze slid to where Robbie strolled across the yard with Lucy. It had been a big step for her after last night, but she'd insisted she had to go outside with the dog or she might never leave the house again. Since there'd been nothing on the perimeter notifications, he'd let her go.

She wore a pair of gray yoga pants, cross-trainers with blue accents against white, and a loose baby blue T-shirt that she'd tied into a knot on one side. The shadows beneath her eyes weren't as bad today, but he'd like it if they disappeared entirely.

He'd gotten up long before she had, as usual. When he'd heard her stirring, he'd started breakfast. A freaking mushroom, tomato, and onion frittata he'd found on YouTube of all things. With parmesan, mozzarella, and fresh herbs from the plants she had on the windowsill.

He never cooked like that at home. He ate omelets or bagels mostly. He did not search for fancy breakfast items, and he'd never felt the desire to make a woman smile by giving her something to eat that wasn't easy and fast. Wasn't like him at all, yet he'd been determined to do it.

They'd eaten at the table in the nook, drinking coffee and making small talk about the party yesterday. Not the dummy and not the threat. She'd had enough of those. She'd slept better than he thought she might, but she'd tossed and turned and whimpered sometimes.

He'd scooted close to her, gently pushed the dog to the bottom of the bed, and stroked her hair while she had her bad dream. If it'd gotten worse, he'd have wakened her. It hadn't and he'd prioritized her sleep over stopping the dream.

He watched her bend to sniff a rose. Her hair was

long and loose, hanging down to her ass, and he found himself wanting to slide his hands into the silk of it and tug her into his arms. It was getting harder to stop thinking about it, especially since he'd lain so near last night and listened to her breathe. He'd ached to touch her, and he'd woken with a raging hard-on this morning that he'd had to take care of in the shower.

He'd spilled into his fist, hips jerking, groaning his release as softly as possible while he supported himself with his other palm against the cool tiles. It'd been a great release but a lonely one.

"Natasha likes her," Ian said, and Dax dragged himself back to the conversation.

"What's not to like? She's brilliant and beautiful."

Ian chuckled. "Tell me you've got it bad without telling me you've got it bad. You're supposed to *play* her boyfriend, not be one."

"Maybe I want to be," Dax admitted, his throat tightening. "When this is over."

Robbie was an incredible woman. He'd kissed her exactly once. He was feeling more than he should at this stage, but damn, how did you fight something like that? Maybe you didn't, and maybe it didn't matter anyway, because she'd been through enough with her ex that she might not be interested.

"You tell her that?"

"No. Figure she has enough shit to deal with right now."

Robbie took the stick that Lucy brought to her and threw it. It didn't go very far, but Robbie laughed as

Lucy bounded after it. His heart did a slow dive in his chest.

Fucking beautiful.

"There'll never be a right time, Dax. Trust me. You either go for it or you don't."

"Got to protect her and find the asshole threatening her."

"Agreed, but you're capable of both. So long as she's feeling the same way. Considering the way she looked at you last night, I'd say she is. But I'm no expert. I danced around Natasha for months, even when I knew she was like nobody I'd ever met before."

Dax laughed. "Yeah, she tried to kill you. That's different."

Ian snorted. "See? Not like anybody else. Robbie like anyone else for you?"

He thought of Tara. What he'd felt for her had been forged through shared experience and companionship. Growing up together gave you a different kind of bond, but that bond was gone now. And he was okay with it. Had been for a long time.

"You know what," Ian said. "Don't answer that. None of my business. You'll figure it out or you won't."

"Wasn't keeping it to myself on purpose. Just thinking."

"The answer will come."

Dax watched Robbie drop to a knee and ruffle Lucy's fur before taking the stick and throwing it again. Robbie was small and vulnerable but strong too. The woman had entire worlds in her head, and she'd enthralled millions with what she dreamed up.

She was too special for the likes of him. That was the answer he kept getting. He was a computer expert, but he was also a warrior. The willingness to commit violence was a job requirement. He was willing because he believed in the mission at BDI.

He came from the kind of family that had often qualified for public assistance but was too proud to take it even when the kids suffered from their pride, and he'd grown up neglected and ignored by the person who should have been a father figure to him. His brother was a criminal, his stepdad was a drunk, and his mother was a sweet soul who wouldn't leave because her husband needed her. He wasn't abusive or mean. He was just an addict who didn't want to believe the truth about himself.

Dax's phone pinged with a text. He glanced at it.

Jared: Laurel Johnson's phone was turned off for hours yesterday. She was in Annapolis at one point, then BWI. She checked into a Red Roof Inn at the airport and flew to Vegas this morning. The day Robbie got the threat and the night someone appeared on the trail cams, her phone was also off for several hours.

Dax repeated the information to Ian. "She's a possibility. She writes thrillers. She'd know she had to do something about the phone. We need to hack the GPS in her car, see where it was yesterday and last week."

"Agreed. I'll tell Finn and Jamie to keep an eye on her in Vegas. It could also still be Sharpe. He's not completely out of the picture, even if he is leaving. Could be headed to the city to meet someone or pick up something. He might return later. I doubt he's ready to give up on Robbie's fortune just because she told him she was done."

"It's a lot to give up, especially if he thinks I'm the only thing stopping him from rekindling his romance. According to Robbie, losing his temper and saying shitty things is his usual behavior. He'll be contrite later, and he might be back to try again. She blocked him so he'll have to appear in person."

Ian grimaced. "Man, I despise anyone who blows up and says stuff like that. And a dude doing that to a woman? Just fucking no. We're supposed to be better than that. Support your woman, encourage her, take a fucking bullet for her. But berate her? No way."

"Copy that," Dax said. He might shout at a woman if she shouted at him, and he might tell her she was being unreasonable, but he'd never call her a cunt.

Not how a man treated his woman. Especially a woman he claimed to love. Trent was a douche who didn't deserve the woman throwing sticks for her rescue dog.

The call ended and Dax went outside to join Robbie. She turned when she heard him, a look of apprehension on her face until she realized it was him.

His heart stuttered in his chest when she smiled. He was wound up as tight as a spring inside whenever she looked at him.

"Everything okay?" she asked.

"Yep. How you feeling?"

She shrugged. "I'm okay."

She bent to take the stick from Lucy, who didn't

want to let go at first. But then she did and Robbie threw it. The dog took off.

"The dummy bothers me. I won't lie," she said. "But you and the guys are looking into it, so I'm trying not to think too much about it. As for Trent, I'm used to his outbursts. He'd shock me if he didn't lose his temper, quite honestly."

A sick feeling uncoiled in Dax's belly. "Did he ever hit you when he lost his temper?"

She shook her head. "No, never. He yelled and said shitty things, but he never lifted a hand to me."

Dax was glad to hear it. She answered too readily for it to be a lie, and she didn't avoid his eyes any more than usual. "Did you and Trent ever take naughty photos?"

She stopped in mid-motion from where she was about to take the stick from Lucy again. Her eyes were wide. "What? Why? Is there a photo of me naked out there? Is that what he was talking about?" A riot of emotions chased over her features. "I'll kill him. Seriously. If he releases nudes of me to the press, I'm going to go after him with guns blazing."

Dax gripped her by the shoulders. "Hey, calm down. I didn't find anything like that. It's just that Trent has photos of him and Kimberlee on his phone and computer, so I wondered. Wanted to be sure he didn't have something he could use to embarrass you."

Red flared in her cheeks, over her neck and collarbones. Her T-shirt had a scoop neck, and it showed a bit of skin where it draped loosely across her chest. If she leaned forward, he'd see her cleavage and the swells of her breasts. He'd like to see that.

She'd glanced away like she always did, but now she met his gaze again. "He wanted to make videos of us in bed and take photos, but I wouldn't do it. He got mad about that, too. Said I wasn't adventurous enough. And when my first book came out and people called me the Queen of Steam, he laughed. Then he'd tell me he was only joking. But I know he meant it. He stopped trying to get me to do it after a while. Guess Kimberlee wasn't so reluctant."

"Doesn't look like it."

"You looked at their photos?"

"Not once I knew what they were. I skimmed them pretty quickly. I was looking for the photo of you. The one from the box."

"Oh." She picked up the stick and tossed it. "Did he have it?"

"No. He might have gotten rid of it. I could find if it'd ever been resident on his computer, but that would take longer and require a different script."

"Are you a hacker or something?"

"Yes," he said, because there was no reason to lie. He'd told her the first night that he was an IT expert, but he hadn't elaborated. "I cloned one of his friend's Facebook accounts and sent a link. He clicked it, and a script opened that fed me the contents of his devices."

"I hope you gave him a virus. Asshole."

He wanted to laugh but didn't. "Nope, sorry. I only wanted to look at the contents."

"Too bad," she grumbled. "Gah, I wish I'd had those cameras installed earlier. I just never needed anything like that before. If I'd had them, we'd know who did it. There'd be no searching Trent's computer, or looking for my old stalker."

He wasn't going to point out that a world famous author with a rabid fandom should've always had a security system that consisted of more than an adorable beagle and a shotgun. "That's mostly true, but if they covered up their features the way the person on the trail cam did, we might not know."

"Right," she said with a frown. "I googled Green Berets, by the way."

"What did you learn?"

"That you're pretty badass. You can jump out of a plane, rescue people who've been taken hostage, swim for miles, infiltrate enemy targets and take them out before they even know you're coming, and a million other things that would make normal humans sob from exhaustion." She gave him a cheeky once-over that he enjoyed. "I'm impressed, Mr. Freed. Tall, dark, handsome, badass, cooks a mean steak and omelet, and knows how to curl a girl's toes with a kiss."

"That's not all I know how to do."

He could see her pulse thrumming in her neck. He told himself not to, but he reached up to stroke a finger over it. She didn't pull away. Her mouth parted and her nipples budded, pressing into the soft fabric of her loose shirt.

Sliding a hand to her hip and tugging her toward him was as natural as breathing. Lowering his head to kiss her was vital to his continued existence.

Which of course meant it was also the precise moment his phone chimed with a perimeter alert. With a groan, he fished it from his back pocket and pulled up the cameras.

A car rolled slowly toward the house. Dax turned the screen. "Anyone you know?"

The apprehension in her expression melted. "It's Autumn."

Dax slipped the phone in his pocket again. *Fuck.* "I thought she'd get here later this afternoon."

"Oh no, not Autumn. She has lists of things that need to get done, and she's very precise.

"Sounds like a drill sergeant."

Robbie gave him a smile. "I better go greet her."

She turned to walk away then stopped with her back to him. He didn't know what she was planning, but suddenly she turned to rush back to him. She threw her arms around his neck, hauled him down to her level, and pressed her mouth to his.

When she let go, she flashed a grin, her cheeks glowing as she took a step backward. "I've been wanting to do that so bad. You have no idea. Thank you for staying with me last night, Dax. I know it wasn't easy, but it made all the difference."

All he could do was nod. Took him a moment to find his voice, and then it sounded raspy as hell. "My pleasure, Robbie."

She pointed toward the house and then waved her hand around. "I have to go say hi."

"I know."

But they kept staring at each other until the sound of a woman's voice greeted Lucy. The dog had taken off for the side of the house where Autumn had parked. Robbie swallowed. "I really have to go."

He nodded, unable to keep up with the range of emotions that crossed her face before she turned and jogged away. He wished they had more time alone. But they didn't.

Her assistant had arrived, and Vegas was tomorrow.

Chapter Twenty-Three

ROBBIE WAS DISTRACTED AND REGRETTING SHE'D TOLD Autumn to come to the farm today. But since they were leaving tomorrow, Robbie hadn't wanted her assistant to feel rushed with everything they needed to cover. First, Autumn delivered mail and packages that had been collecting at her house. She'd gone through them all, noted the ones Robbie should respond to personally, provided a record of responses she'd sent as Robbie's assistant, and set aside anything concerning. Those she gave to Dax along with any recent emails she'd printed that she thought he should see.

They also had to discuss Robbie's social media plan for the next quarter, and Autumn wanted to take a few pictures of Robbie to use when she posted. They'd do them outside or in her office so no one paid too close attention to the differences between Autumn's house and hers.

It was a lot to cover, but Autumn was efficient and prepared. She had a clipboard with a checklist, and she was currently busy going over everything she thought Robbie needed to know for the conference. Unfortunately, Robbie was having a hell of a time focusing on any of it.

All she could think of was Dax and the way his shoulders filled out his T-shirt. Today's shirt was rust-colored with three buttons that opened at his neck. She liked those shirts with the buttons. She wanted to press her mouth to the skin in that opening, wanted to see if he tasted as good as he looked.

She and Autumn were at the kitchen island, and she could see him through the glass doors that led outside. He sat beneath the pergola, feet propped on an ottoman, earbuds in. He was clearly having a conversation since his mouth moved from time to time. Singing would have been more rhythmic.

He'd nearly kissed her earlier. Her heart had almost pounded out of her chest when he'd dragged her toward him and lowered his head. She'd wanted it so badly that she'd ached. But then his phone chirped and it was over before it began.

Yet she was still thinking about it—and thinking about what might have come next. The truth was that she wanted to lie beneath him as he moved within her, her naked body tangled with his, both of them lost in pleasure. She was aware she might have unrealistic expectations about sex with him, but she wanted it anyway. It'd been too long, and she wanted that feeling again, even if it wasn't as spectacular as her imagination.

When Robbie realized that Autumn had stopped

talking, she dragged her gaze from Dax to find her assistant watching her with an arched eyebrow.

"What?" Robbie asked.

Autumn shook her head. "You're daydreaming, but I don't think it's about Damian and Velvet." She turned to look out the window. "He's very attractive. Are you sure he's really a bodyguard, or did Daphne hire a model to pretend to be a bodyguard?"

Robbie laughed. "You mean to pretend to be my boyfriend? But no, he's real. I've met the people he works with. BDI is an elite protection agency, run by the kind of guy I'd describe as dark and intense. I talked to him briefly, and I had more questions than answers by the time I was done. Now that's a man who could be a vampire if they existed. Then there's his wife, who is really the most interesting person. Anyway, yes, Dax is real and he's sexy and I'm pretty sure he's a big part of the reason I've started writing again."

Autumn's mouth dropped open. "You didn't tell me you were writing. You've been blocked for months."

"I know. I wasn't sure it would last, so I didn't say anything. But it's been a few days, and the words are still coming."

"He is *not* Damian LeBeaux."

"Of course not. But I think having him around brought Damian back. I've spent too much time on my own. My choice, I know, but it hasn't helped my work. Being around people again has."

It was hard to admit since most people still made her uncomfortable, but Dax wasn't most people. And neither were his friends. She'd enjoyed their company once she'd eased into it. And she'd found herself thinking even more about her book and where it needed to go.

Maybe she needed people in her life if she was going to create. Being alone certainly hadn't worked. Autumn and Daphne had been her only friends for so long that it was strange to think she might be ready to expand her circle a little bit. But she'd *enjoyed* herself yesterday, before they'd come home and found the dummy swinging from the tree.

Autumn tidied the papers on her clipboard. Robbie thought she might be annoyed. Or maybe hurt. Autumn had been the only person she'd spent any time with in the past couple of years. Robbie spoke to Daphne often, and Daphne came to visit once a year, but it was Autumn who had been there whenever she needed something.

When Robbie was writing *The Vampire King*, it was Autumn she called when she needed to talk through plot or scene issues she didn't want to disturb Daphne with. Autumn had always been a great sounding board. Still was.

She listened, offered her thoughts, and asked pertinent questions that got Robbie back on track. And she made Robbie's life smooth as silk when it came to fielding the business side of being an author—interview requests, reader mail, scheduling, social media.

"I was only kidding about the model thing," Autumn said. "He *is* very pretty, but he was also very businesslike when he called me about your reader mail. Still, I don't want to see you get hurt again. I'm concerned. I've seen the way you look at him. It's like you're off in dreamland or something."

"I know. I'm not falling for him or anything, don't worry. He's a good guy, and he's doing his job. I find him a little inspirational, but that's not a bad thing. Trust me, I know better than anyone that romance novel heroes aren't real."

No matter how much she wanted them to be.

Autumn looked solemn. "So true. The last guy I went out with went to the restroom during dinner and didn't come back for half an hour. He was watching a basketball game on his phone. I only know because I heard a guy telling his girlfriend at the next table. They kept shooting me pitying looks."

"Oh wow. What a jerk! You actually waited for him to come back?"

"Mm-hmm. I finished dinner, ordered dessert, and asked for the check. When he returned, I handed it to him and left."

"Yikes."

"Yikes is right." Autumn looked grave. "Be careful, Robbie. Really. Men are shit."

"I know," she sighed. "Trent actually thought he could come back after everything he did."

"What? No way."

Robbie told her the basics.

"Wow. He's got some nerve."

Robbie sipped the sparkling water Autumn had poured for her. "He does at that. But so do I for once. I blocked his ass."

"Good. So what about the book? Are you getting somewhere, or is it another false start?"

Robbie tamped down a flare of irritation. She told herself she was being overly sensitive because she'd been blocked for so long. Autumn was asking what anyone who knew her well would ask.

"It's not a false start. I have almost thirty thousand words. I'm still discovering the shape of the book, but I like where it's going."

Autumn looked surprised. "Wow. So will they get back together or not?"

"Maybe," she replied, reluctant to discuss Damian and Velvet's reunion just yet.

"You know I'm always ready to talk it over if you need a sounding board."

"I know. And I appreciate it. I'm not ready to discuss it yet, okay? I haven't even told Daphne what's happening."

Autumn nodded. "I understand." She removed a sheet from her clipboard and set it aside. "Why don't we discuss the itinerary for the book tour? We fly to LA after the signing in Vegas, then it's on to Seattle for a day before Denver…"

Robbie tuned her assistant out. She didn't want to discuss another second of the conference, the tour, or her writing, but she nodded along anyway. Every word about the trip made dread pool inside. She didn't know if it was dread of the next couple of weeks of travel and socializing or dread that Dax and his people still didn't know who was behind the threats.

She wanted them to find the person and put a stop

to it. But if they did, Dax would leave. The idea of him not being there when she woke up in the mornings made her insides tighten.

Still, she had to acknowledge reality. He might have slept beside her, and he might have taken her to see his friends, but she was only a job for him.

DAX STAYED out of Robbie and Autumn's way. Robbie had told him they had a lot to discuss and she didn't know how long it would take. She'd seemed resigned rather than happy. He'd wanted to tell her she didn't have to spend time discussing anything if she didn't want to, but it wasn't his place to get in the middle of her business.

Autumn gave him a box with recent letters and emails that she'd flagged as being especially nasty. Dax spent time looking through them, growing increasingly frustrated. There was nothing specific to go on. Most of the missives were from people angry about Damian and Velvet's broken relationship. Some were from people who thought she was a terrible person and should stop writing immediately. And at least one was from a lady who'd been told by the aliens that she needed to warn Robbie they were planning to invade the planet and wanted her to convince all the human women of child-bearing age to welcome the aliens into their beds so they could create a new super race of hybrids.

Dax wondered what the hell that lady was smoking, but he didn't think she was the person who'd driven all the way to Mill Landing—from Arizona, no less—and left a box on Robbie's piano.

Dax shoved the box of letters away and raked a hand over his head. It had been a week and he was no closer to answers than he had been when he'd arrived. Her stalker might have returned, or Trent could be playing some kind of sick game to punish her or push her into his arms again, or a crazed fan had gone to a lot of trouble to find where she lived and was smart enough to avoid detection while he or she left notes and dummies for Robbie to find.

The good thing was that whoever was doing all these things wasn't likely to follow Robbie around on a ten-city tour. If Laurel Johnson was the stalker, and the person leaving threats now, then they'd encounter her in Vegas. But not beyond that. She'd have to return to her home in Waldorf, which made Dax decide it was a good idea to station someone from BDI at Robbie's house for the duration of her absence. Quietly, in case the person was watching the house. Maybe they'd get a break and Laurel, or whomever, would approach again. Maybe they wouldn't be so cautious if they thought Robbie was gone.

Dax made arrangements with BDI HQ to send out their newest operative, Roman Rostov, aka Kazimir Rybakov, who'd recently moved to the US from Russia. Then he got up and headed for the kitchen. It was late afternoon and he was hungry, so he thought he'd grab a sandwich.

Robbie and Autumn were standing at the island, chopping onions. They looked up when he entered.

Robbie's gaze softened as she smiled at him. Autumn looked a touch wary, as if she didn't quite trust him. He wasn't sure why, but they'd only just met in person and he knew he could seem intimidating. Plus Autumn had been around when Trent left, so she knew the kind of hell Robbie had been through. Maybe she thought he was after Robbie's money, too. Good for her for being wary. He wasn't offended at all.

"We're fixing enchilada casserole for dinner," Robbie said. "Hungry?"

"Hell, yeah. Need any help?"

"Maybe open a bottle of wine? I could use a drink."

"Sure. Autumn, you want a drink too?"

"Yes. Thanks."

Dax opened a bottle, poured two glasses of red, and grabbed a beer for himself. He thought about leaving but decided he wanted to stay and observe the two women together. Robbie had told him that Autumn started working for her five years ago. She was twenty-six, single, and she'd worked at the University of Maryland as a secretary. She'd wanted extra money to take care of a house she'd inherited from her mother, who'd taught at the University before she died.

Autumn left her job at the University three years ago to do freelance work as an assistant for other authors, too, but Robbie was her primary client. She worked from home and made a good living. Dax knew because he'd checked. The house was in her name, located on a quiet street in an area within walking distance to restaurants and clubs. She had no debt, and she lived within her means.

There were no red flags about her behavior or situation. She was indispensable to Robbie, and she did her job well. Dax suspected she was one of the people in Robbie's will. Since only Robbie's attorney knew the contents, it wasn't likely that Autumn wanted to kill Robbie for an inheritance she didn't know about.

Robbie picked up her phone and music began to fill the room from the Bose speaker on the counter. She'd chosen an 80s station, which kinda surprised him. She and Autumn belted out everything from Madonna to The Clash to Prince as they chopped, cooked, and assembled a cheesy dish that turned out to be pretty freaking delicious when it was all said and done.

The three of them sat at the kitchen table in the nook and ate dinner, talked, laughed, and drank together until Autumn unsuccessfully stifled a giant yawn. Dax glanced at his watch. It was a little after nine. There was a lot to do tomorrow, but they didn't fly out until the afternoon.

"I'm so sorry, but I got up early today and ran errands before I headed this way. I think I need to hit the sack."

Robbie clasped Autumn's hand as the woman stood. "Thank you, sweets. I appreciate everything you've done to get me ready for this shindig."

Autumn kissed her cheek. "It's what I do. Don't get up. I can find my way upstairs."

"Goodnight," Dax said as Autumn walked away. She threw him a smile and disappeared into the hallway.

"Isn't she lovely?" Robbie asked.

"She is," Dax said. "But you're lovelier."

Her gaze softened. She didn't look away, which made a hot feeling swell in his chest. "You don't have to say that. She's tall and willowy, and she has all that gorgeous red hair."

"Yes, but I'm not attracted to her. I'm attracted to you." He pulled in a breath. "When this is all over, I want to take you out."

She smiled. "On a date?"

"Yes. You okay with that?"

Her gaze dropped, but he thought it was shyness rather than an inability to look at him. "I am."

He was ridiculously pleased with her answer. "Good."

"Dax…"

"Yes?"

"Will you sleep with me again tonight?"

His dick throbbed to life. God, she was killing him. "Yeah, if that's what you want."

"But you don't want it, do you?"

He swallowed. Fuck it, he was telling her the truth. Better that than letting her think up her own reasons, which he was sure would not be flattering to her at all. Even if he had just told her he wanted to date her. "That's not it, babe. I want more. I want to sleep with you naked, and I want to make you come. I want to taste your pussy, and I want to hear your moans in my ear as I slide my cock into your body. But now's not the time for that. I know it, but it doesn't stop me wanting it. Or feeling like being beside you but not *with* you is torture."

"I want that, too. I've been thinking about it all day," she confessed in a quiet voice.

She moved to sit on his lap. It was a bold move for her, but he didn't stop her. When she threaded her fingers into the hair at his nape then slid them against his scalp, his cock went from semi-hard to full granite.

She smiled. "Am I shocking you?"

"In a good way."

Her laugh was throaty. "Kiss me. Please."

Maybe he shouldn't have done it, but he was powerless to say no. He spanned the back of her head with his palm and tilted her face down. She moaned as he fitted his mouth to hers. She tasted like wine, but he'd watched her drink and knew she'd paced herself. So had he. Neither of them were impaired.

She shifted in his lap, feeling him. Making him groan.

"Take me to bed, Dax," she whispered against his lips. "I don't care if it ends up being disastrous, right now it's what I want."

He reared back to look at her. "Disastrous? How so?"

"I'm a romance writer. I've built this up in my head. If it's not all that good, if it sucks, then I'll berate myself later."

Dax laughed. "Well, fuck me running, that's not what I thought you'd say."

Though he shouldn't, it was too fucking late for him. He couldn't deny his reserved writer when she was being so bold. He stood in one fluid motion, hauling her up with him. Then he carried her through the house, Lucy on his heels, to the wing where their bedrooms lay.

Lucy ran in front of him to hop onto the bench at the foot of the bed. Ollie was sprawled dead center of the comforter. They both watched Dax and Robbie with expectant faces.

"Sorry, gang," Dax said. "This is private."

He carried Robbie into his room and pushed the door closed with his foot.

Chapter Twenty-Four

MAYBE THE WINE *HAD* LOOSENED HER INHIBITIONS, OR maybe she'd just let herself get entirely too worked up over the past two days thinking about the kiss they'd shared. Regardless, Robbie had no fear about what was happening between them.

Dax slid her body down his, wrapping her arms around his neck as he set her on her feet. Every inch of him was solid, hard, and beautiful.

He skimmed his fingers down her forearms, her upper arms, then around to cup her ass so he could drag her against him. He was already hard, and Robbie had to bite her lip to keep from moaning.

"I've been thinking about this for days," he said, his voice raspy with need. "Wanting to get you naked and show you how gorgeous I think you are."

"I want you naked, too. I've been imagining…" She reached down to cup his groin, and he cursed.

"I thought you'd be shy," he said with a laugh.

"Oh, I am. I think I've had enough wine to think

I'm a sex goddess though. Better take advantage of me now."

He gently took her hand in his and stepped back. Robbie made a sound of protest, but he shushed her.

"If you're only doing this because of the wine, then I think we need to stop."

"I had three glasses of wine in four hours, Dax. You poured every one of them. I'm not drunk." She tugged her hand free and cupped him again. He was big and hard, and an arrow of desire shot straight into her deepest core.

"Jesus," he said, swallowing. She couldn't agree more.

"You do realize I've had sex before, right? I understand how it works. I'm awkward in social situations and reserved when I don't know someone. But I know you. Or it feels like I do. We've been living together every day for the past week, and I know you aren't the kind of guy to force yourself on me. I really, *really* want to know if you know how to use what God gave you or if you're just pretending you do."

He snort-laughed. "Nothing like a little performance pressure to make a guy question his ability." He pushed his hips forward, into her hand, and his cock hadn't gotten any smaller. She took that as a good sign.

He gently removed her hand from his groin. Then he tugged her shirt up and over her head. "Anything you don't like before we get started?"

Anticipation uncurled within her. "Not a fan of butt stuff, I gotta say."

"No butt stuff. Check."

"What about you?"

"Same. Also, no teeth in the delicate areas. Not a fan of that."

Robbie couldn't help but laugh. It should be awkward to talk and laugh, but it wasn't. She appreciated that he asked. "No teeth. Understood."

He stepped into her, pressed her back against the closed door. "How about we stop talking for a bit? I want to kiss you, babe. And then I want to do unspeakably naughty things to your gorgeous body."

Robbie shivered. *Unspeakably naughty.* She liked that. He was only her second sexual partner ever, but she wasn't telling him that yet. Not until she was sure it wouldn't freak him out and make him quit out of some misguided nobility.

Dax lowered his head and their mouths met. He kissed her like a man starved, and she arched her body into him as his hands cupped her ass and squeezed. Then he grabbed her wrists and pushed her hands over her head.

"Keep them there," he commanded.

Robbie closed her eyes and did as he said. He pushed the cups of her lacy bra down until her nipples were bared, her breasts sitting high as the bra shoved them up and together.

"Beautiful," he said as he pinched both her nipples with his thumbs and forefingers. Robbie kept her eyes closed as a moan escaped her throat.

When Dax licked one of her nipples, she gasped and dropped her hands to his shoulders. He stopped what he was doing and she opened her eyes to meet his glittering gaze. "Hands above your head, Robbie."

She shot them back up, and he laved her nipple again before sucking it into his mouth while softly pinching the other one.

Her pussy couldn't get any wetter or any more sensitive. She wanted him to touch her there so badly, but she also wanted him to take his time and strum her senses into a frenzy.

"You okay?" he asked when she made a noise that might have been halfway to a sob.

"Yes! I just—I want more."

He chuckled, then took her mouth in another hot kiss. Robbie tilted her head back as he took everything she had to give. Her breasts were exposed, her nipples wet from his mouth, and her pussy ached with need.

He slipped his fingers into the waistband of her yoga pants and pushed. He didn't push them all the way down, but let them cling to her thighs after he'd exposed her. He kept kissing her as one palm roved over her breasts, her belly, and down to her mound. Then he wrapped his fingers around her wrists with the other hand and held them above her head. She wanted to put her arms around him, but he didn't let her.

Dax cupped her mound in his big hand and squeezed just enough to send lightning streaking through her body. Robbie gasped into his mouth, and he made a very male sound of satisfaction.

He skimmed his fingers into her wetness, over her clit, and her hips arched toward him, seeking more. It'd been so long since anyone had touched her there. So damned long. She wanted to beg him to finish her right now, but she bit the inside of her lip and didn't.

Dax broke the kiss, his mouth skating to her ear. "Should have mentioned this earlier, but I didn't bring condoms with me on this job. Wasn't planning on this kind of thing. We can still have fun, though. I'm gonna make you feel good, Robbie. Promise."

"I have an IUD, and I haven't been with anyone but Trent in, well, years." What she meant to say was *ever*, but she still couldn't confess it to him. It sounded far too pitiful.

His thumb rolled over her clit, and she choked back a moan. "I'm clean. We have to test yearly for the job. I also haven't been with anyone bare in years."

"I want you inside me, Dax. If you're okay with it."

For once in her life she wanted to make the reckless choice to have wild, hot sex with a gorgeous man, and she didn't want any reason not to go through with it.

He gazed down at her, his expression intense. "I want that too. But not if you have any reservations."

"None. Please, please, please—I'm dying here."

He grinned. "We can't have that."

He let go of her wrists and she put her hands on his shoulders. He dropped to drag her pants and underwear the rest of the way off, then unsnapped her bra and pulled that off too. He didn't move to do anything else, though, and she began to feel self-conscious about him staring at her body.

"Stop," he told her when she tried to fold her arms over her breasts. "I'm trying to decide what to do first. So many damned things I want to do to you."

"I don't think I care so long as you make this ache go away."

He reached behind his back and tugged his T-shirt off one handed, dropping it to the floor. She'd seen his chest twice now, but it was still impressive. Not an ounce of fat on him. Just muscle and more muscle.

"You're so beautiful," she said.

He shook his head. "Think you're confused, babe. You're the beautiful one. Help me with my jeans."

She attacked his belt while he unzipped the denim. "Hang on," he said as the belt loosened. He pulled a pistol from the holster at his back and set it on the dresser beside the door. Then he nodded and she opened the belt and undid the snap.

They shoved his jeans down and off together before he put his hands on her ass and lifted her as if she weighed nothing. Robbie wrapped her legs around his waist, trying to pull herself closer.

"Bed or wall?" he asked.

"Um, both?"

Dax laughed as he lifted her higher, pressing her against the door. And then he lowered her until she felt the tip of his cock at her entrance. Robbie's heart hammered with excitement and a little bit of fear at what happened next. It'd been a long time since anyone had been in there, but she didn't feel like she wasn't ready. Hell, if she got any wetter, it'd be dripping down her thighs.

"I got you," he said softly.

"I know."

He let her fall the rest of the way, sliding inside her

body until she was full of him. They were still a moment as they stared into each other's eyes. Robbie couldn't look away, and Dax didn't either. Then he smiled, and her heart hitched.

"I wondered," he said softly.

"What?"

"If you'd look past me."

She shook her head, but she still didn't break eye contact. It was one of the most intimate moments of her life. She wasn't afraid anymore. Not of him. "Kiss me, Dax."

"I plan to, babe."

He turned and walked them to the bed without breaking the contact between them. Then he took her down to the mattress, pressing her into it with his big, hard body. "Next time it's hot and hard against the door, or maybe bent over the edge of the bed, but this time I want to take you the right way."

Robbie didn't know what the right way was. She suspected that *any* way with Dax was the right way. "Please take me before I explode," she gasped as he dropped his mouth to her breast and sucked a nipple until it was tight and aching.

"I'm taking you, honey. Promise."

"Dax," she said when he kept teasing her nipple. "I'm dying! Expiring on the spot from too much arousal. Make me come. *Please.*"

He laughed against her body, the sound vibrating through her. Right down into her clit. When he reached between them and stroked her, Robbie's back bowed off the bed. She was an aching mass of taught nerve endings, and he was taking his sweet time getting started.

Teasing her mercilessly.

"If you don't start moving, I'm going to write a bodyguard with a little dick and no finesse into my next book."

He laughed again. Then he bracketed her face between his hands, their eyes tangling once more. "I want to watch your expressions while I fuck you. If you have to close your eyes, then close them. But I plan to watch everything that crosses your face."

Her breath caught in her throat. And then he shifted his hips, pulling back before surging inside her, burying himself deep. Robbie gasped in surprise and pleasure as his cock dragged against the nerves beneath her clit when he retreated. She'd never, not once, come when Trent was fucking her. She came before or after with extra stimulation, but not during.

But now, with Dax's body driving hers deep into the mattress, a spark caught and grew into a flame. She unwrapped her legs from his hips, spreading them wide, arching her body into his so that he caught her right where she needed him.

"That's it, Robbie. Use me. Get what you need, baby."

It didn't take long before the tension in her body tightened unbearably. "Dax! I-I think I'm gonna come!"

"Yes," he groaned. "Come for me."

"So close… so close…"

The desire between them transformed into something so raw and physical that all Robbie could do was moan his name and beg him to keep fucking her. Keep pistoning his hips into hers, driving his cock against those nerve endings, winding her body tighter and tighter.

And then it happened. Her pussy clamped around him before the pressure shattered, her release exploding through her in a shower of sparks that made her press a fist to her mouth to keep from crying out too loudly.

"Oh Christ, I'm coming," Dax groaned. "Too soon."

She could feel him swelling inside her, and then his semen shot deep into her for long moments as his hips jerked. Eventually, he lifted onto his elbows to look down at her. "Wow," he said.

"Wow," she repeated, smiling.

He dipped his head to kiss her then pressed his forehead to hers. They were both breathing hard. "I loved every moment of that. I especially loved watching your face as you came. Fucking beautiful."

Robbie felt shy as her release ebbed, but she didn't turn away. She caressed his cheek, threaded a hand in his hair, then skimmed it down over his shoulder before bringing it back to his cheek.

"I'm sorry I closed my eyes. It got intense."

"I'm not sorry. Watching you bite your lip as you gasped, listening to you tell me to keep fucking you just like that as your moans got more frantic? I could do that every day and not get tired of it."

She lowered her lashes. "I don't usually talk like that. It was a first."

He looked extremely self-satisfied. "Good. I like knowing it's something that belongs to us."

There was a scratch at the door and a whine. Dax shifted, and Robbie was shocked at the shivers of pleasure that danced through her. She wanted more, but he pulled out and went into the bathroom. When he returned, he brought a towel to clean up the semen that leaked from her body onto the sheets.

"Maybe we'd better let her in," she said.

"Nah, let's go join her and Ollie in your bed. They're used to being in there with you."

It touched her that he thought of her pets. He already cared more about them than her ex ever had. "Okay."

"C'mon." He pulled her up and kissed her. "Let me watch your pretty little ass walk naked across the room."

He made her glow inside with happiness. She told herself to be careful, but right now she didn't want to be. She gathered her clothes, he gathered his, and they strolled naked from one room to the next. Then they got into bed together, but instead of going to their separate sides, Dax wrapped her in his arms, her back to his front. They fell asleep like that, entwined together, and Robbie was more content than she'd been in years.

Chapter Twenty-Five

DAX WOKE BEFORE DAWN, BLINKING AT HIS surroundings before he recalled where he was. Beside him, Robbie snored softly. Lucy was at the end of the bed and Ollie was pressed to Dax's side. It was no wonder Robbie had a king bed with the way these two sprawled.

He hadn't ever had a pet, so to be in bed with two of them now was something he wasn't used to. But he liked it. Just like he liked being next to Robbie. He reached for her, dragging her into the curve of his body, her ass against his cock. She was the kind of person who could sleep through an earthquake or a tornado, so she didn't wake. He pressed his mouth to her bare shoulder.

He was a thirty-four-year-old man. He'd fucked a lot of women in his life. Not one of them had ever turned him inside out the way Robbie did. She was strong and vulnerable, bold and shy. She was a contradiction in so many ways, and she fascinated him completely. He could spend endless days getting to know her, and he still wouldn't know everything.

He needed to keep her safe. He'd crossed a line getting involved before the mission was over, but it felt right. He waited for the remorse to hit, and there was none. It was right in a way he hadn't imagined it would be. Was he falling for her?

Maybe he was. He tried to remember the way he'd felt about Tara, the feelings he had when they were together. It was *nothing* like this feeling. He wanted to hold Robbie close, and he wanted her to look at him the way she had last night when he'd been balls deep inside her. He wanted that every fucking minute of the day. The wonder, the trust, the joy. He craved it like a junkie craved a fix.

He held her a little bit tighter. He would protect her with every skill he possessed. Find who was threatening her. Make them regret they'd ever dared to terrify her with their threats and their psychological games.

He tried to go back to sleep, but he was an early riser, and no matter how much he liked cuddling with Robbie—and the animals—he had to get out of bed and check the cameras for any visitors in the night.

He returned to his room to shower and dress then made his way to the kitchen to fix coffee. There was a buzzing in his veins that hadn't stopped since he'd gotten inside Robbie. She'd kept eye contact with him for a good couple of minutes before she shut her eyes and lost herself to her own pleasure, and he was still riding the high of it.

He'd loved watching her dark eyes dilate with everything she was feeling. Loved watching her mouth drop open in astonishment, the little gasps and moans in her throat. He'd wanted to take her again when it was over, but he'd refrained. With the journey today, he wanted her to get enough sleep.

He didn't know when he'd get the chance to be with her again, or even if she'd want him again. He hoped she did. Everything about being inside Robbie had been spectacular, but there was so much more he wanted to do to her. Lick her until she came apart. Watch her ride him. Bend her over and fuck her from behind while he wrapped her long hair around his hands.

But not today.

Today was a full day. Before they left for the executive airport and the jet her publisher had chartered, Ollie and Lucy had to go to the pet resort. Robbie wasn't going to enjoy that task. She wouldn't let him or Autumn take them over alone. She had to go, had to say her goodbyes. Dax would be there when she did. He knew she loved them like they were her children. Nothing wrong with that.

Roman would arrive later today, but they'd agreed it would be better if he didn't have to worry about taking care of Robbie's animals while he stayed inside her home and waited to see if someone would make a move.

When Dax reached the kitchen, the first fingers of light stretched across the room, illuminating the island and the person who sat there. Autumn was on her laptop computer, typing something. A cup of hot liquid sat beside her. Tea, since the electric kettle was on the counter and he didn't smell coffee.

She glanced up when he came into view. And then she smacked the laptop closed and pressed a hand to her chest. "Oh my goodness, I didn't hear you coming."

"Sorry. Hazard of the profession." He went over to the cabinet and took out a mug, setting his laptop on the counter so he could fix coffee. Then he got a pod and the creamer. He'd make a cup for Robbie when he heard her stirring, though he didn't expect that to be for at least three hours. "You always get up so early?"

Autumn smiled. She was a pretty girl, a little on the tall side, and slender. She was also an extrovert, which was a great complement to Robbie's introversion. Especially for the next few days when Robbie would need someone super organized to keep her from being overwhelmed.

"I try to. I don't always succeed. What about you?"

"Always. Comes from the military days."

"Robbie said you were in the Army. How did you end up being a bodyguard?"

She picked up her tea and blew on it. He couldn't tell if she was flirting with him or not, especially when she licked her lips before blowing again. She might be, but she was barking up the wrong tree. He'd found the girl he wanted. Now he had to convince her.

"Seemed a natural fit for someone with my skills." He didn't tell her that his computer skills were just as good. He made it a habit not to reveal everything. Good tactics.

"Robbie hasn't been giving you a hard time, has she?"

More like he'd been giving her a hard time. He

wasn't saying *that* either. God knows they hadn't been particularly quiet last night, but they hadn't shouted the roof down either. And Autumn's room was on the second floor at the opposite side of the house. It was a good bet she didn't know Dax and Robbie had spent the night together.

"Not at all," Dax said as he retrieved his coffee. "She understands the need for personal protection."

Autumn nodded. "I agree. She's been living out here alone for years, and she wouldn't get the security system installed. I'm glad you did that for her."

"How did you start working for Robbie?"

She smiled. "I knew her previous assistant. She worked at the college, same as me. When she was ready to retire so she and her husband could move to Florida, she recommended me. Robbie and I hit it off right away."

"You're a big help to her."

"I try. But I worry about her. She was in a bad way when Trent left. The fight over the estate, Kimberlee—all of it took a toll. Her writing suffered." Autumn leaned forward, whispering. "I think *The Vampire King* could have been a better book, but Daphne wouldn't extend the deadline again. She should have taken one look at what Robbie did to Damian and Velvet and given her time to fix it, but it was too late. They crashed the book."

"Crashed the book?"

"It means the publisher has everything already scheduled and ready to go, and the author delivers the manuscript with no time left to make big changes. They crash it into production. Only big authors get to do that, but I think it was a mistake. Robbie didn't do well under the pressure."

"So you don't think what she wrote was good?"

Autumn shook her head. "Not good enough. I have no doubt she'll fix it, and brilliantly. But she would have done it earlier if she hadn't been rushing to turn it in. And now she's had to face abuse from her fans, which Daphne had to expect would happen when she didn't give Robbie enough time. Some of the BookTok reviews have been downright cruel. I don't show her those."

"BookTok?"

"TikTok, but for books. Well, the book side of TikTok. There are so many lovely people in the book community there, but then you have the ones who just love to tear authors apart."

"Send me some links."

She nodded. "I didn't before because, trust me, if a BookToker was coming out here to confront Robbie, they'd video the whole thing and put it up for views. Anonymous threats are not the norm there."

"Got it. I'd still like to see some of these videos."

She opened her laptop and started typing. "That's what I was looking at when you scared me. Sending a few to your email now."

"Thanks."

He usually went over the nightly videos from the trail and house cameras and checked email while sitting at the island drinking his coffee, but he didn't want to disturb Autumn. He snagged his laptop and lifted his cup in a salute. "I'll get out of your way."

"Oh. You don't have to go. It's okay. I was just going to look at some of the workshops happening at the conference."

Dax hesitated, then took a seat at the opposite end of the island. "What do you know about Laurel Johnson?"

"The thriller writer?"

"Yeah."

Autumn scrunched her face, thinking. "I know she lives in Waldorf, and she writes for Spring Books. Daphne isn't her editor, though."

"Have you ever met her?"

"I can't say for certain, but if I was at an event with Robbie or another author, I might have run across her at a cocktail party or something."

"You travel with other authors too?"

"Not anymore. I used to. Mostly I do social media and publicity for my other clients. When I was still figuring it out, I went to a few signings with them. I could have met her there. Why do you ask?"

"Just a line of inquiry. Do you know anything about the Capitol City Writers?"

"Not really. I know they meet monthly. Robbie went to a few meetings, but that was before I worked for her."

"You have any thoughts about the letters she used to get from her stalker?"

Autumn appeared to shudder. "No. They were angry letters for sure, but I don't have any theories. I only got a handful when I took over her mail, and then they stopped. She used to want all the letters people sent to her, but once things got bad with Trent, she told me not to give her anything like that because she didn't want to be tempted to look. So I didn't."

Ollie came sauntering into the kitchen, meowing. He walked straight to Dax and looked up at him then yowled. "So I'm your designated servant now?" Dax asked.

Ollie meowed a little kinder than before.

"Fine."

Dax got up and went into the pantry to get food for the cat. As soon as he returned with it, Lucy was there. He'd left the door to Robbie's room open a crack so they could get out without waking her. Apparently, they were both ready for breakfast.

"You too?" he said to the dog. She whirled at his feet. "Maybe a walk first, huh?"

Autumn was watching him. "They like you. I don't think they ever cared for Trent."

Dax opened the door to let Lucy out, trusting that she'd do her business and come inside for food. "What about you?" he asked. "Did you like him?"

"I only met him a handful of times. He left after I'd been working for Robbie a year. Then he dragged her through two years of hell before the divorce was final. So no, I can't say I liked him."

"What do you think about him trying to get back together with her?"

"I think if he wanted her back, maybe he shouldn't have left her for a younger woman in the first place."

"Do you think he'd threaten her?"

"Definitely. He'd try anything if he thought it would work."

Trent Sharpe *was* desperate. Not for Robbie's happiness, which Dax could almost understand, but for his own comfort. That made him dangerous and unpredictable.

But Dax was more dangerous. Anybody came for Robbie on his watch, he wouldn't be responsible for what he did to them.

Chapter Twenty-Six

The trip to Vegas took five hours by plane. Robbie sat by the window and watched the landscape below for a part of the trip. She read for another part. Opened her laptop to look at her work in progress, but couldn't manage to write so she closed it again.

Dax sat beside her, as cool and unflappable as always. She had no chance at cool because she kept thinking about last night with him. The way he'd lifted her up like she weighed nothing and plunged his cock into her. When her back was against the door, she'd wanted him to fuck her right there until she screamed. She'd written scenes like that but had never experienced it.

But he'd walked her to the bed while still inside her, and then he'd made her come apart beneath him. The way he touched her, teased her—yeah, it was every bit as good as anything she'd imagined for Damian and Velvet. She wanted more. It'd been so damned long since she'd had sex, and even longer since she'd been excited about sex.

Now all she could think about was how long it would take before they were alone in the hotel room in Vegas. He'd kissed her when he'd brought her coffee this morning, but that didn't mean he was open to the idea of having sex again. Maybe he'd decided it was a bad idea after all.

Eventually, the plane landed and a limo took them to the hotel. Robbie and Dax were shown to a suite. Autumn had the room next door. She arched an eyebrow at Robbie when there was only one bed in the suite. Robbie jerked her head toward the couch as if she intended Dax to sleep there. It was a pull-out, which was part of the original arrangements, but she had no intention of asking him to use it. Though maybe it wouldn't be up to her.

Dax seemed to be checking the room at random, moving curtains, lifting up knickknacks. She didn't know what he was looking for, but she tried to focus on Autumn going over her checklist.

"The kickoff keynote—that's you—is at eleven in the morning," Autumn said, reading from her iPad. "There's a Q&A session, then a break for lunch, then your second panel. There will be a question and answer session after that one, too."

Robbie was dreading the questions. Her panic must have shown because Autumn gave her a smile. "I'm screening the questions before they get passed to the author who'll be reading them to you, but it's possible someone will slip extras in. We've talked about what to do if anyone goes off script."

"I tell them I'm not prepared to answer their question if it's about Damian and Velvet because my editor doesn't want me to discuss it."

"Right. You got this, Robbie." Autumn's gaze slid to Dax and then back again. "I'll say goodnight."

It was only five p.m. in Vegas, but they were still on eastern time. It was eight in the evening at home. "You could have dinner with us if you'd like."

"No, I'm fine. I want to walk the strip, and I have plans to meet up with a few friends. Unless you need me?"

Robbie knew that Autumn was in touch with other people who did assistant work for authors. It made sense they'd want to get together when they were all in one place. And it was a relief as well. Autumn's extroversion shone brightly, and her light was a little too intense after a full day of it.

"Not at all. Go have fun."

The door closed and she and Dax were alone. Robbie didn't know what to say now that she had her blessed quiet, so she crossed her arms beneath her breasts and went over to the window to gaze out at the Strip. It was packed with cars and people. The casinos were a spectacular sight with all the lights and interesting features like a pyramid and an Eiffel Tower. Not that she could see everything from her window, but she'd seen a lot of it as they drove in from the airport.

"You want to order dinner from room service?"

"Yes. Definitely."

"It's something else out there, isn't it?"

Robbie nodded. "Overwhelming. Makes me miss my quiet farm even more. Or what used to be my quiet farm before someone started stalking me there."

Dax put gentle hands on her shoulders. She shivered as he turned her. His eyes were full of concern. "You're wound tight, aren't you?"

Not what she'd expected he would say. "It's been a long day and a lot of noise."

"I know, honey."

"What were you looking for? Behind the curtains and underneath things?"

His gaze was unflinching. "Cameras. Listening devices."

Shock vibrated through her. She hadn't considered such a thing. "Did you find any?"

"No."

"Did you expect to?"

"Wasn't sure. You're a celebrity at this conference, and I had to consider the possibility someone bugged the room. They didn't."

"I'm relieved to hear you say that. The idea of someone spying on me…" She shuddered. "I don't like it."

"Most people don't." He dropped his hands from her shoulders and went over to pick up the room service menu. He gave it a look then handed it to her.

She started to say she wasn't hungry, but her stomach growled. "Grilled cheese and tomato soup. But it won't be as good as yours."

He grinned. "Honey, my soup came out of a can. I'm sure this is far better."

Not to her. The hotel's soup might come from a five-star kitchen, personally overseen by the ghost of Julia Child herself, but it wasn't made *for* her by a man who wanted to comfort her. A man who'd held her when she broke down, tucked her into bed, and watched over her while she'd slept.

He hadn't even known her, and he'd seen what she needed. Instead of chalking it up to being emotional over the situation, he'd drilled down to the essentials and realized she was sleep deprived.

But all of that was one hell of a mouthful to say to a man you'd known for a week. A man you'd been intimate with only once.

He made her want to be brave. To put herself out there. But it was hard after a lifetime of thinking you weren't good enough the way you were. That you needed to be fixed so you could behave like normal people did.

"I'd still rather be eating soup from a can at my kitchen island," she said softly.

His smile warmed her. Made little tingles of electricity buzz and pop inside.

"Me, too." He picked up the phone and ordered room service.

Robbie returned to looking out the window. It *was* fascinating. She wished she was the sort of person who could go out there and be a part of it. Who could let herself go and enjoy. But that wasn't her and never had been. She needed a plan, and even then she usually didn't go through with it.

Unlike when Dax had cajoled her into going to Tallie and Brett's place. That had been fun enough that she wondered if she was her own worst enemy sometimes. Maybe putting herself out there a bit more was a good thing.

"Dax?"

"Yeah?"

Her heart thumped. "Are you planning to sleep in the same bed with me tonight?"

"Sleep?" He stalked toward her, slipped an arm around her waist, and dragged her to him. His eyes perused her face, and she found herself unable to look away. Strange, since usually she couldn't hold anyone's gaze for long. "I plan to do a lot more than sleep. Provided you let me."

She felt light as air inside when his lips skimmed her collarbone. "I want to sleep with you, too. B-but I want you to make me come first."

His chuckle against her throat sent tingles of arousal to her pussy. "Oh, I plan to. More than once."

DAX MADE good on his word. After they'd eaten, after Robbie wanted to go checkout the casino—to be brave, she said—they returned to their suite and Dax locked the door. He did another sweep for devices, but there was nothing.

Then he tugged Robbie into his arms and kissed her.

She wrapped her arms around his neck, arched her body into his, and he nearly forgot his own name. He stripped her much more quickly than he intended, then picked her up and laid her on the bed.

"I want to see you too," she said, her eyes bright.

She was looking at him, not past him. Made his heart fucking pound in his chest. He stripped quickly, dropping his clothes into a pile, then crawled onto the bed, his shoulders between her legs. Her eyes widened a little. She whimpered as he spread her legs and slid his thumbs into her slit, opening her. She was wet and ready, her pussy swollen with need.

Dax couldn't stop. He didn't want to. This gorgeous, sexy, amazing woman was hot for *him*. And it made him happier than he'd been in a long time.

The truth was he was falling for a reclusive romance novelist who disliked being around people and wanted to hide in the country. He could live with that. He loved her farm, and her pets, and he loved being with her. So long as she looked at him the way she had last night when he was buried balls deep inside her, he'd die a happy man.

"I'm going to lick you, Robbie. You ready for it?"

She lifted onto her elbows to look at him. So fucking sexy. Her hipbones were a little too sharp, her belly a little too hollow, but she was still beautiful. Her nipples budded into tight peaks that made him stop what he was doing and suck on them instead.

Her hand fisted in his hair as she moaned his name. He sucked one and then the other nipple before he dropped between her legs again. Then he licked her in one long swipe from bottom to top, circling his tongue around her clit as he pressed two fingers into her.

"Oh God," she gasped. "That's amazing."

Dax pushed his shoulders beneath her thighs, lifting her for better access. Then he sucked her clit while he fucked her with his fingers. She was so wet and hot, and his dick ached with the need to be inside her. He wanted to find his own pleasure, but he wanted her to get hers first.

"Dax! Oh, that's… Oh my God…"

She curled up off the bed, her hands digging into his scalp as she arched her hips and ground her pussy against his tongue. He fucking loved it. But he didn't quite give her what she wanted. He stopped sucking and licked around her clit instead. Then he dropped down and replaced his fingers with his tongue, strumming her clit lightly while he licked into her.

She spread her legs wider, thrust her pussy into his face, and he fucking loved every second of it. Loved driving her insane, loved that she was getting what she needed. Loved that she was begging him to make her come.

"I love the way you taste," he told her when he came up for air. "Love the sounds you make and the way you beg for more. Jesus Christ, Robbie, you're so fucking hot."

He swirled his tongue around her clit again, then sucked until her moans turned to pants. She was close when he thrust two fingers into her, but that sent her over the edge. She screamed his name as she came, a hoarse, beautiful sound that made his balls tighten so hard he thought he might come just from the sound alone.

Dax dropped to spear his tongue into her again. He wanted to feel her orgasm, wanted to taste it. She moaned once more, her body shaking as she came. Dax was harder than stone when he crawled up her body. Her eyes blinked open, and he was so fucking glad he'd only turned the lights down and not off.

She smiled, and he kissed her, though he felt anything but tender at the moment. He had an urge to pound into her until his balls exploded. He hooked one of her legs behind the knee and spread her wide. Her other leg wrapped around his hips as he sank into her.

"Fuck, you feel amazing," he said.

"So do you."

"I know you said romance authors aren't really writing about their sex lives, but is it wrong of me to want to inspire you?"

She slid her hands over his chest, his side, then reached between them to cup his balls. "I need inspiring, Dax. Lots of inspiring. Please, please inspire me."

He lowered his head and licked her top lip. "Lucky for you, I'm in an inspiring mood."

He moved then, pulling back until the head of his dick was at her entrance, then thrusting deep. Over and over until her eyes closed and her mouth dropped open. He loved watching her tits bounce, loved the way she arched her hips, seeking her own pleasure.

He loved it so much he didn't want it to stop, but the tingling in his balls told him time was running out for him. He was nearly there when Robbie started to shake beneath him, sobbing his name as she found her pleasure.

That was all it took to make him come hard, jet after jet of semen filling her as he groaned her name into her hair.

Fucking perfect. He could live like this. Die like this.

He squeezed his eyes shut as emotion slammed into him. Being with Robbie was unlike being with anyone else. He didn't *want* to be with anyone else.

When the tremors subsided, he left the bed and got a towel. After he cleaned them both up and they were settled in bed again, he hooked an arm around her and dragged her close. She threw a leg over his and skimmed her palm up and down his abdomen and over his chest. Made his dick start to stir again.

"You're so fit," she said. "Not an ounce of fat on you."

He smiled. "That's not really possible, you know."

"I know. Allow me to fantasize a little bit."

He kissed her brow. "Sure. You can use any part of me for inspiration if you like."

She chuckled. "Don't worry, I will. Though Damian was already pretty hot. But now I have details I don't have to imagine."

"What kind of details?"

She traced one of the lines that formed a V beneath his abs. "This. The inguinal crease. I've looked at pictures, learned the name—which isn't all that sexy, by the way—but I've never explored one in person." Her finger traced up the other side, then over his abs. "It's seriously sexy."

"Then I'm glad I work out."

She sighed as she stopped exploring and rested her hand on his side. "I don't feel awkward when I'm with you."

His chest tightened. "That makes me happy."

"Me too."

He drifted to sleep with Robbie anchored to his side, her breaths evening out, her body relaxing against him. This was what he wanted. Robbie in his arms every night, safe from harm.

Chapter Twenty-Seven

"Is there something going on between you two?" Autumn asked.

Robbie couldn't help but smile as memories of last night and this morning in the shower assailed her. Dax was so damn good at making her let go of her fears, her inhibitions. He'd soaped her body gently then rinsed her, his fingers toying with her clit while she moaned and arched into his hand.

When he turned her around and splayed her legs while pressing her torso against the cool tiles, she'd had no idea what was happening next. Then she'd felt his tongue lapping her clit from behind, and her legs went weak. After she'd come that way, he'd fucked her doggy style, holding her hips as he slammed into her and made her splinter apart yet again.

She'd missed a lot in her life, and it angered her to think about it. She was a freaking romance novelist, and she hadn't had the best sex of her life until Dax Freed. It was a crime.

She blamed herself for not realizing sooner that she and Trent were all wrong. He'd given her what she wanted, which was the freedom to be alone, but he'd chosen her because he'd wanted a quiet, biddable wife and she'd lacked enough confidence to fit the bill. Any spark of spirit she'd shown, he tried to crush, just like her parents always had. He'd tried to crush her creativity too, but he hadn't succeeded. Thank God for that. She didn't know what kind of person she'd be now if she hadn't been able to write her stories.

Whatever it was, she had no doubt she'd be miserable.

"Earth to Robbie," Autumn said.

"Uh, sorry." She dragged in a breath and straightened, a smile she couldn't contain splitting her face. "Yes, there's something going on."

Autumn frowned. "Oh, Robbie. I told you to be careful. This won't end well. You know it won't."

Anger flared, though she told herself Autumn had her best interests at heart. Her friend had been there during the worst. She knew the toll the breakdown in Robbie's marriage had taken. Dax wasn't Trent, though. Even if it didn't work out, he wouldn't treat Robbie like shit. She believed it because of the way he'd already treated her.

Like she was worthwhile. Like what *she* wanted mattered. Nobody in her life had ever done that, other than Daphne and Autumn.

"I know you're only trying to protect me, but I'd rather you didn't automatically assume the worst. Dax is great to me. He's nothing like Trent."

"Respectfully, you don't know that. Trent was great to you at first too, wasn't he?"

Robbie knew what Autumn was saying. And it hurt because she wasn't wrong. Trent had masked his selfishness until after they were married.

"Men are slick when they want something from you," Autumn continued. "They will say anything to get their way, and then when you fall for them, they start to treat you like shit until one day you think that's just the way it's supposed to be."

Robbie touched Autumn's arm. Autumn jerked away with a force that stunned her.

"I know how slick men can be," Robbie said softly. "I don't know what's happening between us other than it feels good, okay? I haven't had sex in so long I thought things had dried up permanently, so I'm pretty thrilled that it all still works as it should."

Better than it ever had, really.

Autumn took a step away and tapped her iPad, sniffing disdainfully. "You barely know this man and you're having sex with him. I hope you know what you're doing."

Robbie had never been so irritated with Autumn before, but she understood why the other woman worried. Robbie hadn't written for a year after Trent walked out. Autumn didn't want to see her go through that again. "Women can have sex for the fun of it, you know. I've been with no one in years, and now here's this gorgeous man who knows how to make me feel good about myself, and I just—I feel hopeful for the first time in a long time."

Autumn closed her eyes and huffed a breath. When she opened them again, whatever shadows that had been in her expression were gone. As if nothing had happened. That was a skill Robbie didn't have. She admired it.

"You're right. I'm sorry. You can sleep with whomever you want, and I'll still be here for you if he breaks your heart, which I hope he does *not*. Maybe you should break his first?"

"Maybe," Robbie agreed, though she didn't want to do anything of the kind. She didn't know what would happen beyond today, but she knew that sex with Dax, sleeping with Dax, felt right. He made her feel in control of her life, not controlled by the pressures and expectations of others.

She wanted more days like that, where the weight of expectation didn't press down on her and make her stumble under the burden.

Dax came out of the bedroom. He'd been on a call and had excused himself while Autumn ran through the morning's itinerary again. As if Robbie didn't know it already. His gaze sought hers, and she met him easily. There was no urge to look away. He smiled. She smiled too.

"You ready to go knock 'em dead with your speech?"

"I think so." She was nervous, but not horribly so. Surprisingly. If she'd had to talk about anything else in the world, she'd have been paralyzed with fear. But she could talk about writing to other writers with the confidence of someone who'd finished a few books and knew what it felt like to dream about stories and hope you found people who wanted to read them.

Dax held out a hand and she took it. He looked amazing in a navy blue suit with a white collared shirt unbuttoned at the neck. He didn't wear a tie, and she knew he had a shoulder holster beneath the suit jacket. He probably had another gun in his waistband. He looked like he could be personal security because of his size, but holding her hand changed the equation a bit.

"I'll be close to you at all times, and Finn and Jamie will circulate and look for any problems."

Her heart thumped. She'd met Finn McDermott, who had the most delicious Irish accent, and Jamie Hayes this morning. She hadn't realized until they'd walked in that Jamie was a woman. She was pretty, with dark hair and a surprisingly curvy figure, and Robbie had felt a little flare of jealousy at how easily she bantered with Dax. It was gone quickly when Jamie clasped her hand and said with genuine warmth how happy she was to meet Robbie.

"Do you expect any problems?"

"Not really. But it's a public place, and this is your first appearance since the book came out. There could be a disgruntled fan or two, especially at the book signing later."

Robbie nodded.

"It's twenty minutes to eleven," Autumn said. "We need to get downstairs and get you into the ballroom where your keynote is being held."

Dax squeezed her hand and they headed for the

elevator. All she had to do was get through the day, then it'd be night and she'd be alone again with Dax.

Heaven.

DAX'S PHONE BUZZED. He wasn't wearing a headset because it would have been too obvious. Since he and his team weren't busting into a terrorist stronghold or taking down drug dealers in their lair, it wasn't strictly necessary. Phone communication worked for the small team and kept them unobtrusive.

He glanced at his screen, then swore at the group message from Jamie Hayes.

Trent Sharpe's here.

Fucking great. He glanced at Robbie. He was sitting at the speaker's lunch table and he had a good view of both her and a portion of the crowd from the seat he'd chosen. Finn and Jamie had the room, but it was habit to position himself so he could see as much as possible.

Robbie stood at the podium, talking with a confidence that made him proud. He hadn't expected it, but she'd shocked him. She was smooth and polished, and she had the crowd eating out of her hand just like he'd predicted. He should have known. Writing was her thing, and these people were writers who wanted to know how she'd achieved her success.

She looked amazing, though he also thought her beautiful back home in her yoga pants and messy buns. She'd dressed with the event in mind, donning a black sheath dress that looked incredible on her. The fabric hugged her curves, not too tightly, but enough to define her shape. Her legs were bare, and she had on a pair of matching patent heels with red soles.

Her jewelry was understated, but he would have expected nothing less. She had a pair of diamonds in her ears, and a gold signet ring on her right hand. She also wore a slim gold bracelet on her right arm. She did not wear a watch.

Her hair was loose today, hanging to her waist in silky chestnut curls. He wanted to spear his fingers into it and mess it up, but that would have to wait until later.

Dax texted Jamie and Finn. *Copy. Keep close to him.*

They both answered with a thumbs up. Then Jamie sent another.

I'll take care of it. I'll follow and see if I can distract him.

Dax hit the thumbs up. Jamie was skilled at playing any part she was assigned. She stood a better chance of derailing Trent than Finn did.

Dax didn't like that Trent had turned up. What was the man playing at by following her across the country? Was he planning to beg her again to take him back? Or maybe he was desperate enough to try something crazy. Dax didn't know what Trent might do, but he wasn't giving him a chance to get near Robbie.

She was talking about her journey as a writer, from the first glimmerings of an idea to snatching time wherever she could to work on her manuscript. She talked of writer meetings, and people who believed in her, people who tried to tear her dreams down, her first book deal and how her life had changed.

She even talked about the breakdown of her

marriage and how sometimes letting go was the best thing you could do even when it hurt. Because when you let go, something better had a chance to happen.

She made eye contact with him when she said that, and his chest tightened. He held her gaze as long as he could before he had to watch the crowd again. The irony of being the one to look away first wasn't lost on him.

She talked a bit longer, then finished with, "Thank you, and never give up."

The crowd got to their feet, clapping and cheering. Dax watched, astounded. He didn't know what he'd expected, but he hadn't expected that. Robbie turned to look at him, her smile triumphant. Holy shit, his girl was a ringer. He'd thought she'd be scared out of her mind, stuttering through her speech, but when the chips were down, she'd risen to the call.

Autumn had disappeared, but another woman came to usher Robbie to one of two armchairs that had been placed on the stage and fitted her with a small microphone. The podium was removed, and Robbie took a seat. A blade-thin woman walked onto the stage, waving to the crowd as she did so. When she took the opposite chair from Robbie, it hit Dax why she looked familiar. He got up and moved closer.

Laurel Johnson was also wearing a microphone, though she hadn't turned it on yet, and she was smiling at Robbie. She didn't have a weapon, and didn't appear crazy. Didn't mean she wasn't, though. She said something to Robbie. Robbie tilted her head. He moved closer so he could hear.

He couldn't see Robbie's expression from where he stood, but he could feel her discomfort in the lines of her body. He prepared to leap onto the stage and throw himself in front of her, but then he heard her voice. "I'm sorry. Have we met before? I have social anxiety, and I often lose details of events after the fact."

Laurel's smile didn't fade. "It's been a few years. Capitol City Writers group. You came to a few of our meetings."

"Oh. Yes. Of course."

"That's all right. A lot has happened for you since then. I'm going to turn on my mic now and start, if that's okay with you?"

"Yes, please."

Laurel turned on the microphone as she shuffled a handful of papers in her lap. The pre-submitted questions, presumably. She welcomed Robbie again, mentioned specific moments from her speech, and asked her first question.

It was all very normal, and Dax felt the tension in his body ease. He started over to where Finn stood at one side of the room. There was a sudden commotion near the doors leading to the ballroom. Someone shouted. Dax reached for his weapon at the same time Finn did. They exchanged a look, and Dax sent a hand signal. Finn nodded as he broke for the doors.

Dax sprinted to where Robbie stood on the stage with Laurel Johnson. He wrapped an arm around her, pulling her in close where he could protect her.

"What's going on?" she asked, her eyes wide.

The shouting continued and the crowd shifted

toward the doors. "I don't know, but Finn and Jamie will take care of it. Ms. Johnson, would you care to accompany us to the exit?"

Laurel Johnson's eyes were wide as well. "I think I should stay—"

Gunshots split the air. People screamed and scattered, rushing toward other exits, a giant mass of humanity that would crush anything in its path.

"With me. Now," Dax ordered, herding the two women toward the closest exit. They had no time to lose. If they didn't reach the door first, they could be swept into the crowd, crushed against the walls, or trampled if they lost their footing.

He didn't know what had happened, who'd fired the shot, or if it was intended for Robbie. None of that mattered at the moment. All that mattered was getting them out in one piece.

Chapter Twenty-Eight

Laurel Johnson's long legs were doing a better job of keeping up than Robbie was in her heels as Dax propelled them along through the back hallway of the hotel. She stumbled and would have fallen if Dax hadn't gripped her arm and held her up.

"Sorry," she gasped.

"It's fine. Keep moving."

He got them to a stairwell. The shouting grew muted as the door slammed behind them. Dax took them up two flights of stairs. Robbie was panting by the time they stopped to gather their bearings. Laurel was breathing hard too. Dax wasn't, but the intensity in his expression made her heart skip a beat.

He snagged his phone and made a call. "What's happening? You and Jamie clear?" If he'd been angry before, he looked murderous now. "Copy. Get her to the hospital. I'm taking Robbie to her room. Let me know what's going on, and I'll get over there as soon as I can."

Robbie's pulse rocketed. "Take who to the hospital? What happened?"

"I should be down there," Laurel said. "I'm chair of the conference committee."

Dax was herding them toward the service elevator. "It's over now. The assailant has been subdued. Hotel security's helping calm the crowd and direct people. The cops are on the way."

"Who's hurt?" Robbie asked.

"Jamie. She was shot. She's alive and swearing a blue streak, but she's in pain."

Robbie's belly twisted tight. "Shot? By who? Was…?" She swallowed. "Was it meant for me?"

His eyes were like chips of ice. "Just get in the elevator when it arrives. We'll talk in the room."

"I'm going back down," Laurel said. "I need to go and do what I can."

Dax nodded. "Of course. I don't think Ms. Sharpe will be returning."

"I have to fulfill my commitment," Robbie said firmly. She was shaking inside, though.

"Babe, I don't think there will be any further events today. The police need to take statements, and there's a lot of people in the hotel. It'll be cordoned off for hours."

Laurel turned her gaze on Robbie. "I'm really sorry this happened. I know you don't do many events, and I was hoping…" Her mouth flattened. "I was just hoping it'd be a nice experience. We worked hard to make it that way for everyone. I remember how quiet you were at the CCW group, and I want to say I'm genuinely happy for your success. You've been an inspiration."

Robbie was touched. "Thank you. I'm sorry I stopped going to meetings."

"You can always come back sometime. We have a lot of new people. We get things done these days."

"I live on the Eastern Shore now, but I'll think about it."

"Good."

"I'd like to speak to you about the Capitol City Writers," Dax said to Laurel. "Will you have time later?"

"Yes, of course." She felt around in her pocket and pulled out a business card. "You can text or call. Are you a writer, too, Mr. Freed?"

Robbie thought he almost cracked a smile. "Not quite."

Her gaze dropped. His jacket was pushed back and his pistol grip was visible in the shoulder holster. Understanding dawned. "Ah, of course. So that part of the speech about something better happening after your marriage failed wasn't real?"

The heat of embarrassment flared in her veins. Robbie could feel Dax as a solid presence beside her. She didn't want to look at him, because if she did, her tongue might twist and stay that way. She kept her eyes on Laurel, determined not to look past her or glance away. "Oh no, it was real."

Laurel smiled. "Okay, then. Good. I'll see you later, Mr. Freed."

"Dax."

"Dax. Thanks for your help. Again, I'm sorry things went wrong."

She walked away, and Dax shepherded Robbie into the elevator. As the doors closed, he hooked an arm around her and anchored her to his side. His lips pressed to her hair, and a shudder went through her as she flattened her palm against his belly, needing to feel him. Needing to reassure herself he was real.

"I'm glad that part of the speech was real," he said softly, his mouth against her hair. "I still want to take you out on a date when this is over."

"And I want to go. What happened in there, Dax?"

"A few more minutes. Promise."

The elevator slowed to a stop and the doors opened, letting them out on their floor. They had to walk a distance because the service elevator was located farther from their room. Robbie stopped and took her heels off while Dax waited for her. When they reached the suite, he palmed his keycard and swiped it against the reader. The light turned green and he pressed the handle.

The room had been made up since they'd left. Robbie went over to the couch and sank onto it, grabbing a bottle of water from a tray as she went. She twisted the top and drank. Her nerves were partly shot. Not entirely shot, because she still didn't know what'd happened.

Dax came over and sat on a chair nearby. Not beside her, but where he could face her. He leaned forward, arms on knees, hands dangling.

That couldn't be good.

Robbie blinked, swallowing the bile that threatened. "Tell me."

"Trent's here."

"Here? In Vegas?"

"In the hotel."

She considered it. "He knows people in the industry. If he wanted to shop some kind of tell-all about our marriage, this might be a place to start."

"I don't think that's what he wanted, Robbie." He blew out a breath and dragged his hand down over his face. "There's no good way to say it, but he shot Jamie. She went to intercept him before he could make a scene. I don't know how he got the jump on her, but he did."

Robbie was frozen. Utterly frozen. "I... Trent *shot* her? That's not... like him."

She couldn't get her mind around it. Just couldn't.

"It is now, honey. I'm sorry."

Robbie wrapped her arms around her body and curled her legs beneath her. She was numb. Utterly numb. "I just... That's not the man I knew."

"People do crazy things when they're desperate. He's broke, he's lost his trophy wife, and he's about to lose everything that's left. The bank won't loan him another dime, his creditors are calling, you blocked him and won't speak to him. I think he came here to get your attention."

"B-but..." Her throat felt like it was made of broken glass. "I don't understand. He was going to shoot me?"

Dax took both her hands in his. She hadn't realized how icy they were until that moment. His were like brands. "I don't know, but it's possible. He—fuck, there's no easy way to say this, Robbie."

Her insides crystallized into ice as well. "Tell me. I need to know."

"He was shot by hotel security. He's alive, but Finn says it doesn't look good."

"Oh my God."

"He was someone you loved. I'm sorry."

She shook her head. Tears welled. "I did love him, but not for a long time now. I just—I can't reconcile that he would do something so terrible."

Someone pounded on the door. "Robbie!"

"It's Autumn," she blurted needlessly, because Dax was already moving to let her in.

Autumn rushed into the room, looking a little wild. "Oh my God, are you okay?" She dropped onto the couch beside Robbie and rubbed her shoulder.

Robbie swallowed, nodding. "I'm fine."

"I went to make some arrangements for the book signing, and when I heard gunshots…." Autumn closed her eyes. "My God, it scared me to death. The elevators are packed or I'd have been here sooner."

Robbie wrapped her fingers in Autumn's and squeezed. "I'm glad you're okay. I… Dax said it was Trent."

Autumn's eyes widened. "Oh shit. Why? Why would he do that?"

"I don't know."

Autumn went over to the bar and started pulling out bottles. "I need a drink."

Dax's phone rang, and he walked into the bedroom

to take it. Robbie couldn't move. She kept thinking of that moment when the shouting broke out, then the gunshots. It was hard to reconcile that it had been Trent doing the shooting. Had he been trying to get into the room where she was speaking? Had he been planning to kill her? Why? *Why?*

She shouldn't have blocked him. She should have kept texting with him. If he'd thought there was a chance, he wouldn't have done such a thing. If she'd let him down easy, maybe he'd have accepted there was no chance of them getting back together again.

Autumn reappeared with two glasses and thrust one at Robbie. "Vodka tonic. I think you need it as much as I do."

Robbie took the drink and swigged a mouthful. Dax returned and knelt in front of her. "I need to go check on Jamie. It might be a couple of hours, but you'll be safe here. Don't leave this room, and don't open the door for anyone." He glanced at Autumn. "Neither of you steps foot outside this room, okay?"

Autumn nodded. She'd already downed half her drink. "I don't think the signing's happening now anyway. Even if it is, I don't want to go."

Dax's look was fierce as he cupped Robbie's jaw in both hands and made her look at him. "Listen to me, honey. It's not your fault. Not. Your. Fault."

The tears she'd been holding back welled up again. One slid down her cheek. He wiped it away with his thumb. "Sorry," she whispered.

He leaned forward and kissed her. Softly, gently. She wanted to burrow into his arms, but she refrained.

Barely. She felt safe when he held her. Like the world couldn't touch her. That he knew what she'd been thinking when she hadn't said a word about it only strengthened the feeling.

Oh my God, she *loved* him. The feeling slammed into her, left her gasping in shock on the inside.

But it was true. He knew her in a way nobody else did. He knew who she was, and what was important to her, and he didn't think she needed to change. He thought she was perfect the way she was. He was fierce and beautiful, the best man she knew.

She wanted to tell him, but the time wasn't right. And maybe she wasn't quite brave enough anyway. Even if she found the courage, there were too many words to be said and they weren't alone. He had to focus on other things right now. His teammates needed him, especially Jamie Hayes.

"I'll be back, Robbie. We'll talk then. You're gonna be okay, you hear me?"

"I know. Please let me know how Jamie is when you see her. Tell her I'm s-sorry it happened."

He looked like he wanted to say more, but he nodded. "I'll tell her. She did her job, Robbie. She doesn't blame you."

She clutched the cold drink in her hand. "Okay. Go, Dax. We'll be fine. We'll watch a movie or something, and we won't go anywhere."

He kissed her forehead. "Be back as soon as I can."

When the door closed behind him, Robbie shut her eyes and lay her head against the cushion.

"Your ice is melting. Let me refresh your drink."

Robbie looked up at Autumn standing over her. Then she handed her the glass.

Autumn went back to the bar. "There's some potato chips over here. Want a bag?"

"Sounds good."

Autumn returned and gave her the drink and chips. Then she sat at the opposite end of the couch and tore into her own bag. "Maybe we should order room service. I'm starved."

"Then we'd have to open the door. I don't think Dax would approve."

"Probably not. Fine, I'll just eat everything in the bar."

Robbie gulped a big swallow. She might regret it later, but getting a little bit drunk now would surely ease the knot of tension sitting like a stone inside her gut.

Autumn raised her glass. "Here's to day one. A rousing success so far."

Robbie didn't feel like laughing, but she managed a smile at the sarcasm. "Cheers," she replied, lifting her glass in salute before taking another drink. The alcohol burned through her, leaving a warm glow in its wake.

A few more swallows and this day might just be bearable.

IT WAS a short trip to the ER where the ambulance had taken Jamie. Dax texted Finn, who met him outside and took him to the small private waiting area that'd been designated for them while a doctor cleaned and dressed Jamie's wound.

Trent Sharpe had procured a Sig Sauer P238, a compact .380 caliber single-action pistol. Thankfully, he hadn't loaded it with hollow points or Jamie would be a lot worse off than she was. The round that hit her was a full-metal jacket round. It'd gone through her upper arm, missing bone, and kept on going until it embedded into a pillar. Jamie was hurting and pissed, but she'd be fine.

"Any idea what happened?" he asked Finn after they'd discussed Jamie's wound.

"Jamie said she misjudged the situation. Sharpe stepped out of the room after she saw him. She went to intercept, but he'd gone into the restroom. She waited for him to come out. When he did, she approached. He reached into his pocket but she thought he was going for a phone. By the time she realized he had a gun, others had seen it and started shouting. He was trying to rush the ballroom door when she tackled him. He fired wildly, and one of the rounds hit her. Another bystander was hit as well. He's in surgery, but the prognosis isn't good. When Jamie let go, Trent was still scrambling for the door. The crowd had scattered toward the exits. Security called for him to stop. When he didn't, one of the officers shot him."

"Jesus," Dax breathed. "You get near him?"

"He wasn't conscious when I went over. I'd be surprised if he survives. He was hit in the torso, about two inches below the heart."

"Fuck." He didn't care if the motherfucker died.

He cared how it affected Robbie. She already thought it was her fault that Trent had fired a weapon and hurt people. How was she going to take it when he died and they had no answers for why he'd done any of it?

"How did our guys miss that he was on the move?" Finn asked. "I was so focused on Jamie that I didn't ask when I spoke to Ian."

"They were tracking the GPS on his phone, but he canceled his service. Or the carrier turned it off because he couldn't pay the bill. It cut off yesterday."

They hadn't had eyes on Sharpe because following him wasn't high priority, but they'd been plunged into darkness on his movements when he'd lost his cell phone service. BDI was still working on piecing together his path, but he'd used a stolen credit card to get a budget flight to Vegas. He hadn't appeared to have any plan beyond getting to Robbie.

Dax was still shaking inside over how close he'd been. Had he been planning to kill her? Take her hostage and threaten her? Or was it as simple as a high profile murder-suicide because he was out of options and wanted to punish her?

"Shit. Piss-poor timing," Finn said.

"Understatement."

"How's Robbie holding up?"

"She's in shock. When I left, she was drinking a cocktail with Autumn." He scrubbed a hand over his head. "I can't figure out what Trent's plan was. He didn't leave the photo for her because he wasn't on the Eastern Shore at that time, but he could have had an accomplice. Though who would do that and keep it quiet?"

"He could have paid someone and didn't tell them what it was. Gave them the key, said to be sneaky and not tell anyone."

"True. So then he approached her house in the middle of the night with a 1911 and either wimped out or thought better of it, started trying to get back together with her, hung a dummy in a tree when she wasn't as receptive as he'd hoped, then used someone else's money to fly to Vegas, procure a weapon, and start shooting? What the fuck is the sense in any of that?"

Dax had been through the man's phone and computer thanks to the script in the link Trent had clicked, and he'd found no trace of the altered photo. Not even a photo of Robbie sleeping that Trent might have used to make the composite in the first place.

Finn shook his head. "No clue. But where's the sense in ditching your rich wife for a gold digger in the first place, then going and spending every last dime you got in the divorce settlement? I'm thinking the sharpest thing about the dude was his last name."

"No kidding." How had Trent ever let go of a woman like Robbie? If Dax was lucky enough to have her in his life the way Trent had, he wouldn't ever give her a reason to doubt his devotion. "I really don't think he did those things. Not all of them, anyway. There's still the matter of the stalker, and the specific word choice in the letters. I don't think Trent was detailed enough to think of copying the phrasing. I think he was desperate, and I think he thought it'd be a lot easier to win her back. He thought she was still alone, and likely to stay that way. Finding me there threw him."

He needed to know more about Laurel Johnson and the other woman who'd been in charge of the writers group. Just because Laurel had been with him and Robbie when the shooting started didn't mean she hadn't written the letters and made the threats. She'd also turned her phone off during the times when someone had trespassed onto Robbie's property and placed the box with the photo and hung the dummy, and during the night when someone approached the house. Though she seemed to turn it off most nights, so that didn't mean anything. The other two did.

"Yeah, fuck. This case has too many potentials."

Dax's gut churned. "Yep."

The door to the waiting room opened and a nurse in scrubs walked in. "Are you waiting for Jamie Hayes?"

"Yes," Finn and Dax said together.

"Lucky girl," the nurse said, smiling. "She's going to be fine. The doctor cleaned and dressed the wound, and the bleeding is under control. We've given her a nice dose of morphine, and we'll be keeping her a while for observation. She's asleep now, but she'll be able to have visitors when she wakes. She can probably go home in a few hours."

"Thank you," Dax said. "We're both grateful."

"Yes, thank you," Finn added.

The nurse eyed them both, then winked. "Like I said, she's a lucky girl. I need one of you to fill out some forms for me, please."

"I've got it," Finn said. "I know you wanna get back to Robbie."

"Thanks. I'll see you both at the hotel later."

Dax decided to find Laurel Johnson before he went up to the room. He texted her and she responded that she was in the bar. He found her sitting with a group. She got up when he approached, and he motioned for her to join him at another table so they could talk in private.

"You wanted to ask me about the Capitol City Writers. What do you want to know?"

Her smile was friendly. Didn't mean she wasn't a psychopath underneath it.

"Robbie said she remembered two women who ran the group. One of them was an English professor named Michelle, and the other was a woman named Laura or Lori."

He already knew she'd been in the group when Robbie went because she'd talked about it earlier, but he wanted to clarify.

"That's right. Laurel is my pen name, but my real name is Laura. I wanted to jazz it up a little while still making it something I would answer to. You'd be surprised how many authors take pen names and then don't answer to them at conferences," she said, laughing. "Anyway, yes, Michelle left the group a few years ago after things got a little weird."

"What do you mean by a little weird?"

Laurel looked troubled. "She was a good friend, but she started being paranoid about her work. Accusing people of stealing her ideas even when it was obvious they hadn't, ranting about editors and agents she'd never met, saying her daughter stole her manuscripts and shredded them or sold them to other writers, which was ridiculous. Her daughter would come with her sometimes to meetings, before things went wrong. She was just a teenager then." Laurel sighed. "It was pretty awful, really. I think Michelle had a personality disorder, but I don't know what happened to her. I haven't heard from her in years. Why do you ask?"

"Robbie had letters from a stalker when she first published, and for the next few books. They ceased coming, but there have recently been some new threats made, and I'm investigating all possibilities."

"You don't think it was her ex-husband behind the recent threats? I heard he wasn't expected to survive."

"It might have been him, but I've got to ask."

Laurel folded her arms and nodded. "I'd say Michelle was capable of letters, definitely. She was very critical of Robbie's work when she brought it to the group. Truthfully, I don't think she liked romance novels. She was an English professor at the University of Maryland, so she was a bit of a snob about literature and what constituted it. She didn't like my thrillers either, but she never directly said so."

"Do you have any contact information for her?"

"I'd have to look when I get home again. Her surname was Skerritt if you want to try and find her that way. Otherwise, I can send what I have when I'm home."

"I'd appreciate that." He gave Laurel his email address then texted the name to Ian.

"Oh," Laurel said as he stood. "Something else."

"Yeah?" He still wanted to know why her phone had been turned off at key moments when Robbie was being threatened, but there was no good way to ask. Besides, if she was the one stalking Robbie, then he wanted to catch her at it. Catch her and make sure she never got a chance to do it again.

He'd be sorry if it was Laurel though. She seemed decent and hard-working, but he knew that didn't always mean anything. His stepdad had seemed that way at times, then he dove into the bottle and didn't come out for long periods while their lives went to shit.

"Michelle lived in College Park. She had a house there with her husband and daughter. Her husband had a different last name from her, though. Pinkerton, I think."

The hairs on the back of Dax's neck stood at attention.

"No, Pinkney. That's it. He was a Pinkney while Michelle was a Skerritt."

Chapter Twenty-Nine

Robbie couldn't open her eyes. They were so heavy. So very heavy.

But something wasn't right. She'd been on the couch in her suite, drinking with Autumn, but now she was hot. It had been cool in the suite. She'd been icy, but that had been a reaction to everything that'd happened.

What had happened?

Oh yeah, gunshots. Dax rushing her out of the room. Trent shooting people…

Robbie moved her head back and forth, trying to rouse herself. What the hell? Was she on the floor? Had she passed out in the bathroom? She really should *not* have accepted that second drink.

"Dax," she mumbled. "Dax."

There was no answer, no footsteps.

"Autmmmm… Autmmmmmm."

Still nothing. Why couldn't she talk? Had she gotten shit-faced? Where was Autumn?

She tried so hard to make herself open her eyes, but

it wouldn't happen. She let herself sink into slumber again. It was easier than trying to wake up.

"MICHELLE SKERRITT!" Dax shouted into the phone as he ran for the elevator. "Where is she now?"

He had to consider that she was involved, that her daughter might be helping her. All this time, the stalker had been close. She'd never been a stranger. Never been an angry reader. She'd been *right fucking there*.

On the other end of the line, Jared and Ty were working to find the information while Ian barked orders in the background. The elevator doors opened and he ran inside, hitting the floor number and jamming the button for the doors to close.

They took their sweet-ass time sliding together, but soon the elevator was moving. He kept watching the floors tick by, praying nobody got on with him, feeling cold sweat slide down his spine.

Autumn Pinkney. She lived in College Park, in a house she'd gotten from her mother. She'd worked for Robbie for five years and never said a word about her mother or the Capital City Writers. Hell, she even drove a car with sixteen-inch tires. He'd never considered her. Not once.

She'd pretended not to know Laurel Johnson when he'd asked, though she had to have met her since Michelle sometimes took her teenage daughter to meetings.

Why hadn't Laurel recognized Autumn? Or had

Autumn managed to avoid the other woman entirely? She hadn't been in the room during the speech and hadn't been present to get Robbie set up for the Q&A session. She'd claimed to be working on the signing event later, but that was clearly a ruse so she wouldn't have to encounter Laurel.

"Michelle Skerritt, PhD," Ty said. "Forty-nine, currently a resident in Willow Brook Psychiatric Hospital. I can't get information on what the diagnosis is, but she's been committed for the past three years. She's not allowed off the premises at all. Before that, she was still at home."

He recited the address. Dax already knew it was Autumn's. *Fuck.*

"Her husband left seven years ago and filed for divorce. Michelle kept the house, he got the joint property in Pennsylvania. Daughter is Alicia Autumn Pinkney—fucking hell, Dax. She's twenty-six, single, currently lives alone in the house she transferred into her name with a power of attorney. According to this, Autumn is five-eight, with brown hair and brown eyes."

"She dyes her hair red and wears green contacts," Dax said, his heart hammering as he remembered the way she'd rubbed Robbie's back earlier. Offering sympathy. All of it a lie.

She'd been in Robbie's home. Many times. Hell, she'd probably gotten a key made or swiped one of the extras Robbie had in a drawer in her office. For five years, she'd been biding her time. Why?

The elevator opened, and Dax bolted down the hall, sliding to a stop in front of the door. He informed Ty, then shoved the phone into his pocket before drawing his weapon. He swiped his keycard, praying he wasn't too late.

He told himself the door would open and Robbie would look up and smile. His heart would do a slow tumble into his stomach, and relief would overwhelm him. Autumn would be there, blinking in shock. She had no reason to think he was onto her. Not that he knew what her plan was or why, but he could only pray she hadn't yet set it into motion.

He pushed the door inward and peeked around it. The room was empty. Two glasses sat on the coffee table, leaching moisture into the polished wood. He entered, then checked the bedroom and bathroom. No one was there.

Dax's stomach dropped. He snagged his phone from his pocket. "They're gone."

He tried to be brutally clinical as he surveyed the suite. Robbie's handbag was gone, which gave him hope. If she had her phone with her, they could track it. That hope died when he discovered her phone on the couch, wedged between the cushions.

"Her phone's still here," he said, picking it up and swearing as he clutched it tight.

"We'll track Autumn's," Ty said. "Jared's calling Finn."

Dax wanted to *do* something, but there was nothing he could do until he had information. It felt wrong not taking immediate action. He wanted to run after her, but where would he run? Autumn could have taken her anywhere.

His stomach squeezed tight.

Jesus Christ. Her stalker had been under his nose all along. Michelle Skerritt might have written the early letters, but there was no way she'd written anything recently. It was all Autumn. Not Trent Sharpe, not Laurel Johnson, not a random, angry reader.

Autumn Pinkney, Robbie's treasured and trusted assistant. Her friend. Yet another person in her life who'd betrayed her.

He wanted to shout the walls down he was so fucking pissed. And scared. He was definitely scared. Robbie trusted him, and he'd let her down. He thought of Lucy and Ollie in the pet resort waiting for her to return. He thought of her house with the beautiful yard and the faded tobacco barn she wanted to renovate for horses someday. She was quiet and awkward, but she was the kindest, sweetest person he knew.

He loved her. It hit him like a freight train going eighty. He fucking loved her, and he'd do anything to get her back. When he did—not *if*—he wasn't wasting another moment examining his feelings or keeping them inside. He'd lost Tara because he couldn't express himself, but he wasn't doing that with Robbie. Maybe she wasn't in love with him, and maybe his heart would shatter into a million pieces, but he vowed if he got her back, he was telling her. First thing he said would be those words.

"Not getting a signal now," Ty said, "but Autumn's last location was southeast of the city in the vicinity of Eldorado Canyon. Cell strength isn't good. There might be a lack of towers, or she could have turned off the phone."

"She had to have rented a car," Dax said. "I'm headed down to the concierge desk to find out if she made any arrangements. Send me a photo of her so I can use it."

"Doing it now. Jared says Finn's on his way. Jamie's still knocked out, but she's doing fine."

"I'm on the move. Let me know if you find anything else."

"Good luck, Dax."

HER HEAD HURT. This time when Robbie tried to open her eyes, they stayed that way. Daggers jabbed her temples, but she was determined to figure out where she was. It was still hot. Couldn't be the bathroom floor if it was so hot. The suite was air-conditioned, but she was sweating buckets. That wasn't right.

There was a bright shaft of light coming from a window, and dust motes danced in the air. Robbie blinked. Was she dreaming?

Except the heat felt very real, and so did the sweat. She tried to push herself upright, but her hands were tied.

Panic wrapped around her heart and squeezed. What was happening? Had her stalker found her? Had Autumn opened the door and someone hurt her before they kidnapped Robbie? Or maybe she'd been kidnapped too.

Did Dax know yet? Oh my God, if Dax didn't know, she was in big trouble. She could die. Whoever had done this would kill her, and she'd never see Dax again. Never get to tell him that she loved him. That he'd actually made her believe in heroes. Not the fairy-tale kind like she wrote about, but the kind that had your back and believed in you.

Believed you weren't flawed because you were awkward or quiet, believed you hadn't lost your talent, and believed you were strong despite your own belief you were weak.

Simply believed. That was worth more than all the money in the world. And she hadn't told him.

A door creaked open then slammed closed on rusty hinges. A screen door? Robbie tried to focus on the shape silhouetted against the glaring light.

"About time you woke up."

"Autumn? Is that you? Oh my God, did you get away from them?" Another happier thought filled her. "Are you here with Dax? Is this a rescue?"

Autumn snorted. "Sorry, Robbie, not a rescue." She came over and hunkered down a few feet away from where Robbie lay on the hard floor. "Nobody's coming to get you. This is it. End of the line."

"What? What are you talking about?" Robbie shifted until she could prop herself against the wall at her back. Her head swam, and bile rose in her throat. God, she felt like she'd consumed the entire bottle of vodka.

"I'm talking about you. You ruined *my life*. Ruined my mother's life. Ruined *everything*," Autumn snapped. "Before you came along, she was doing good. She hadn't been sick in a long time. She was writing again, running the Capitol City Writers with that idiot Laura. Helping people *write*. But you showed up and you took advantage of her generosity. You pushed her too far, and she broke again."

Robbie's mouth was dry, her throat tight. Every word was like a knife in her heart. Confusion hung over her like a fog that wouldn't lift. She didn't know what Autumn was talking about, but she heard the hatred. Felt it.

Autumn. *Her friend.* Or so she'd always thought.

"I-I don't know what you mean, I swear. Whose generosity?"

"*My mother's!*" Autumn shouted. "Michelle Skerritt!"

"I d-didn't know."

"Of course you didn't. I was at those meetings, and I saw you. You didn't even remember me when you hired me. Always so focused on yourself and your anxiety. Poor little Roberta Sharpe, so shy," she said in a high-pitched voice. "Yet you're the one who makes millions with your awful writing and your plagiarized ideas."

"I never stole anything from anyone," Robbie blurted before she thought better of it.

Autumn closed the distance between them and slapped her across the face so hard her head rocked back and hit the wall. Her cheek stung, and tears sprang to her eyes.

"Damian LeBeaux and Velvet Asbury. My mother was writing those characters when you arrived. Not those stupid names, of course. But you read her story about an immortal vampire and his soulmate, and you took her idea. Then you broke them up in the last book! What the hell were you thinking? How could you ruin everything like that?"

Robbie couldn't speak she was so shocked. Autumn was red with anger, her eyes flashing. She didn't sound sane, and yet Robbie had known her for five years. She'd always been efficient and done her job perfectly. But this? It was crazy.

Michelle Skerritt had never been writing about a vampire. If she had, she hadn't shared it with the group. Robbie would have remembered something like that. Hell, she'd have been thrilled to have someone to talk to about vampire books.

Michelle had been tall, thin, with attractive features and a blond bob. She was the English professor who'd looked down her nose at most of the writers in that group. She'd written about relationships. Mothers, daughters, husbands, sons.

Broken relationships. Dysfunctional ones. Her pages were filled with ennui and sadness.

There hadn't been an immortal character *anywhere* in her stories. Robbie didn't remember a lot about the woman's writing other than it contained a lot of flowery sentences, which Michelle had once called lyrical when someone challenged her on it.

She thought about the letter she'd gotten when her first book came out. *You won't get away with it. I'll tell the world.* Every letter from her stalker had that phrasing. They contained vitriol about her story, about her, and about readers having terrible taste if they liked her writing. They also accused her of stealing her ideas from better writers.

Michelle Skerritt had been a literary writer who considered romance novels trash and a waste of good paper. She'd said as much at least once in Robbie's hearing. That was part of why she'd stopped going. Robbie truly had never had any idea Michelle had become obsessed with her to the point she literally thought she'd been the one writing about Damian and Velvet. It never crossed her mind.

Robbie knew if she tried to defend herself, if she said any of that to Autumn, she risked another slap. Or worse. Clearly, Michelle had suffered from mental illness. Did Autumn as well?

Robbie remembered a sulky teenager with headphones sitting in a chair separate from the group. She'd had brown hair, not red, and she'd stayed on her phone most of the time. She hadn't been interested in anything they were doing. Robbie had a hard time reconciling that kid with the woman before her, but they were obviously the same person.

"What are you planning to do with me?" she asked.

Autumn paced back to the other side of the room, then whirled. "Not sure yet. I'm improvising. I had to because you got all hot and bothered over that bodyguard, who finally fucking left you alone with me for a while. Jesus, Robbie, after everything Trent did to you, you had to go and fall into bed with this guy?"

Robbie wasn't going to argue. She would lose if she tried because Autumn had all the power in this situation.

She thought back to the day Dax showed up at her farm. "Did you leave the photo of me in the coffin?"

"Of course I did. I was also the person on the trail cam that night, and I hung the effigy from the tree a few days later—that was supposed to be you, by the way."

Her heart ached. "Why? Why would you do any of those things?"

Autumn ignored her. "I sent the most recent letters because she can't. She's not even supposed to read your books, but someone snuck her a copy. Not me. They're bad for her." Autumn made an animal sound in her throat. "I was so fucking angry—I wanted you to feel like she does. Like the walls were closing in and no one could save you. I wanted you paranoid and afraid. I never thought you'd get a damned bodyguard though. It's not like you to let anyone in, but Daphne made you. Fucking Daphne."

Autumn paced into a shaft of sunlight, then out again. Robbie realized that Autumn was crying.

"My mom doesn't even know me anymore. Can you believe that? *You did that to her.*"

"I'm sorry," Robbie said, because it seemed like she should. She'd say whatever it took to pacify Autumn. To get Autumn to let her go. Or to delay long enough for Dax to find them.

If he found them. Robbie shivered. If she had her phone, he could track it. But she didn't. Autumn wouldn't have brought it. Despair swelled into a hard knot inside.

"You aren't sorry." Autumn went over and snatched up the leather satchel she always carried that had her tablet and any documents she was working on. "If you want to make it right, you can sign this letter that says you did it. The doctors say she'll never recover, but she will if I make you admit what you did. She needs you to be accountable."

Autumn yanked a piece of paper out of the satchel and advanced on Robbie. "Sign this, admit you stole her work, and I might let you go."

Robbie recoiled as Autumn dropped to her haunches in front of her. The paper shook in her hand. Robbie looked into her eyes. Really looked. What she saw made her heart drop and her throat seize up. Autumn looked wild, like she might leap on Robbie at any moment. The polished demeanor of her assistant—her friend—was gone. Or maybe that had been the act and this was the real Autumn, finally set free to say the things she'd kept inside.

"I… I can't sign it with my hands tied."

Autumn's gaze dropped. Her face twisted. "You want me to let you go so you can try and escape."

Robbie shook her head. "No. I swear. Where would I go? I don't even know where we are."

Autumn studied her. "You're still feeling the effects of the valium. I'll untie you, but if you try anything, I'll shoot you."

She went over and picked up a pistol off the table near one window. "The beauty of flying a private charter is you can bring your gun with you." She stroked it lovingly. "It was my dad's. Before he left us. It's the only thing I have of his."

Autumn picked up a knife, the blade gleaming in a

spark of sunlight that shafted into the room. Then she advanced on Robbie, knife in one hand and pistol in the other. "I'm going to untie you, and you're going to sign this paper that says you stole my mother's work. You try anything, and I won't hesitate to kill you."

Fear hot-footed its way across Robbie's skin. If she signed the paper, she might be as good as dead anyway. And if she didn't? She closed her eyes and leaned against the wall. "I'm sorry, I need a minute. I feel… kinda sick."

"It's the Valium mixed with the alcohol. You'll be fine."

"I know. I just… I need a few moments to breathe." What the hell was wrong with her? First she'd wanted Autumn to untie her, and now she thought if Autumn did so, she'd kill her as soon as the paper was signed.

Think, Robbie.

What would Velvet do? She wouldn't simply wait for her king of the night to swoop in and rescue her, though she'd been known to do that, too. When the enemy was a powerful immortal. Even then, she used her wits to distract them. Just long enough for Damian to arrive.

"I-I need to pee."

"Pee where you are. I don't care."

"I might get urine on the paper when I sign. I'm so weak I could drop it. That wouldn't be good, would it?" Her heart pounded like mad.

Autumn's brow scrunched. "What do you want me to do? Carry you to the bathroom?"

"Not carry me. Help me get there. Then I'll sign."

"You can fucking sign now if you don't want me to shoot you."

Robbie swallowed. "Shoot me and I can't sign a damned thing. You won't get my confession at all if I'm dead. Is that what you want?"

Autumn looked furious. And trapped. "You don't hold the cards here, Robbie. I do."

"All I want is to pee. Then I'll sign your paper. Hell, I'll record a video if you want me to." That idea popped into her head at the last second. It was a good one, though. If Autumn took her up on it, she'd have to use a phone. If she'd turned it off, she'd have to turn it back on again. That would give Dax and his team a way to find her.

Or so she hoped.

Robbie bit her lip as Autumn sucked in a breath. It was a long shot, but it was the only one she had. If Dax knew she was gone, if he was looking for her, if he was searching for her through cell phones, he might get Autumn's signal. Especially if Robbie flubbed her lines a few times and Autumn had to keep the phone on.

"Fine. I'll help you to the bathroom. But no bullshit. I won't hesitate to cut you. And I'll keep cutting you until you do what I want. You can live a long time with bleeding cuts, you know."

As if to punctuate the point, she dragged the leg of her pants up to her calf. For the first time ever, Robbie saw the fine silvery scars on Autumn's leg. They were too uniform to be the result of an accident.

She lifted wide eyes to Autumn. Her eyes were hard as rocks. "Cutting relieves the pain. You'll see."

Autumn tucked the gun into her waistband. She kept the knife in one hand as she grabbed onto Robbie and tugged. It took some doing, but Robbie managed to get to her feet. She was groggy as hell, and her stomach threatened to heave whatever was in it. She clutched Autumn, who grunted angrily as she walked them toward the restroom. Robbie wanted to grab the gun, but she was too woozy to do it. Even if she did, Autumn could overpower her easily.

Once they made it there, Autumn cut the zip-tie around Robbie's wrists.

Blood flowed back into her arms, making her want to cry out at the pins-and-needles sensation. If she'd thought she was going to get the jump on Autumn somehow, she'd been wrong. She could barely feel her arms as the blood flowed back in. What she could feel, hurt.

She hiked her dress up and dragged her underwear down, not bothering to hold back the dry sobs that racked her. She hurt, and not just her body. Her heart hurt. She wanted Dax. So bad. She wanted to burrow into his arms and not come out for a week.

More than that, she wanted to tell him she loved him. Even if he didn't love her, she wanted to say it. Just take that chance and go for it. She'd never been bold, other than in the pages of her books, and she was regretting it now.

"Fucking get it done, would you?" Autumn said.

"I'm trying. It would help if you weren't looking at me."

Autumn's jaw worked. But she backed out of the

room and shut the door. It wasn't like there was anywhere to go, so it wasn't a huge risk. The window was too small to climb out. However, there was a plunger. If Robbie could remove the handle, she could use it as a weapon.

She managed to pee while she worked the handle free of the rubber cup. Then she got herself together again. If she came out swinging hard, she could connect. And if she missed?

If she missed, it might be the last thing she ever did.

Chapter Thirty

Dax sped through the desert, heading for the pinpoint on the map. Finn sat beside him in the silver Jeep Ian had procured for them, monitoring Autumn Pinkney's location. Ty Scott was on the phone from DC, running the program that had a lock on the signal.

They were heading southeast, tracking the last known location of Autumn's phone. Occasionally it pinged a tower, but the signal was spotty. She'd probably put her phone in airplane mode, thinking that was enough to eliminate tracking.

It wasn't for his team. Her signal was weaker, but it was still there and still traceable. They'd left pavement behind miles ago as they traversed a twisty dirt road between rocky cliffs that led toward the Colorado River.

There were no signs of life where they were. Nothing but dirt, rock, and scrub for miles. Occasionally, they came across a rusted out vehicle, sometimes with bullet holes, but there were no signs of life in those either. Dax kept driving. He wasn't stopping for anything until they got Robbie back.

It was still daylight, which could be a problem when they got closer. He'd worry about it then.

After a half hour on the dirt track, Ty said, "There's an old mining town up ahead, but there aren't a lot of people who live there. Beyond the town, there's a small RV park with some rental cabins scattered over a few acres headed toward the river. Autumn's signal is coming from the back of the property."

"Copy," Finn said, looking over at Dax. Waiting for a decision.

"I don't wanna wait. I think time is critical. Michelle Skerritt's in a mental hospital, and her daughter's been pretending to be Robbie's friend for five years. She has an endgame in mind. I think now that she's finally made her move, she won't waste any time when she gets what she wants."

"Agreed," Finn said. "How you want to do this?"

"I say we drive in slow and look for the rental car. Once we've found it, we can keep going, then double back on foot."

"Works for me."

Dax's gut churned as they rounded a turn and came upon a brown valley dotted with a few weather beaten homes and trailers. There was a gas station sign, but as they got closer they realized it wasn't a gas station at all. It was just a sign someone had put up in their yard. Dax drove slowly through town, continuing to the RV park, his heart pounding harder with every passing mile.

From a distance, the park looked like it'd been abandoned, with only a few old RVs scattered across it. He could see the metal roofs of cabins dotting the landscape, and he prayed that whatever Autumn had in mind, she hadn't done it yet.

There was a weathered building with a car sitting at the front of the park, and Dax stopped so Finn could go in and get information. He returned a few minutes later, dropping into the seat and nodding.

"She's here. Hasn't left since she drove in a couple of hours ago. A young woman traveling alone, but if Robbie was lying on the backseat, the lady inside wouldn't have seen her from where she's sitting."

Dax's belly twisted. If Autumn had disposed of Robbie before she got to the park, he'd lose his fucking mind. He'd take her down if that was the case. No mercy.

His thoughts must have shown on his face.

"She's there," Finn said firmly. "Don't think like that."

Dax nodded. "Trying to be realistic. She couldn't have planned this. She couldn't have known Trent would show up, or that Jamie would get hurt and I'd go to the hospital, giving her an opportunity to kidnap Robbie."

"No, she couldn't have known any of that. But she has to *want* something or she wouldn't have done it. She's waited five years. Why? If all she wanted was to kill Robbie, she could have done that at any point prior to now. She's had opportunities."

"That's why I can't figure it out. Why *now?*"

"Dunno, man, but that's not our department. All we gotta do is go get your girl and bring her home."

His girl. He liked that. "Yeah."

Dax drove slowly toward the cabins, searching for a glimpse of a green sedan. Something flashed in the distance—and then a flame shot skyward before enveloping one of the cabins. Dax floored the SUV. A woman with red hair was silhouetted against the cabin, watching the flames licking the walls. A gas can lay at her feet. She turned as they rocketed toward her, her eyes widening a split second before she sprinted toward the open car door that sat nearby.

"Fuck, don't let her get away," Dax shouted as he skidded to a stop and ripped off his seatbelt. He didn't have time to go after Autumn. He had to get inside the burning cabin and find his woman. Robbie might already be dead, but he wasn't going to let her burn. He had to hold her one more time.

"Dax!" Finn shouted as he reached the front porch. Flames licked up the sides of the building, across the roof, racing to consume the wood.

Dax kicked the door open, took a deep breath, and leaped inside the flaming building. Smoke choked the breath from him, and his eyes stung so badly he couldn't see anything. Heat surrounded him, singeing into him, until he wanted to run.

But he couldn't. He *had* to find her.

"Robbie," he choked out. *"Robbie!"*

He dropped to a crouch, searching. He could see a little better since the smoke was rising. But it would soon choke the life from him. If he didn't find her, he'd die.

But so would she. If there was even the smallest hope she was still alive, he had to get to her.

A few feet away, something moved. His gaze lasered onto it. *A hand.*

Dax scrambled for her. She was on her back, eyes closed, blood staining one side of her face. He didn't have time to check her. Instead, he hefted her up, threw her over his shoulder the way he'd been trained, and darted for the wall of flame that used to be a door.

Fire licked at his legs, his arms, but then he was through into the clean air again, stumbling forward until he could lay her down on the ground and check for signs of life.

"Jesus Christ," Finn said before he took off for the SUV and the First Aid kit there. Autumn Pinkney screamed and cried from where Finn had left her. She was on the ground, arms and legs bound together like a calf at a rodeo.

Dax didn't fucking care about her.

"Robbie," he said as softly as he could with the smoke still burning his throat. "Robbie."

Her eyes fluttered but didn't open. He checked her pulse. It was there, but faint. Irregular. Fading.

Finn returned with the kit. Dax shook his head and started chest compressions.

"Don't you fucking leave me, Robbie," he ordered as he pressed down over and over.

He could feel the tears streaking his face, but he didn't care. All he cared about was making sure she lived. Making sure she knew how he felt.

"You listen to me, Robbie. Lucy and Oliver need you. I need you." He gulped in a breath. It came out as a broken sound he didn't recognize. "I fucking love you, do you hear me? I love you, Roberta, and you'd better not leave me. I can't—I can't do this without you, do you hear?"

He kept doing the compressions. Finn knelt and checked her pulse. In the distance, the sound of a helicopter grew louder and louder. His team would have called for emergency assistance, but he didn't know if Robbie would live long enough to get it.

"Her pulse is stronger," Finn said. "It's working."

Dax recognized the sound he made as a sob. He didn't care that his teammate was there to witness it. "That's it, Robbie. Breathe for me. Let your heart beat for me. Mine beats for you. Don't make it beat alone. Please don't make it beat alone."

ROBBIE'S THROAT HURT. Her eyes stung. And her head was fuzzy. She had to wake up, had to get out. Was that gasoline she smelled?

She remembered standing in the bathroom, gripping the plunger handle tight, gathering her courage. Then she'd opened the door and lunged at Autumn, swinging for all she was worth. She'd missed, and despair had bloomed in her soul. She was too slow from the drugs, too clumsy, and Autumn was fast.

She hadn't stopped swinging, though. She'd even managed to land a blow, but harmlessly on Autumn's side. Autumn had cried out, but she hadn't stopped fighting.

And then the plunger handle was ripped out of her grip and she was pushed onto the floor.

"You stupid bitch," Autumn had hissed. She'd closed a pen in Robbie's fingers, then thrust the paper at her. "Sign it, and I won't kill you for that."

"No," Robbie had said hoarsely. It was the only thing she had left. Her only way to fight.

"Sign. It."

"*No.*"

Autumn had screamed. Then she'd stood and kicked Robbie. Robbie curled up, putting her hands over her head, and Autumn kept kicking and kicking, hitting her with the handle, screaming in rage.

That was the last thing Robbie remembered other than the smell of gasoline.

She had to wake up, had to get out. *Now, Robbie!*

"Honey, shh, it's okay. Don't fight. You're safe now. You're safe."

She stilled, listening. Dax? She wanted to speak, wanted to open her eyes and look at him, but nothing happened. Was it really him, or was she hallucinating? Hearing his voice because she wanted to, not because he was really there.

She knew she needed to fight, but in the next moment, liquid heat flowed into her veins and she didn't want to fight at all. She just wanted to sleep.

Black Velvet

HE DIDN'T LEAVE her side other than when he had to. Dax sat beside Robbie's bed in the hospital and watched over her. Sometimes he slept. He ate when someone brought him something. He managed to brush his teeth because someone thought of that too.

Finn checked in at regular intervals. Jamie did as well. She'd been discharged and she was fine. She wore a sling, and Finn was a bit overprotective of her, but she bore it with good humor.

Dax took calls from his team because he knew they were concerned. Ian could have ordered him to leave and get some rest, but he didn't. Probably because he knew he'd have a fight on his hands. Dax wasn't one to disobey orders, but he figured that was the one he'd draw a line in the sand on.

He never had to, though, because it never came. Ian Black knew what it was like to be in love with someone, and what it was to almost lose them. He knew the special kind of hell Dax existed in right now.

Robbie was physically fine. Her body was healing. Autumn had kicked and hit her repeatedly, bruising her all over, fracturing ribs. There'd been no swelling on the brain, but Dax didn't know how long she'd been unconscious before he'd started chest compressions. If it was too long, with her pulse that irregular, there could be permanent damage. They wouldn't know until she woke.

He'd been waiting for two days now. She'd tried to surface a couple of times, but she'd thrashed and moaned so badly the nurses had sedated her again. Dax talked to her a lot. He told her about his life in Florida, how he'd always felt unworthy because of the way his stepdad treated him, but that he didn't feel that way with her. With her, he felt like he belonged. Couldn't explain it, but it was as true as the sky being blue or the sun being hot.

He didn't know if she heard him or not, and he knew he'd have to tell her everything again when she was awake, but for now it felt good to say it. Cathartic. He told her that Lucy and Ollie missed her and couldn't wait for her to come home. He called the pet resort daily and gave her reports. There were pictures, too, because the staff texted them to him. He showed her, even when she couldn't see them.

He held her hand. Her cold, small hand that had typed over a million words and made so many people happy. Her room was filled to bursting with flowers and balloons and get well cards from fans and friends alike. He didn't know how the news had gotten out about her being in the hospital, but he was glad to see that people cared.

It was after midnight on the third day when Dax let go of her hand and lay back in the recliner beside her bed to try and get some sleep. He slept in fits and starts. At one point, he dreamed about fire licking the walls and ceiling. He jerked awake, blinking at a white tiled ceiling, his heart pounding.

When he turned to look at Robbie, to reassure himself she was still there, she was gazing back at him. Maybe he was still dreaming, but he lowered the recliner and stood beside the bed, praying he wasn't.

"Hey," he said softly.

"I hurt," she said.

He took her hand gently. She squeezed his fingers, but her grip was weak. To be expected. "I know, honey. I'm sorry."

"Am I dreaming, Dax? Or are you really here?"

"I'm here, Robbie." Something hot and wet dripped onto his hand. Fuck, now he was crying. He swiped away the tears and bent to press his lips to her forehead. "I love you."

Her eyes closed, but they didn't stay that way. When she opened them again, they glistened with moisture as she tried to smile. Her face was still bruised from where Autumn had hit her, but her tiny smile was the most beautiful thing he'd ever seen.

"I love you, too," she whispered, her voice hoarse from the smoke inhalation. "My hero."

His heart was full. Not only because of the words she said, but because she was *there*. She was still his Robbie. "Welcome back, honey. I've missed you."

Chapter Thirty-One

ROBBIE WAS IN THE HOSPITAL FOR A WEEK. BY THE TIME she was released, her body didn't ache nearly as badly—though the bruising looked terrible—and her throat didn't hurt so much when she talked.

She sat in the back of an SUV with Dax as Finn drove them to the airport. Dax had suggested they stay in a hotel suite for a few days so she'd have more time to heal, but she wanted to be home. He hadn't argued. Her fingers were twined in his, and she leaned against him, taking comfort in his strength.

When Finn drove up to a big jet on the tarmac, she blinked in disbelief. Whenever she chartered anything, it was usually small, but this was a 737. It was white with a black tail and gold lettering that said BDI.

"We're using your company plane?"

"One of them," Dax said. "Ian wouldn't hear of anything else."

Robbie sniffled. She'd only met the enigmatic Mr. Black once, but she liked him. She liked all the people she'd met who worked with Dax, as well as their partners. Lovely people.

They'd sent her flowers and cards while she was in the hospital. She'd been touched by their thoughtfulness for someone they'd met once. Her parents had predictably left annoying voice messages hoping she was feeling better and then saying they'd like to talk about necessary renovations to their condo whenever she felt like calling.

She hadn't called yet, and she wasn't planning on it until she was stronger. Daphne had threatened to fly to her bedside and keep a mother hen watch on her if she didn't do as she was told. Between Daphne and Dax, there was no way she could have misbehaved even if she'd wanted to.

There was still much about the day Autumn had kidnapped her that she didn't know. She knew that Trent had died from his gunshot wound. He'd had a letter in his pocket from the bank repossessing his boat, and though nobody could be certain, it seemed as if he'd been planning to storm the room to kill her and then himself. The last brutal act of a desperate man who refused to take responsibility for his own choices, but wanted attention for his final act, nevertheless.

It saddened her and angered her, too. That he would blame her for his own faults so much that he wanted to murder her as punishment leached away any sympathy she might have had for him. She'd apologized to Jamie for getting her shot, but the woman waved her off and told her it was part of the job. Robbie wasn't responsible for anyone else's actions.

It was comforting, and yet she'd always wonder if she could have done anything differently.

They left the SUV behind and boarded the jet. Finn and Jamie led the way, Finn talking and Jamie seeming irritated if the way she gestured at him was any indication. Robbie didn't know why. She leaned toward Dax once she was seated and whispered, "What is going on with them?"

Dax glanced over. Jamie was gesticulating with her free arm, and Finn was shaking his head. "Don't know. Want me to ask?"

"No!" She realized he was grinning at her. "Rotten man."

Dax kissed her cheek. Even that little gesture had her insides melting. She wanted to be with him so badly. Naked, in bed, his body moving inside hers. Reminding her she was alive. It wasn't happening anytime soon, though. Too much bruising and pain. Dax wasn't going to touch her so long as she winced every time she moved.

"I think he's sweet on her," Dax said, keeping his voice low. "Not sure if she feels the same."

Robbie watched them. Jamie sat down and Finn reached over to buckle her seatbelt. She glared but didn't stop him. "It's possible. She didn't shove him away."

"Hard to buckle a seatbelt with one arm in a sling."

"Not impossible."

"True." He brought their linked hands to his mouth and kissed the back of hers. "I love you."

She never got tired of hearing that. Her entire being

felt as if it had been suffused with light when he said it. She needed that so much. "I love you more."

"Not possible, babe."

She lifted her other hand, though her body protested the movement, and palmed his cheek. It felt so good to touch him. "Okay, not possible. I can never thank you enough for running into a burning building for me."

He looked tortured for a moment, but it passed. "You don't have to thank me. If I hadn't saved you, I'd have lost me, too."

Her heart squeezed hard whenever he said things like that. But she understood the feeling because her last thoughts before she'd blacked out had been about him. She'd hoped he would find her, but if he didn't, she'd hoped he wouldn't blame himself.

Robbie nibbled her lip. Every time she'd asked about Autumn since she'd awakened, he'd told her they'd talk about it later. She was getting tired of waiting.

"You still haven't told me about Autumn. I know you captured her, but not what happened. Is she in jail? Will I have to press charges? I think it's time I know, Dax."

He nodded. "You're right. I didn't want you thinking about it when you were in the hospital trying to heal, especially when you had to process Trent's death. Though you aren't a hundred percent yet, I think you're strong enough... Autumn isn't well, honey. She's in a psychiatric facility for now, but she'll be charged if she's released."

"Her mother's in a facility, too. I think." She'd gathered that from what Autumn had told her about the doctors saying she'd never recover, and about someone sneaking her a copy of *The Vampire King*. You wouldn't have to sneak a copy to a woman who had the freedom to buy one online or in a store. But she didn't know she was right until Dax confirmed it.

"Yes. Michelle Skerritt was in and out of hospitals for years, but she was committed three years ago. She seems to have been obsessed with you, probably because she knew you before you published. When your book took off, she fixated on it and you. You had the life she wanted, and she hated you for it."

She'd already told him that Autumn had tried to make her sign a letter saying she'd stolen Michelle Skerritt's work and passed it off as her own, but she'd refused to do it. The accusation still made her mad, though she was sympathetic to the fact the woman had a mental illness. Didn't make it any easier for someone to accuse you of not doing the hard work you knew you'd done.

"I don't know if Autumn's mentally unstable like her mother or not," Dax said. "To be honest, I think she's probably a psychopath. She's charming and efficient, and she made herself a part of your life for years before she took action. She changed her hair and her eye color, and she started using her middle name to hide who she was."

Robbie was sad for Autumn, despite what she'd tried to do. "She said she wanted me to feel the walls closing in like her mother had. To be paranoid. That's why she left the threats she did and why she wrote the letters after her mother couldn't."

He nodded. "She confessed to everything, though I don't think she meant to. She was ranting when Finn took her in, though she's calm and in control now. That's why I think she's a psychopath, but I'm not an expert. I just know she's not right in her mind. We have her DNA from the sweater she used on the dummy, so no matter how she tries to retract her statements, we have evidence she was there." He squeezed Robbie's hand. "She didn't want you to be happy. She wanted you miserable and lonely, and she wanted you scared. She left the rose and the blue box because her dad gave her mother a rose and a blue box for their anniversary a few weeks before he left them for good."

Robbie knew now that Autumn had duplicated a key to the house. That was how she'd gotten in that day. Whether or not she'd left the door open on purpose was something Robbie didn't know and probably never would.

"I think she did it because her mother didn't recognize her anymore. That's what set her off."

"I think that's likely. We found the picture of you sleeping on her phone. She took it a few months ago. The alteration was done recently."

Robbie shuddered. "She came to stay for a weekend. We were brainstorming social media posts and promo ideas for *The Vampire King*. God, when I think that she hated me so much for all that time—she could have murdered me in my bed instead of snapping a photo."

"She didn't just want you dead, though. She wanted you to suffer."

It hurt to think someone could harbor such hate for you. Especially someone you'd considered a friend. "She didn't like that I was falling for you. She kept telling me I had to be careful, that I should remember what Trent did to me. She could see that I was happy for the first time in a long time, plus I was writing again. I think maybe she wanted to take all of that away from me before she did anything else."

He kissed her hand again. "I agree. Autumn wanted to terrorize you and make you feel alone. It's possible she would have left it at that if you'd broken the way she wanted. But you didn't, so she took her chance when it came."

Autumn had drugged her cocktail, then taken her into the desert to force her into signing the confession. She'd flown into a rage when Robbie tried to stop her with the plunger handle then lost control when Robbie still wouldn't sign. Robbie had wondered why Autumn didn't just shoot her instead of kicking and beating her, but Dax had told her that the gun didn't have a firing pin. It was a war souvenir, picked up when her dad had served in Desert Storm. It didn't work on purpose.

"I'm glad you found us when you did."

She didn't remember the trip out to the desert, but Dax had told her where they'd been. The middle of nowhere on a dirt road. How Autumn had found the place was anyone's guess, but Robbie suspected she'd been doing her research before they'd ever left home. Just in case.

"Understatement of the year, babe. I only wish I'd found you sooner. Before she hurt you."

"I know, but it's not your fault. You saved me."

He jerked his chin in a short nod, his expression

hard. "She's lucky Finn took her down. I wouldn't have gone so easy on her."

Robbie squeezed his hand. "You wouldn't have hurt her. Because you're a good man and you believe in justice."

"Honey, if she'd succeeded in killing you, nothing would have stopped me from taking payment in kind then and there."

He was so fierce. For her. She loved him for that. No one had ever had her back like he did. Loved her like he did. She smiled at him, her heart light and free.

"Enough of that, Dax. Let's talk about something happier."

He smiled back, though she could see the churning emotion behind his eyes. "You aren't looking past me," he said softly. "That's a happy thing."

She wasn't, and she didn't want to. "I can't see anything but you when you're in the room. You're all I want."

"Fuck me," he growled. "I can't wait for you to feel better. I want to get you alone and do dirty things to you."

She giggled. "I want that so much. You have no idea."

"Bet I do. Shit, talk about something else or I'm going to get a hard-on."

"Oh dear… Hey, I know—who do you think's going to be happier to see me? Lucy or Ollie?"

"Lucy. But Ollie feels it in his heart, he just doesn't show it."

She loved that he knew her pets so well. "I think you're right."

"Lucy's easy to love. Ollie's harder because he's stand-offish, but I like that cat. We have a bond."

Robbie laughed. "Do you now?"

"We do. We're going to do more bonding, too. You watch. Ollie's going to follow me around like a dog."

"Oh, I don't doubt that at all."

She was happier than she'd ever been and looking forward to spending all her days with the man at her side. She wanted to experience everything with him. She would never take another day for granted again. She wouldn't be afraid to put herself out there, to try new things and meet new people.

He had given her that. The belief that she could. It changed everything. She'd fought back against Autumn's attempt to force her into signing a lie, and she'd kept fighting even when the old her would have given up and done what someone else wanted just to make the situation go away.

She'd stopped believing in heroes because they didn't exist, but she'd been wrong. Until she believed in herself, she couldn't believe in anyone else. She did now.

Dax Freed was her hero for making her see the truth. He always would be.

Epilogue

"Come on, woman," Dax said. "We're going to be late."

Robbie hustled out of the master bedroom, fastening an earring as she sashayed toward him, hips swinging enticingly. His jaw hit the floor as he took in her curve-skimming turquoise dress. It hit below the knee and it was still the sexiest fucking thing he'd ever seen.

She had on pointy heels in what she'd said was a nude color, and her hair was slicked into a beautiful bun at the nape of her neck. A few stray hairs escaped, but he thought that was by design because they framed her face perfectly.

"I'm coming. Jeez, what's your rush?"

"Our date. It's our first date and you're already running late."

She stopped and put her hands on her hips, gaping at him. Then she laughed. "You idiot, we've been living together for three months. How can this be our first date?"

"Because you've been writing for most of it, and we've never gotten dressed up and gone out."

"We've gone to people's houses. Brett and Tallie. Ian and Natasha. Jared and Libby. And we've gone out to eat."

"In jeans. For backyard cookouts." He flourished a hand up and down his body. "I'm wearing a suit."

"I see that. You look extremely handsome in it, too."

"Don't flatter me, babe. I don't want to get stuck making love to you instead of taking you out like I'm supposed to."

She sauntered toward him, her eyes going all dewy. "And really, would that be such a bad thing?"

Her palms came up to rest on his chest. He gazed down into her beautiful brown eyes and felt himself start to weaken. "Yes," he said, as much for himself as for her. "It would be bad. I made you come three times this morning. What am I? A sex machine?"

She laughed as she turned away to get her purse. "Well, yes. And I love that about you, by the way."

She made him want to take her back to bed. He was only her second lover, but he was determined to be the best. Not that he didn't believe he was anyway, but he had a reputation to uphold.

Still, if he wanted to show her the evening he'd planned, they had to go. Now.

They patted Lucy and said goodbye to Ollie—who still wasn't following him around like a dog. The silly animal seemed to consider him a personal servant able to fetch meals and scratch chins, so that was progress of a sort.

"Where are we going?" Robbie asked when they were in his truck and moving down the long driveway to the road. "You never said."

"Still not saying. You'll see when we get there."

"Oh, mysterious. I like it."

He reached over and took her hand in his. He loved the feel of her skin, the way simply touching her made sparks flare in his soul. In the three months since they'd returned to Maryland, she'd bloomed. Her body had healed, the bruising fading away to nothing, her ribs knitting together again.

Her spirit had healed, too. He'd been worried about that. Robbie had been abused by people she'd loved. More than once. Her parents had always treated her like she was flawed when she was perfectly normal, just introverted. Trent had taken advantage of her love and thrown it in her face when he'd left her for another woman and then took half her estate. When he couldn't worm his way into Robbie's life again, he'd tried to kill her.

And Autumn. Dear God, Autumn Pinkney. She'd pretended to be a caring friend before she'd snapped and nearly succeeded in her plans to kill Robbie. It still woke him up in a cold sweat some nights, the memory of that wooden cabin going up in flames and knowing Robbie was in there. Some nights he dreamed he didn't reach her in time. Those were the worst.

But she was here, and she was safe, and he wasn't letting anyone get to her ever again.

The angry emails from fans had tapered off, though they still happened occasionally. He'd been screening them for her while she'd been writing. She'd written like a madwoman within days of their return. So much so that she'd finished her book and turned it in to Daphne with only a few days to spare.

She'd recently hired a new assistant, a woman that Laurel Johnson had recommended. So far, it seemed to be working out. Robbie was in touch with Laurel, and she'd promised to go to a Capitol City Writers meeting one day soon as a guest speaker. He'd asked if she was sure, and she'd nodded firmly and said she was. He couldn't deny that she was a great motivator when she talked about being a writer. That she wanted to do it again, without prompting from her publisher, was a wonderful thing. He was behind her all the way.

They drove through Mill Landing. When he turned onto a side street and parked in front of an old building on the corner, she turned to look at him with big eyes. "What's this?"

"You'll see."

He came around to help her exit the truck then led her to the glass door of what used to be an old general store. The windows along the front were rippled with that aged look of old glass. The door creaked as he opened it. The wooden stoop was worn down from years of foot traffic. It was a great building, and currently unused.

Inside, a round table was set with a cloth, glasses, and silverware. There were bread plates and knives, too. The candles were lit, and three people in chef and waiter uniforms waited for them.

"Dax," she said wonderingly. "What have you done?"

He went over and held out a chair for her, then bent to kiss the soft skin beneath her ear. "You expressed admiration for this building before. I thought you'd like to see inside."

It was spectacular, with wood panels that went up two stories and a coffered ceiling. There was a catwalk around the entire top floor that opened to the room below. The interior needed a bit of TLC, but it was still beautiful.

Dax spoke to the staff then joined Robbie at the table. A string trio entered from the back and started playing in the corner they'd set up for themselves.

Robbie's eyes were misty as their waiter came to offer water and wine. The chef and her assistant left to prepare the meal in the restaurant next door.

"This is… Oh my God…" She craned her neck to look around the room. "Words fail me."

He chuckled. "Words have failed the famous author? Oh dear, what will the world say?"

She grinned at him. "Not permanently, you gorgeous man. I love old buildings, so thank you for doing this."

"Ah, but I haven't told you the rest of it yet." He lifted his glass in a toast. "To Roberta Sharpe's next book. May it be a rousing success."

She clinked with him and sipped. "Thank you."

"You didn't tell me what you called it."

Her eyes crinkled happily. "*The Vampire's Queen.*"

"Is that a hint?"

"Maybe it is."

"You aren't going to tell me?"

"Won't it spoil the book for you?"

"Nah, I'll read it and love it regardless."

"Okay, yes, Damian and Velvet are reunited. I think people will love it. I hope so anyway."

"They will. Wouldn't it be great to have a launch party here?" he asked, looking up at the paneled walls.

"Oh, you mean like a cocktail party? It'll need some more cleaning for that, but we could hire people. So long as the owner will rent it to us, I mean."

He loved that she went straight to making a plan. The old Robbie would have looked panicky before saying she'd really rather stay home. She wasn't suddenly an extrovert or anything, but she seemed to enjoy getting out now and again. She chose her people to mingle with, and she always seemed to have fun.

"I have another idea," he said. "The building's for sale. You told me that if you hadn't been a writer, you'd want to own a bookstore with hand-picked books and discussion groups that met regularly. Why not turn this into a bookstore? You don't have to run it. Design it. Stock it. Start your book groups. Hell, you could probably get Tallie and the others to come. Hire people to run it, and then you'll have this space to come to whenever you want. Stop in and surprise people. Do something for the town and get the bookstore of your dreams at the same time. Maybe not the way you always thought, but close enough."

Her jaw had dropped as she stared at him. "You

remember the things I say when I've had two glasses of wine and I'm just babbling?"

"I remember everything about you, Robbie. You're my woman."

She tilted her head back and pressed her fingers beneath her eyes. "Dammit, I don't want to cry. It'll mess up my eyeliner. Why are you so damned amazing, Dax Freed?"

"Because I love you, babe. You're my everything. And I want to give you whatever your heart desires. If it desires a bookstore, then I've found the building for you. And if it doesn't, that's fine too. We're still going to have an amazing dinner together, and we're also going to dance while I hold you close and whisper naughty things in your ear."

She sniffled. "I can't believe I got so lucky. The day you knocked on my door and demanded a house tour was the best day of my life. Not that I knew it then."

He took her hand and gently pulled her up into his arms so he could sway her around the room until the food arrived. "Every day with you is my best day," he whispered in her ear.

She hugged him tight. "Marry me, Dax. I want you to marry me."

He stopped swaying her and looked down into her beautiful face. "Did you just steal my thunder?"

She grinned cheekily. "Maybe I did. But I know you'll wait a long time to ask because you don't want me to think you're after my money. Hell, maybe you'll never ask because of it, so *I'm* asking *you*."

His heart was so full it hurt. "Woman, you didn't ask. You told me," he teased.

She shrugged. "I know what I want and I'm going after it. So will you or won't you?"

"Oh, I definitely will. But I'm signing a prenup. I want you to know it's you I want."

"I already know that. Believe me, I know."

She kissed him, the music played on, and the pieces of his life fell into place like tumblers in a lock. His heart and hers were made to fit together. Always.

Bonus Epilogue

THANKSGIVING DAY

"LOOK," Dax said as he came into the kitchen. "I'm being followed."

Ollie sauntered behind Dax, stopping when he got level with Dax's legs. Robbie arched an eyebrow. "It's the kitchen, Dax. Of course he followed you in."

Dax rolled his eyes. "Watch."

He turned and walked out again. The cat looked at her then swiveled his head to look at Dax. He licked a paw. Then he sauntered in the direction Dax had gone.

Robbie snorted. "You're feeding him treats," she called as she peeled potatoes for the Thanksgiving feast they were having with friends later. A house full of people were arriving in a few hours with dishes to share. Robbie couldn't wait. It was the first time they'd ever hosted a big meal, and she was simultaneously nervous and excited.

Dax reappeared, looking offended. "I am not. How dare you, lady."

Ollie was on his heels. Dax bent down and picked the cat up. Robbie expected a struggle to ensue, but Ollie butted his head against Dax's chin and started to purr.

"You are freaking kidding me," she said. "What did you do? Feed him treats from your lips?"

"What? No, of course not. Yuck. He loves me, don't you buddy?" Dax scratched the cat's chin. Ollie closed his eyes and purred loud enough to wake the dead. "See?"

Robbie shook her head. "Okay, fine. You've charmed our cat."

Dax grinned at her. "Our cat? You mean *my* cat."

"You two are ridiculous," she teased. "Come help me with these potatoes. I need to check the turkey."

"You mean come peel them while you peer at the turkey and pronounce it's coming along?"

"Something like that."

Dax gave Ollie a last scratch and put him on the floor. Then he took over peeling while Robbie checked the turkey. As predicted, it was coming along.

"Do you want me to peel again?" she asked.

"Nah, I got it. Sit and relax. You worked late into the night."

She did, and it felt great. She was writing her new fantasy romance and having so much fun. Daphne had green lighted the project after proclaiming *The Vampire's Queen* a perfect ending to Damian and Velvet's story.

She thought about publishing under Lucy Oliver,

but ultimately it was Roberta Sharpe who had the audience. She would always be Roberta Sharpe on books, but she was Robbie Freed in real life. She'd married her hero in September, at the courthouse, because it'd felt right. They'd had a big reception a couple of weeks later with their friends, held at Mill Landing's newest bookstore called—what else? Lucy & Oliver's Books.

Daphne had flown down, and Robbie had invited some of her new friends from the CCW. Laurel Johnson had turned into a great friend, and she and Robbie talked often. Being published by the same publisher had been their common ground at first, but being writers was their ultimate common ground.

"What else are we fixing?" Dax asked.

She loved that he asked and that he participated. That was the kind of man he was. He still had a dangerous job, and she still worried about him when he went away, but she wouldn't change who he was the same as he wouldn't change who she was. That's why they worked.

Respect and mutual understanding.

"Well, I found that recipe for sausage dressing I planned to make. And I thought you were fixing your famous macaroni and cheese. I heard Ty ask specifically for it."

Dax laughed. "Yeah, I am. It's a little odd for Thanksgiving though, don't you think?"

Robbie shrugged. "Nah. It's about eating what you like, and lots of it."

They spent the rest of the morning preparing, then Dax helped her set the long farm table she'd purchased a long time ago with dishes, silverware, and glassware. She'd had Tallie come and create the centerpiece that ran the length of the table a few days ago. There were small pumpkins, leaves, acorns, and greenery that she'd woven together with candles of different sizes until there was a magnificent display down the center of the table. It was like something out of a magazine, and it made Robbie happy to look at it.

She changed into black trousers and a soft cream sweater with low-heeled booties, dabbed on perfume, then went to join Dax in the living room so they could greet their guests when they arrived.

When she entered the room, Dax was at the piano. Robbie watched him curiously as he put his hands over the keys. He shot her a smile then launched into *Moonlight Sonata*. She had to scrape her jaw off the ground.

"Are you kidding me right now?" she asked. "You *play?* Why didn't you tell me?"

He grinned at her. "I'm a one-trick pony, honey. This is my best song."

It was incredible to her ears, but she wasn't exactly musical. She'd bought the piano because she loved the way it looked, and she secretly wished she knew how to play, but she would never learn.

Yet here was her husband of two months playing freaking Beethoven like a pro.

Robbie went over to the bench and stood beside him with her hand on his shoulder. His fingers were long and beautiful, and they moved across the keys like they had a memory of their own.

"I'm so impressed," she breathed. "And irritated you

didn't tell me you could play. What else are you keeping from me? The coordinates to Santa's workshop? The secret recipe for KFC?"

He laughed as he stopped playing and tugged her down beside him. "You're so funny, Robbie." He huffed a breath. "I didn't tell you because I wasn't sure I wanted to play again. Piano holds associations for me, not all of them pleasant. My mom teaches piano, and I was her favorite guinea pig. My brother never learned because my stepdad thought it was for sissies, but I spent a good part of my childhood practicing while Sean got to play."

"Oh, Dax. I don't like that man, no matter that he was nice enough the time I met him."

"I know, baby. I don't like him either."

"Your mother never said a word."

"She wouldn't. I kind of had a big meltdown when I was fourteen and had to be the star in her recital. I was a total asshole, and Mom cried. She fought to keep her piano whenever my stepdad was broke and wanted to sell it for booze and rent money. I knew it meant something to her for me to play. I'm not proud of how I acted. I apologized later, and she said it was okay, but she told me I didn't have to play anymore. She said she wouldn't force me, and she wouldn't ever mention it again if I didn't bring it up. So I didn't. She kept her word."

His fingers moved over the keys, teasing out such beautiful notes that her heart ached. For the beauty and for him. "Thank you for playing for me. It's so lovely."

"It's rusty," he said. "Mom would make me do remedial finger exercises."

"It's beautiful to me." She kissed his cheek then wiped the lipstick away with her thumb. "I love you, Dax. You're so amazing. Strong, tough, and protective, but then you can do something like this that takes a soft hand. I am continually impressed by you and so happy you agreed to be my husband."

He grinned. "Flattery will get you everywhere, Mrs. Freed." He glanced at the grandfather clock as it started to chime. "But later. Right now we have to get ready for our guests."

She stood and he joined her. The doorbell rang not five minutes later, and they went as one to welcome their friends into their home.

It was a Thanksgiving filled with laughter, a few tears from the newest little Black, a short piano recital from Daria Black, a proposal that no one saw coming, and lots of love and way too much food.

Much later, they lay in bed together, tired from the day but not too tired to make quiet, sweet love. When it was over, they cuddled together under the covers, naked and happy. Robbie sighed as she traced the defined muscles of Dax's torso.

"Damian LeBeaux has nothing on you," she said. "I thought I'd made the perfect hero. Then I met you."

His fingers were in her hair, playing softly. "You have no idea how honored I am when you say things like that."

She kissed his chest and licked her way around his nipple. She was too tired for more, but she still loved to hear his breath hiss in. "I'm going to keep saying them. Every day. Until I run out of words."

He tugged her head back and fused his mouth to hers until her body melted. "I don't always have the words like you do, but I have this. And I plan to keep showing you how I feel every day we're together. You're my other half, Robbie. If I were an immortal vampire, I'd choose you."

At that moment, Ollie jumped onto the bed and let out a very loud yowl that had them—and Lucy—bolting upright, startled out of their wits.

They laughed until they cried, Ollie settled down, Lucy went back to sleep, and then Robbie threw an arm and leg over her husband. Minutes later, they were both out. It'd been a long day and a perfect night.

There were many more to come.

———

Books by Lynn Raye Harris

HOT Heroes for Hire: Mercenaries
Black's Bandits

Book 1: BLACK LIST - Jace & Maddy

Book 2: BLACK TIE - Brett & Tallie

Book 3: BLACK OUT - Colt & Angie

Book 4: BLACK KNIGHT - Jared & Libby

Book 5: BLACK HEART - Ian & Natasha

Book 6: BLACK MAIL - Tyler & Cassie

Book 7: BLACK VELVET - Dax & Roberta

The Hostile Operations Team ® Books
Strike Team 2

Book 1: HOT ANGEL - Cade & Brooke

Book 2: HOT SECRETS - Sky & Bliss

Book 3: HOT JUSTICE - Wolf & Haylee

Book 4: HOT STORM - Mal & Scarlett

Book 5: HOT COURAGE - Noah & Jenna

The Hostile Operations Team ® Books
Strike Team 1

Book 0: RECKLESS HEAT

Book 1: HOT PURSUIT - Matt & Evie

Book 2: HOT MESS - Sam & Georgie

Book 3: DANGEROUSLY HOT - Kev & Lucky

Book 4: HOT PACKAGE - Billy & Olivia

Book 5: HOT SHOT - Jack & Gina

Book 6: HOT REBEL - Nick & Victoria

Book 7: HOT ICE - Garrett & Grace

Book 8: HOT & BOTHERED - Ryan & Emily

Book 9: HOT PROTECTOR - Chase & Sophie

Book 10: HOT ADDICTION - Dex & Annabelle

Book 11: HOT VALOR - Mendez & Kat

Book 12: A HOT CHRISTMAS MIRACLE - Mendez & Kat

The HOT SEAL Team Books

Book 1: HOT SEAL - Dane & Ivy

Book 2: HOT SEAL Lover - Remy & Christina

Book 3: HOT SEAL Rescue - Cody & Miranda

Book 4: HOT SEAL BRIDE - Cash & Ella

Book 5: HOT SEAL REDEMPTION - Alex & Bailey

Book 6: HOT SEAL TARGET - Blade & Quinn

Book 7: HOT SEAL HERO - Ryan & Chloe

Book 8: HOT SEAL DEVOTION - Zach & Kayla

The HOT Novella in Liliana Hart's MacKenzie Family Series

HOT WITNESS - Jake & Eva

7 Brides for 7 Brothers

MAX (Book 5) - Max & Ellie

7 Brides for 7 Soldiers

WYATT (Book 4) - Max & Ellie

7 Brides for 7 Blackthornes

ROSS (Book 3) - Ross & Holly

Filthy Rich Billionaires

Book 1: FILTHY RICH REVENGE

Book 2: FILTHY RICH PRINCE

Who's HOT?

Alpha Squad
Matt "Richie Rich" Girard (Book 0 & 1)
Sam "Knight Rider" McKnight (Book 2)
Kev "Big Mac" MacDonald (Book 3)
Billy "the Kid" Blake (Book 4)
Jack "Hawk" Hunter (Book 5)
Nick "Brandy" Brandon (Book 6)
Garrett "Iceman" Spencer (Book 7)
Ryan "Flash" Gordon (Book 8)
Chase "Fiddler" Daniels (Book 9)
Dex "Double Dee" Davidson (Book 10)

Commander
John "Viper" Mendez (Book 11)

Deputy Commander
Alex "Ghost" Bishop

Echo Squad

Cade "Saint" Rodgers (Book 12)
Sky "Hacker" Kelley (Book 13)
Dean "Wolf" Garner (Book 14)
Malcom "Mal" McCoy (Book 15)
Jake "Harley" Ryan (HOT WITNESS)
Jax "Gem" Stone
Noah "Easy" Cross
Ryder "Muffin" Hanson

SEAL Team
Dane "Viking" Erikson (Book 1)
Remy "Cage" Marchand (Book 2)
Cody "Cowboy" McCormick (Book 3)
Cash "Money" McQuaid (Book 4)
Alexei "Camel" Kamarov (Book 5)
Adam "Blade" Garrison (Book 6)
Ryan "Dirty Harry" Callahan (Book 7)
Zach "Neo" Anderson (Book 8)
Corey "Shade" Vance

Black's Bandits
Jace Kaiser (Book 1)
Brett Wheeler (Book 2)
Colton Duchaine (Book 3)
Jared Fraser (Book 4)
Ian Black (Book 5)
Tyler Scott (Book 6)
Dax Freed (Book 7)
Finn McDermott
Thomas "Rascal" Bradley
Jamie Hayes

Mandy Parker (Airborne Ops)
Melanie (Executive Assistant)
Natasha Black, aka Calypso, aka Athena
? Unnamed Team Members

Freelance Contractors
Lucinda "Lucky" San Ramos, now MacDonald (Book 3)
Victoria "Vee" Royal, now Brandon (Book 6)
Emily Royal, now Gordon (Book 8)
Miranda Lockwood, now McCormick (SEAL Team Book 3)
Bliss Bennett, (Book 13)

About the Author

Lynn Raye Harris is a Southern girl, military wife, wannabe cat lady, and horse lover. She's also the New York Times and USA Today bestselling author of the HOSTILE OPERATIONS TEAM ® SERIES of military romances, and 20 books about sexy billionaires for Harlequin.

A former finalist for the Romance Writers of America's Golden Heart Award and the National Readers Choice Award, Lynn lives in Alabama with her handsome former-military husband, one fluffy princess of a cat, and a very spoiled American Saddlebred horse who enjoys bucking at random in order to keep Lynn on her toes.

Lynn's books have been called "exceptional and emotional," "intense," and "sizzling" -- and have sold in excess of 4.5 million copies worldwide.

To connect with Lynn online:
www.LynnRayeHarris.com
Lynn@LynnRayeHarris.com

Made in the USA
Middletown, DE
13 May 2025